TEMPTING IVY

A YOUNGER MAN ROMANCE

AMY J. HEART

COPYRIGHT

Tempting Ivy: A Younger Man Romance
Copyright © 2018 by Amy J. Heart

All rights reserved.

Cover design by Aubrey at A.T. Cover Design.

This book is a work of fiction. Names, characters, places, and incidents either are products of the author's imagination or are used fictitiously. Any resemblance to actual persons, living or dead, events, or locales is entirely coincidental.

ISBN Paperback: 978-0-6483392-7-4

PROLOGUE
NICO

To celebrate her sixteenth birthday, my mom visited a Roma fortune-teller who lived in the ruins of a decaying castle, a day's train ride from her Hungarian village.

With her heart beating wildly, Mom listened to a prophecy about a stubborn guy who didn't believe in love and his fated mate.

Many years later when I was twenty-four, and it was almost too late, she handed me a piece of paper and made me read it, and I found out that pigheaded idiot was me.

My mother had transcribed the Romani woman's exact words to her, and this is what they said…

Listen closely sweetheart, for what I tell you shall come to pass. You are young, but you must never forget.

I see three important men in your destiny, but only one who truly matters.

The dark farmer's love is steady and strong, but you will not want his goodness.

The blond voyager's beauty is blinding, and you will follow him far from home. This stealer of joy will crush you, but he will not take your heart. You will keep it safe for the third man. And for him, you must wait a long time.

Your only child is the one you see clearly, and you'll name him after your grandfather, Nicholai.

Your boy has a difficult path, for he refuses to acknowledge the truth. He believes only in beats of wild music and discards tender pulses of the heart, locking his soul up tight.

The woman with the key to opening it is older. Yes. So very much older than he.

One day your son will surrender. One day he will understand—only love has the purest pulse and a beat that is ever true. Far truer than any song. Hers are the lyrics he must follow, for the cup of her happiness is his to drink.

Her happiness is his. You understand?

That day, he will need your honesty, and you must tell him the truth about his father.

Because your son is the man who matters.

Your son, Zsofia, is the one.

If only I'd been ready to hear those words sooner, long before I met Ivy, then I might have been smarter and not acted like a jackass and fucked it up. But that's what I do best —fuck things up. And I can write some kickass songs, too.

Yeah, I'm pretty good at that.

1

IVY

Drunk Ivy

"So, do you want a tequila sunrise?" I yell over the thump and crash of the band. I gaze around at the sweaty crowd packed into our favorite dive bar, Silva's, then glance back at my friend Mia. She looks a little blurry.

"No, thanks!" she says. "I plan to stay sober."

Beams of light flash purple and white over the enraptured faces pointed at the stage. The hypnotic beat makes my stomach churn, and everything appears in soft focus, like a weird dream. Or a nightmare.

I stand swaying gently in the center of the audience, bass

pounding through my chest, the bodies pressed tight against me keeping me upright.

"Shit," I yell in Mia's ear. "I don't know how this has happened, but I think I'm very, very drunk."

Scowling, Mia shakes her head at me. Long, platinum pigtails bounce around her cute pixie face. "Hmm. I wonder if it might have something to do with the five cocktails you've guzzled?" she grouches. "That's why I'm staying sober tonight. Someone has to look after you."

"I'm fine," I lie, making a mental note to keep the slurring to a minimum.

"Listen, Ivy, I've known you almost three years now, and I've never once seen you wasted before. This is disturbing. And, please, what's with the tequila sunrises? You don't even *like* orange juice."

"That's true. It has been known to make me... um... make me..." I'd better not finish that sentence. If I do, she might not want to stand next to me.

Mia's frown grows as she latches onto my crimson velvet tunic, pulling me close so she can yell in my ear. "Make you *what*, Ivy?"

Not telling. Not telling.

I point at the band rocking out on stage. "Wow these guys are great." I may be trying to divert her attention, but I'm not lying.

The four-piece garage rock outfit is killing it up there with their heavy, melodic riffs, an intoxicating beat, and about the sexiest looking guy I've ever seen growling out emotional vocals. His longish messy hair, dark-angel scowl, and bulging tattooed biceps are doing exciting things to my insides.

I'd love a closer look at him. And also for my vision to be working a little better. I hate alcohol.

Not falling for my distraction, Mia shakes me hard. "Orange juice makes you *what?*"

"Vomit."

"Wrong answer." She reaches for my glass. "Gimme that."

Pouting, I bat her hand away. "No. I haven't finished it yet. What's happened to you tonight? You're meant to be the fun one."

"Ivy, you're having enough fun for both of us. If I had any idea that you'd start to sound like a toddler, I'd never have suggested alcohol might help you feel better. This is freaking me out. You're normally so sensible."

She's right. Getting smashed really isn't my scene. My mom—who is a total embarrassment—boozed her way through my childhood, snoozing during ballet performances and school plays. Any event a normal parent would be wide awake for and snapping thousands of photos, she was there snoring loudly in the back row. Or trying to sleep with my male teachers. Even the married ones.

As a result, I'm deeply scarred and spend too much time worrying about what people think of me. It's an old habit. And growing up with a drunk for a mother, I tend to steer clear of alcohol. No matter how bad things get. But at work today, I cracked.

I'm an artist, and I do mixed media portraits of people with tragic backstories—paintings with all sorts of weird things stuck on them. In two months, I'm having my first exhibition at the art gallery where I work.

Honestly, I love Mad Wolf Gallery and adore hanging out with all the other artists employed there. It's the owner, Kendra, who increases my blood pressure and leads me to drink. Today, she looked at my exhibition folio, wrinkled her elegant nose and informed me that I had a lot of work to do if I didn't want to get laughed out of town. Nice one boss. Impressive way to mentor and nurture your artists.

Oh, who cares about Kendra? Another tequila sunrise and I'll forget she even exists.

I'm all set to complain to Mia that I'm the mature one here tonight, tell her she should loosen up, act her youthful age and have some fun when the music disappears, replaced by a screech of feedback.

The sizzling-hot singer yells through the mic, "We're Granddad. And you guys are awesome. Be bad and have a great night."

I wouldn't mind being bad with him.

Disappointment settles in my chest as the band leaves the stage. I was hoping to stare at that guy a lot longer and continue my discreet drooling.

As I swing around to push my way to the bar, orange juice swishes in my belly.

"I need some air," I say, clutching Mia's arm. "I'll be right back."

"I'll come with you, so you don't get lost and stumble all the way down to the foreshore and drown. I can't have that on my conscience, can I?"

"Stay there. Honestly, I don't feel sick at all, just a little fuzzy. I'm only going out into the alley to star gaze for a minute. I'll be back before you know it. Promise."

Her mouth opens, a protest working its way out. "Ivy—"

"Oh look, is that Up Void getting ready on stage?" I yell, cutting her off.

To say she's obsessed with the next band's singer is like stating that dogs quite like being patted, or cats are okay with having their ears scratched—the understatement of the century.

Desperate for a glimpse of her crush, she scrutinizes the roadies fiddling with leads and amps.

With Mia suitably distracted, I tug the hem of my dress lower and push politely through the squeeze.

A classic White Stripes' tune distorts through the speakers, battling to be heard over all the excited chatter and laughter. I feel jealous of the hyped-up crowd and wish I was madly anticipating the next band, too. But I'm not.

I'd rather be tucked up in bed with my Kindle like the semi-old person I am. When did I become so boring?

Heaving a big sigh, I push open the back door. I'll get a big dose of fresh air, then head home. I think I've had all the excitement I can handle for one night.

Which, believe me, isn't much.

2

NICO

Not an Asshole

I have no idea why I'm thinking about the dumb prophecy my mom's been going on about for years while I stand on stage after the gig packing up gear. The one concerning my alleged fated mate. It's ridiculous. Whenever she brings it up, I just laugh my head off and go about my business, because I'll never do something stupid like fall for a girl.

Ever.

I know for a fact there's no such thing as true love. Heartbreak and disappointment—that's about all there is.

Why else has Mom cried for my shit-for-brains father every night since he ran out on us when I was a baby?

She's had a hard life, a Hungarian village girl bringing up her bratty kid all alone in America, working three jobs to keep us alive. The last thing I want to do is make her unhappy, but as I help roadies push amps around and unplug leads, lyrics rattle around my brain about lying deadbeat losers and broken-hearted single mothers.

I'm turning Mom's pain into a song. And I can't help wondering, does that make me an asshole?

"Hey, asshole. Get a move on. Up Void's roadies are busting my balls to get our shit off the stage."

Okay, so maybe our guitarist Linc thinks I'm an ass. But he hates everyone, so I'm not too worried. And I reckon there'd be at least a few girls who agree with him. I'm not known for being a sweetheart to chicks. If I'm too nice, they get ideas and try to insert themselves into my life. And who wants to be saddled with a girlfriend? Not me right now. And probably not ever.

"Your balls can relax, man," I say as I drop wound-up guitar leads into a bag while scanning the crowd for the hot redhead I had my eye on during the show. I've got a thing for lanky brunettes, so I was amazed to find myself seeking out the curvy girl again and again during our set. Seems like she's missing in action now though. I fucking hope she hasn't already left.

"I'm done, Linc. Just gotta drop this last load in the van. Line up a whiskey for me at the bar."

His cynical gaze tracks over the buzzing crowd. "This is gonna be one of the last times Up Void play a fuckhole joint like this. They're already too big for it."

"It's good we got the support again. The crowd went apeshit for us."

"Yeah, well it sure helps that you're tight with South. Keep on sucking up to their singer, won't you?" Linc flicks spikes of black hair out of his face and jumps off the low stage into the crowd.

After zipping up four duffel bags crammed with gear, I fist bump an Up Void roadie and plunge down into the sea of drunk folk.

I make slow progress because people want to talk, so by the time I reach the rear exit, my arms are heavy with exhaustion. Finally, I push open the metal door that leads to the alleyway, a blast of cool air waking me up.

Rain splatters my face as I open the van door and throw the bags on a messy mountain of band equipment. There's a loud crash and a yelp behind me. I whip my head around and see a girl bent over, giggling as she picks up a trash can she's obviously collided with. Very nice ass.

When she notices me, she straightens up, covering her mouth with one hand and waving at me with the other.

Awesome. It's the chick I've been staring at all night. "Oh, it's you," I say as I head straight for her.

She stiffens and looks behind her. "Who?"

"You. The hot redhead."

She covers her mouth again and laughs, patting her mane of flaming locks like she's checking it's still attached to her head. "You seem very flamil... flamiliar... whoops." She snorts loudly. "Shit. I can't talk properly. I meant to say *famil-*

iar. Do I know you?" Her voice is low, a little husky, and a lot sexy.

"No. But you should," I say. Yeah. I'd definitely like to get to know her a little—find out just how soft her skin is. And being a redhead, is she covered in freckles? I'm close enough to touch her now and, fuck, she looks even hotter than she did from the stage.

She sways against the brick wall, dark-red dress inching up her creamy thighs. She tugs it down. I watch her fingers smooth over her skin.

"What exactly do you mean by *know you*? As in the biblical sense?" She slaps her palms over her mouth like she can't believe what came out of it.

I laugh. "Sure. Yeah. What a good idea."

She has a heart-shaped face and sweet, doll-like features. The deep bow in her upper lip gives her a permanent pout. It does something to my gut. And my dick.

"I don't know why I said that. I'm not normally so—"

"Drunk?"

She nods enthusiastically. Like she's impressed by how observant I am. It's not that hard to tell she's three sheets to the wind. Or maybe a whole laundry basket full.

Her big eyes get even rounder. I can't tell what color they are out here, but I'm thinking something light. Maybe blue or green like mine are.

The back of her hand slaps my chest hard. "Oh, yeah! I *do* know you. You're that singer from inside. The cool band guy."

Shit. She *is* a bit drunk. But still very cute. And exactly what I need in my bed tonight.

"Yeah. That's right. I sing and play rhythm guitar."

"I really liked Granddad. You're great." She lists dangerously to the left, then rights herself. "What was I saying? Oh… Granddad. Yep. Fantastic."

I glance at the back door of the club, expecting to see some old dude doddering out. "So, whose granddad is great?"

"Your band. You've got really good… um… songs."

"Thanks. But what about the granddad?"

A frown crinkles her forehead. "Your band, silly."

I lean closer, get a whiff of her scent. Something sweet like oranges. "What about my band?"

"Aren't you called Granddad?"

I try not to crack up, but fuck that's funny. My laugh echoes loudly around the alley. "We're called *Burntbad*, not Granddad. Man, I really should learn to speak more clearly through that mic, huh? So I'm guessing you came to see Up Void tonight, not us."

"That is unfortunately true. You see, my friend is madly in love with their singer," she says, looking guilty. "That what's-his-name. You know that blond guy?"

"South. Yeah. Figures. Who isn't into him?"

She presses her palm back on my chest and leans in. "Sorry. We had no idea who the support band would be tonight. But, don't worry, I'm sure there are lots of people who're in love with you too."

I bite back a grin as her eyes widen comically. "You're very pretty in a mean bad-boy kind of way."

Shit. That's the first time anyone's used the word pretty to describe me. Hot. Bad. Prick. They're the kind of words I'm used to hearing from girls. And I've definitely heard mean a time or two before.

Glancing down at her hand clutching my t-shirt, I step forward. She steps back until she's pressed against the wall. The brick right next to her head feels rough as I press my palm into it and dip my head close.

"So, I'm pretty, huh? And also mean? Sounds a bit like you're trying to insult me."

"Well, there's hardly any light out here, but I'm fairly sure you're gorgeous. Also, you look sort of grumpy. In a hot way, of course."

Huh. Good answer.

"Why can't I quit talking?" she asks.

"I don't know. Want me to try and help you stop?"

"Please. If you've got any ideas, I'd love to hear them."

"I'll have to show you. Just let me know if it's not helping and I'll stop right away."

As her frown deepens, my mouth takes hers, and I breathe in her confusion, drink down her shocked gasp and ragged sigh as she melts against me.

The traffic noises disappear. I no longer feel the rain falling on my skin. Instead, internal sounds rage, rocking and rolling and hammering at my skull. My gut tightens, a heavy bassline pounding through it. Music moves my breath in and out of my lungs.

Words flash. Urgent. Crazy ones.

Images flicker of flames and burning pyres. Hot skin

flecked with sweat. Red hair curling. Sweet lips smiling. And over the Friday night street sounds, horns blaring, the sound-check inside the club, three words pulse through my blood.

Need.

And *take.*

And *more.*

Fuck, I'm hard as granite.

I taste alcohol.

Sharp.

Something fruity.

Sweet.

And her.

More sweetness.

Her fingers dig into my arm. I cradle her jaw, angle her face, and press deeper. This is insane. I fuck enough girls to not react like a school kid ready to detonate at first base. So why are my hands shaking? Why do I want inside this girl so badly?

Somewhere back on planet earth the hinges of a metal door screech. Someone laughs. A guy. It's deep, gravelly, loud. And it's fucking Linc.

"Oh, hey! Sorry, man," he says. "Didn't realize you were engaged in important business out here."

Shooting him daggers, I say, "And now you do. So why the fuck are you still standing there flapping your mouth?"

He laughs again, probably because I'm huffing words out like I've just sprinted around the block five times. And then he salutes me and kindly does as requested and fucks off.

Now. Back to those juicy lips.

"Who was that?" hot-redhead whispers.

"No one. Just our lead guitarist. Linc."

"Oh. He seems nice. Kiss me again?"

"Sure." The rain pelts down harder, drenching my hair as I stare at her lopsided smile. "I like the way you think." Shit my voice is raspy as fuck. Must be all the yelling I did onstage. "But do you realize we're getting soaked out here?"

I wonder if she's wet where it really counts, beneath her clothes. Because I am ready to rock, and it's taking super-human control not to slide her velvety dress up and find out.

"We should go inside," I say. Because if we don't, any second now, I'm gonna try and fuck her right here in the alleyway. And even though it's not a good idea, I can't seem to get the thought of doing it out of my head.

Sure I've fucked girls rough against dirty walls before, but this one's drunk, and I'm mostly sober. I'm not a big enough of an asshole to take advantage of the situation. No matter what Linc thinks.

A cat yowls and we watch it scramble past, chased by an even scrawnier looking dog. We smile at each other for way too long, but for some reason, I don't want to stop.

"Come inside with me," I say, breaking the spell. "The band's got a tab at the bar. I'll get you a drink." Maybe that's a bad idea, too, because I think she's had more than enough. But, then again, who am I to judge?

Usually, I don't mind getting wasted. Just not tonight. A support with Up Void is a serious opportunity. Those guys are going places fast. There's no way I'd risk fucking it up.

"The rain isn't bothering me at all." She drags my head

down. "So, I'd like more kissing, please. You have such nice lips. So soft."

I groan, my breathing instantly turning ragged. This girl makes my blood wildfire-hot.

My tongue strokes slowly as I kiss her, trying to keep the pace easy. But, man, I want to do the exact opposite. Forget my conscience. Be the asshole I was born to be—my father's son—and kiss her hard. *Fuck* her hard. Right here. Right now. But, instead of charging ahead, I pull back and start talking.

"What's your name?" I ask, my fingers playing through her silky hair.

"Ivy."

"Ivy, huh? It's nice. Old fashioned." I consider her sulky lips, the dip in her pointed chin. "But, I don't know, Ivy has an edge. It sounds dangerous, and you don't feel that way. Maybe Ruby would suit you better—with all this red hair." I curl a flaming strand of it around my fingers.

"How would you know whether I'm edgy or not?" Scowling, she untangles my fingers and shoves my hand away. "For all you know, I could be just as dangerous to get close to as the plant. Maybe that's exactly why my mom called me Ivy, Mister Cocky Britches. Because I'm poisonous."

I choke on a laugh. "Did you just call my pants cocky?" I sense some parental-issues rising, so I'm pretty keen to change the subject. "In case you're interested, my name's Nico. You live around here?"

"Not far. I work at Mad Wolf Gallery, a few blocks away next to the warehouse apartments. Mia and I come here sometimes after work because it's so close."

"Oh, you mean the gallery near the beach?"

She nods.

"My friend Angelo lives in that posh warehouse complex in the same street. I used to have some other friends who lived there too. But they're out on a farm now, busy being do-gooders. But you've probably seen Angelo around. Good looking rasta dude?"

Ivy scrunches up her face. "I think I've seen him. My boss, Kendra, probably knows him. She's the reason I'm in this pathetic state tonight."

"A little buzzed? Why, what did she do to you?"

"She was her usual intimidating, patronizing self. And she told me my work would never be ready for the exhibition I've got coming up in a couple of months. Called my paintings juvenile. And try hard."

"She sounds like a bitch. So, you're an artist?"

"Uh-huh. I do mixed media. Collages. That kind of thing."

"I don't really know what that is, but I'd like to hear about it. Hey, I've got an apartment out past the old brewery, where the scenery gets a little seedier. It's cool though. You should come and check it out."

She gives me a narrowed side-look, so I rub her hip softly, staring at her lips, and say, "We can finish what we started here. How about we catch a cab to my place right now?"

With her gaze roving over my face, she chews on her thumbnail. My chest tightens while I wait for her to decide.

Say yes. Say yes.

"Okay, but you'll have to meet my friend Mia first. She'll probably want to photograph you and put your number in her contacts. Maybe even take a video of you answering a few personal questions."

I laugh and lean closer, brush my lips over hers.

For a few outstanding seconds, she kisses me, and then breaks away. "I'm serious, Mister Rock Star."

"Fine." I pull back so she can see my eyes, to show her that I mean no harm. I only want to make her feel good. "I'm okay with that. But I need to get closer to you, Ivy. I'm writing songs right here, right now from just touching you. What's gonna happen when I'm inside you? I'm thinking full-blown symphonies. Angels and trumpets."

She huffs a laugh. "Boy. No wonder you musicians have legions of girls following you around everywhere."

"Yeah? Well, tonight, the only person I want to follow me is *you*."

She gets a funny look on her face, like she's trying to figure out a problem—me—I guess.

"Okay. Let's go for it, then. I hardly ever do anything spontaneous. I'm usually all about the planning. Tonight I'm gonna change that up."

She tugs her dress down again, grabs my hand, and tows me toward the club.

All signs of post-gig fatigue have disappeared.

Ivy's got me firing on all cylinders.

3

IVY

He's a Baby

"**W**here have you been, Ivy? I've spent the last twenty minutes picturing you choking to death on puke," complains Mia when she catches me exiting Silva's restroom after leaving Nico at the stage door to collect his stuff.

"I told you before I didn't feel sick," I yell.

As I walk toward her, grungy band posters blur at the edges of my vision, the hallway lighting harsh and unforgiving. Images swirl through my mind. A dark alleyway. Tousled hair. A lush mouth, complete with a sexy lip piercing. Eyes soulful and heartbreaking.

Physically, that Nico guy is all my teenage fantasies

wrapped up into one super-dangerous package, but luckily, I've given up acting stupid over attractive men. They usually turn out to be disappointing creatures anyway, and I'm far too old for the drama of dealing with another one. Right now, all I want is his body.

"As you can see," I say when I reach Mia. "I'm fine."

Actually, after my surprise make out session with the hot-singer guy, I'm more than fine. Whole body on fire, I remain in a lusty daze, and I can't wait to get back to those lovely lips of his.

"I've been outside kissing the singer from Burntbad," I yell over the noise of the roadies checking sound levels in the band room. I'm obviously still a bit on the drunk side because as she reels backward in amazement, I grab her skin-tight, black top and pull her close. "And guess what? I'm going to have sex with him. Now!"

Her eyes bulge. "*Here?*"

"Oh, not right here and now. But tonight. At his apartment!"

"*No.* Really?"

"Oh, yes," I confirm proudly.

Over the last six months, I've been on a few dates and even had actual sex a handful of times. There was the animal massage therapist Mia set me up with, a nerdy video game designer who picked me up at the gallery, and an accountant I met through Tinder. All disasters. And not one of them got my juices flowing like that guy did out there. *Nico.* Just his kisses, the sound and feel of his breath panting over my skin was enough to make me disregard my cautious never-go-home-with-strangers rule.

Mia shakes my shoulders hard.

What? Wrapped up in visions of rock-boy splendor, I'd almost forgotten she was here.

"But that's so unlike you, Ivy. You're sensible and for an artist, strangely conservative."

I give myself a mental slap and drag my attention back to my frowning friend. "But, Mia, how could I not? He just swaggered on up to me, spoke a few words in his yummy voice, and the next thing I knew, we were getting it on. Wait until you get a load of the eyes on this guy! It was a bit dark out there, but I had no trouble feeling how hard and hot his body is. I'm talking world-class sex machine. He looked good on stage, but up close he's perfection. I need to paint his sexy face. Do you think you could snap his photo for me without him noticing?"

"No! And I hope you won't try and paint him tonight. Getting your rocks off should be your number one priority." Looking past my shoulder, Mia smirks. "Don't turn around, but that premium pleasure machine is strutting his way over here right now."

"Good. I told him you'd want to meet him before we leave. You can advise me if he's mentally unsound or not. I was too turned on before to notice."

She squeezes my arm. "Holy smokes. I think my panties just went up in flames. You're right. The closer he gets, the better he looks."

Nodding and smiling smugly, I turn to check out the guy

who I'm hoping will be the provider of numerous orgasms over the next few hours.

Oh, wow. He's totally yum. The strap of his canvas bag molds his band t-shirt close to his muscular chest. He's wearing pale denim jeans, a cocky smile, and as he approaches, I can't help but notice how flawlessly smooth his skin is. Much, much smoother than mine, actually.

When he reaches my side, his beauty illuminated clearly in the bright hallway, my smile vanishes clean off my face. Crap. This guy is a baby. Or at best an extremely well-developed teenager.

Shoving his hands in his pockets, he chin tips Mia then gives me a devastating crooked grin. With dimples!

The heart attack I'm about to have has struck me speechless. He's freaking gorgeous. And so shockingly young that I can't move, only stare in wonder at those eyes. They're huge, green, almond-shaped gemstones, framed by the longest lashes I've ever seen on a boy.

His gaze roaming my face, his expression grows confused. He must have noticed the crow's feet around my eyes and realized that I'm old enough to be his... his what? His Aunt? And he's about to run away screaming.

Mia's gaze bounces between us like she's assessing the happy couple at one of the pet weddings she photographs. Her side job is quite lucrative. Rich people are crazy. And when they love their pets, they're often willing to spend a fortune on things like dressing them up in silly bridal clothes and paying Mia big bucks to document them looking foolish.

She sticks her hand out at the boy-man. "Hi, I'm Mia. I love your band."

He shakes it. "Thanks. Name's Nico. So, Ivy said you might want to ask me some questions. Or make like... a little video before we leave."

She laughs. "I'm not a complete ogre. But I wouldn't mind photographing your license as a safeguard."

"Sure. I get that." His hand delves into his back pocket.

"Wait," I say.

He pulls a black wallet out, thrusts it at Mia, and then turns back to me. "You ready to go?"

Mia locates his license and snaps a photo.

Ready? For what—me to drop him back at his parents' house? It's not a school night, but I wouldn't be surprised if he has a baseball game on in the morning.

Mia, bless her, clicks a few shots of Nico's bonny face, pretending to aim for the Breeders poster on the wall behind him.

"How old are you?" I ask.

Mia's face twists so hard, I can see it in my side vision. Disapproval radiates from her. And, unbelievably, she's pissed at me, not the pretty scowly-faced boy.

"What?" Nico leans closer, eyebrows raised like he missed the question. I believe I spoke quite clearly.

I cross my arms at him. I can't tolerate people who pretend to be slow. "You must have noticed we have a signifi-cant age gap issue going on here."

Wearing an offended looking frown that makes my underpants area buzz, he says, "Hey, I'm not that young. I'm twenty-four."

"Well, mister, I happen to be thirty-four, and I think—"

"So what? Big fucking deal."

"*Big deal?* Did you not hear me properly? I am *ten years* older than you. Ten! You're a baby. And if you think I'm interested in sleeping with a child, then your soft head isn't screwed on right."

"Women hit their sexual peak in their thirties and forties, men do so in their twenties. We couldn't be more perfectly matched."

"In *bed.*"

"Sure. Yeah. Absolutely," he nods enthusiastically.

Mia sighs and hands his wallet back. "I don't think you'll be needing me for this shit-show. Message me, Ivy, if sanity prevails and you end up leaving with him. Nice to meet you, Nico. Good luck. You'll be needing it."

He steps closer. Too close. "Listen, don't overthink it. Let's just leave now, Ivy. Come on."

I point at Mia's departing back, wave my hand at her twenty-five-year-old butt. "Wouldn't you rather go home with her? She's about your age, you know."

Frowning, he looks too. Then shakes his head at me. "No. I wouldn't rather leave with your friend. You'll do just fine."

"Hi, Nico," says a sweet voice.

He sighs heavily.

A girl with long, honey-brown hair bounces at my side. She's cute, perky, and practically drools all over him as she slops a kiss on his cheek. "Great show tonight."

"Hi, Felice," Nico says, flicking a quick glance her way.

She tugs on his arm, drawing his attention back. "You guys are *so* good. Dead Heart totally rocked. What a brilliant song! I love the riff and your voice, the way it—"

"Hey, thanks. Listen, can you give me a minute? I'm talking to my friend Ivy here about something important."

She checks me out. "Oh, hi, Ivy. Sure. See you at the bar later, Nico?"

He shrugs a noncommittal shoulder.

I'd give almost anything to be her age right now. Trying to conceal the jealousy souring my gut, I smile as she gives him a saucy wink, and then rolls her seductive hips away.

"Or what about Felice? Wouldn't you rather sleep with her tonight than old Grandma here?"

He laughs. "No, I really wouldn't and—"

"That's because you've probably already had her."

Guilt flashes over his stupidly attractive face, and then he stalks forward, backing me against the wall. "Can you stop interrupting for a second and let me fucking speak?" He braces his forearms next to my head and bends close. He's tall, of course.

"You're sexy as hell. There's no one else I want to touch tonight but you, Ivy. Believe me, you're all I want."

My heart melts momentarily at his earnest expression, the intensity in his voice. Then I will it to freeze against this beautiful boy who makes me want what I can't have. And, even knowing he's too young for me, I *do* still want him. Desperately.

Warm hands frame my face, and my nipples instantly

harden. His eyes fix on my mouth before his own zooms closer. "Come on, Ivy. You want this, too. I can feel it."

He's not wrong. His lips brush mine, making my traitorous heart shudder and my head spin.

I pull away. "I'm in no state to know what I want. I'm drunk. And I rarely do this... drink much I mean."

"No? Why is that?"

I'd prefer not to tell him, but I start talking anyway. "My mom slurred her way through my childhood—she was a constant embarrassment—so I'm not into drunk people. Which is a shame because, tonight, that's exactly what I am. A drunk person. And I'm sorry, but I can't do this with you. It wouldn't be right."

Defeat narrows his emerald eyes. "Fuck," he says under his breath. "You've got me with the drinking thing. I don't want you to regret a moment of what we do together."

There is no doubt I'm still affected by the tequila sunrises, because before he can even think about walking away, I grip his arm and blurt out, "Wow. Your eyes are incredible. They're so—"

"Green. Yeah. So I've heard."

They're stunning. The jade color glows brightly offset against his long lashes, the dark eyebrows that make him look a bit angry, his sun-kissed tawny hair. Just looking at him is enough to break my heart. Crumble my defenses to dust.

"Shit. I'm sorry, Nico. I know I'm giving out mixed signals. It's ridiculous. I'm the one who's acting like a child.

Why don't we be friends? If I run into you again, I don't want it to be awkward between us."

Those serious eyebrows draw down. He's not happy. And fair enough, too. He'll have to work his sexual ju-ju all over again, bust his moves on some other girl now. No doubt he'll be surrounded by hopeful participants within seconds. The mental image of him ramming Felice hard, his brow creased in concentration as he fucks her, mocks my tender heart. I'd love to know what it feels like to be that close to him.

It's so unfair. Why didn't I meet him five years ago? No! That's the alcohol doing the thinking, because then he'd only be nineteen, and I would still be… older.

This is terrible. I didn't know I had cougar tendencies. Taboo desires. But *are* they taboo? Probably not these days but imagine what people would think of me. An old hag with a gorgeous young stud. I'd be laughed at just like my mother always was for chasing guys who didn't want her.

I wish I didn't care, but I do. I'll never allow myself to be reduced to the punchline of a joke like my mom was.

Feedback screeches from the band room. A miked-up voice shouts, and the crowd screams like harpies.

Nico strokes my cheek with calloused fingertips, lips twisting, his hand drops to his side. "Sounds like Up Void's onstage. I'm gonna go watch them. You should come check them out. They'll make you want to live dangerously. Ever thought, sweet Ivy, that a slice of reckless living might be just what you need?"

He makes it two steps away, then turns back. "We've got some more gigs coming up here soon, and it sounds like you'll be sober the next time we bump into each other. So, take this as a warning, Ivy—this isn't finished—I'll be coming for you."

Crap.

He mustn't have noticed the tiny wrinkles blooming around my eyes. No matter. When he sees me in broad daylight, I'm sure he'll break his legs running in the opposite direction.

4

NICO

Mad Wolf

On a sunny afternoon, exactly one week after I first met Ivy, I find myself standing across the street from Mad Wolf Gallery wondering what the fuck's got into me. I should be at work, but I haven't stopped thinking about her or that dumb fated mate prophecy my mom's been going on about forever.

But, hey, I'm not clueless—I know the prophecy is bullshit. Ivy is the first 'older woman' I've bothered to look at twice, and she couldn't be less interested in me. That fortune-teller didn't know what the hell she was talking about. Cougar-fated-mate my ass.

Still, cougar crap or not, nothing will stop me from trying

to change this chick's mind about getting down and dirty with me. I need to fuck her. And soon. Before I go out of my mind.

So, I guess that's decided then. I'm going in. And if she's not at work, it'll be a recon mission. A chance to gather information.

Ducking around traffic, I head for the impressive glass-fronted building across the road. The warehouse has rustic wooden sides and an awning covered in metal-cast paw prints, wolf skulls, and assorted bones. Looks cool.

Feet planted on the pavement out front, I stare through the window into a massive room dotted with bizarre sculptures and colorful paintings that stand out bright against the white walls. There's a tall silver desk near the entrance, and guess who's standing behind it? Yep. Ivy.

Wiping my palms on my jeans, I take a slow breath to settle my pulse. That's weird. I have no idea why my hands are sweaty. Before I push open the door, I run rough fingers through my hair. I don't know why. It always looks the same. Like a windblown fucking mess.

She looks up as soon as I enter, her eyes flaring wide, pale skin flushing.

"Hey," I say, strolling toward her casually like I stop by her workplace every day.

"Hi." Her pen drops onto a pile of papers. "It's Nico, isn't it?"

"Sure is." Nice one. Pretending she's almost forgotten me. I put my hands on the desk and press my hips against the front surface so I'm close to her.

While I study her features, she flicks a panicky gaze around. Other than a well-dressed elderly couple transfixed by a painting of storm clouds, it's just us in the vast gallery space.

Frowning, she says, "So, what are you doing here?"

"You're even prettier than I remembered." Her silver-gray eyes widen as I lean in and inhale deep. "Man, you smell real good. What is that? Perfume?"

"No it's a herbal shower gel called Fleur de..." She trails off and shakes her head, waves of red hair streaming everywhere.

Shit, she's even got a smattering of pale freckles. Not many. Just enough to make her sweeter. And sexier.

"I'm sure you don't want to know what brand of soap I use."

"You'd be surprised by what I want to know about you." Right now, I'm thinking everything. I want to know it all.

She shuffles papers around but doesn't speak. Maybe she hopes I'll disappear quietly if she just ignores me. That won't be happening anytime soon.

"This is a cool place," I say, gesturing around the room like I own it.

She looks at my mouth, her papers, then back at my mouth again.

"So, how can I get you to talk to me? Or give me one of those hot smiles I remember from the alleyway the other night. You're killing me here with the silent treatment." My voice echoes loudly, bouncing off the walls.

"Shh. Pipe down."

"What for? I'm not saying anything wrong."

"Going on about me killing you! What's that supposed to mean? And what are you doing here anyway?"

"I came to see you. Isn't that obvious?"

"But why?"

"I want to invite you to our gig tonight."

"*Why?*"

"Well, scientific research confirms that if you catch live music regularly, it helps you live longer. So, I'm looking out for your health."

"Really?" Her scrunched up nose suggests she doesn't believe me.

"I've almost got like a photographic memory. Kind of. I remember lots of random facts."

"Mostly useless ones?"

"Yep," I say with pride. And maybe a little embarrassment.

"Nico. Why are you really here?"

I lean closer and lower my voice. "I wanna see you in the crowd, Ivy. I want to look at you while I'm onstage sweating and burning up and imagining what it'd be like to fuck you."

She slaps her palm over her mouth then lets it fall onto the papers. "You're wasting your time," she whispers. "I'm not going to sleep with you. And maybe smut talk from a stranger is something that girls from your generation find irresistible, but I certainly don't."

Huh. "So are you a time traveler from the fifties or you just don't like it when guys shoot straight?"

"No. Honesty is good. But don't expect me to be

impressed with your *cocky-pantie-melter* attitude. It's repulsive."

Okay. She's not playing games or thinking about getting it on with me. I need a different approach.

"Alright. Sorry I misread the situation. It's just I've been reliving our alleyway session, thinking about kissing you, and I hoped that maybe you were into me too. Guess it was just the alcohol turning you on the other night, not me."

Red flushes over her face again. "I don't normally drink."

I stick my hand out for her to shake and give her a wide smile, the one that shows off my dimples. I hate them, but girls are always commenting on my face craters. I'm not ashamed to use them to my advantage.

"Friends, then?" I ask. Something like indigestion burns in my chest while I wait for her to speak.

Finally, she smiles and takes my hand, her eyes popping at the colorful tatts ranging over my arms. "Yes. Friends is a good idea."

I give her hand a quick, firm shake before fisting my own deep in my pocket. "So, *friend*, any of your art on these walls?" I ask, trying to ignore the zap I got from touching her. The one that shot straight to my dick.

"Yep. It's just something little, though."

"Will you show me it?"

"Do I have to?"

"No." I push away from the desk and amble to the nearest wall. "I reckon I can guess." I go straight to the stupidest thing I can find. A painting of the beach. It's pretty good.

Except that all the bathers are wearing clown costumes. "This one yours?"

She laughs. *"No."*

With Ivy at my side, I move along the row of artworks, inspecting them and attempting to make her laugh.

I point at a bronze sculpture of a reclining naked woman. Broad sweeps of smooth, shiny metal make me want to touch, but the black penguin perched on the woman's head is a little off putting. Fucking ridiculous. "How about this? You strike me as the bird watcher type."

Ivy's laugh is louder this time. "If you spent the rest of the day looking, you'd never guess which one it is, Nico."

Fuck, but my name sounds good on her lips. I want to feel it whispered hot in my ear, and then moaned into my mouth.

"Yeah I would. Just watch me find it."

Expression wary, she crosses her arms over her chest, drawing my gaze to her tits.

Damn, she looks hot. The little black dress hugs her body just right. Why did I ever think curvy girls weren't my type? I've never wanted someone in my bed so badly as I do right now.

"So how are things going with Burntbad?"

"Good. We're gigging at least three nights a week at the moment. Our booking agent is getting an east coast tour together for later in the year. Should be lots of sweaty fun." I swap to the opposite wall, quickly examining all the framed work. Rectangles and squares filled with wild splashes of color, jarring textures and tones.

"Can you live off your band earnings?"

I laugh. "No way. I manage a cafe at an organic nursery. That's how I eat and pay rent."

Her mouth drops open. "Do you really?"

"Yeah. The Heaven and Earth garden center. I've worked there since I was a kid. Ever been there?"

"I've heard of the cafe. Mia's had lunch there. She says it's very cool. And you *manage* it?"

I bring the dimples out again. "Yeah. I know it's hard to believe, but my brain works quite well." There's a different look in her eyes now. It's clear she no longer thinks I'm a complete deadbeat. Good. That's progress.

Boots squeaking on the parquet floor, I spin and bend, narrowing my eyes at a painting about the size of my laptop screen in the bottom row.

Half a woman's face appears in a dreamy wash of purple and tangerine watercolors. The girl's dark gaze bores into me in an accusing way. Torn up pieces of black and white photos —legs, arms, and who the fuck knows what else—add texture and unsettle my stomach. There are words written in cursive script where the rest of the girl's face should be.

I squint to decipher the tiny letters. It's a poem about being lost. Not fitting in to the norm. I dig it.

"*This* is yours." I grin over my shoulder at her before turning back and soaking in her painting—collage or what-ever the hell it is.

"Nope," she says, her face once again flushed red.

"You fucking liar." I snort.

She laughs, and then lets out a big sigh.

"It *is* yours. And I bet you're a Diane Arbus fan."

"Yes! I love her work." She looks impressed by my skills of observation. "How could you tell?"

"It's the vibe in this picture. You're into misfits. It's great. I like it a lot."

She rewards my compliment with a genuine smile. Fuck, even her teeth are pretty.

"Well, Kendra, my boss isn't very fond of it. But she has a policy of displaying at least one piece from all the artists who work here, so she has to suck it up. But notice how hidden away mine is?"

"She's jealous for some reason."

I get that smile again. I have a feeling she has no clue how sexy it is.

"So, Nico, how do you know about Diane Arbus?"

"I've got one of her photographs at home."

"Something you cut out of a magazine. Which one?"

"The sad-looking Christmas tree in the living room. And it's not a cut out or a print. It's an original."

Her jaw drops.

"A guy my mom cleaned for, rich dude. He gave it to her. He was a friend of Diane's."

"No way! Oh shit. Wow! Can you bring it in? I'd kill to see it."

"Nope. If you wanna touch it, you'll have to visit my place. It's too precious to take out anywhere." I'm lying. I'd be happy to take it on a three day hike up a mountain. But I'd be even happier to have Ivy inside my pad. Alone. Where she can stop staring at my lips like she's doing now and just fucking touch them already.

"Come and have a drink with me after the gig. Meet the guys. You'll see I'm not so bad. And we'll make a date for you to come and see the Arbus. Maybe even tonight, if you're keen."

"I can't. I'm helping Mia at a wedding. Another time maybe. But, so we're clear, it would just be as a friend."

"Didn't you say she worked here with you? So, is she like a wedding planner or something?"

"Not exactly. I'll show you her art. It might help you understand the full wackiness of what she does."

As we cross the room, the tapping of her heels hypnotizes me—along with the sway of her hips.

We stop in front of a hilarious portrait of a bulldog and a Siamese cat, both dressed in full wedding regalia. The cat sure looks pissed about the frilly veil draped over its sleek white fur.

"So she's an animal photographer," I say.

"Not quite. She's a *pet wedding* photographer."

She laughs at my expression.

"*Real* weddings?"

"Yep. The sumptuous nuptials of the pets of the rich and stupid."

"Fuck me." *Please, Ivy*, I add silently. Anytime she wants, I'll be ready.

The phone at the desk rings out shrilly, and her heels go clack, clack, clack as she rushes to answer it. I watch her play with her hair while she talks.

When she ends the call, I go over and try the dimples again. "Can I ask you something?"

"Of course."

"I need the truth." I take a big breath. "So if you can't give it to me, just say pass. Okay?"

"Well, it depends on the question, but I'll do my best to answer honestly."

"So…" My boot makes squeaking noises as I kick it over the wooden floor. "Do you like me at all?"

Her eyebrows slant upward. "Oh! Sure. You seem like a nice enough guy. Bit full of yourself. But, I think you've got a good sense of humor. So… yes, I'd have to say that I do like you."

That's not what I meant. Is she pretending not to understand?

"But, do you *like* me, Ivy?"

She stares at my mouth as though she's lip reading.

"You haven't thought about kissing me again?"

"No, Nico. You need to give up on that idea. Given the age difference, it would be very inappropriate. And I'm sure there are plenty of girls who'd like to kiss you. I mean look at you."

Now we're getting somewhere.

Pulse pounding, I dip my head close and whisper, "How do I look, Ivy?"

She tries to step away, but I put a gentle hand on the back of her skull. I'm not stopping her from moving, just suggesting she stay put. Stay close so I can feel her tremble. Hear how uneven her breathing is. Smell her skin.

"Start talking. What about how I look?"

Rosy lips parted, she raises her head and meets my gaze. My heart stops beating.

"Oh stop it. You know exactly what you look like. You're beautiful and you know it."

Yes. Finally, she's admitting I affect her in some way. I can't prevent a satisfied smile from spreading slowly. It probably confirms I'm a cocky bastard.

Palms on my chest, she pushes me away. "But that doesn't mean I'm going to sleep with you. I want a serious relationship. Kids someday soon. Not a dirty fuck with a gorgeous man-child. And I hate to think where your dick has been."

What? *Shit.*

So, I'm not only conceited, but I'm also a man-whore. That kinda hurts, so I laugh like she's made a joke to hide the fact that her words make me sad. And she nods like I've just proved every single one of her not-very-nice theories about me.

"This is all a joke to you, isn't it?"

"No! You turn me on, Ivy. What's so wrong with admitting that?"

"You're only out for kicks and thrills. And I think you're loving the challenge of a girl saying no to you. You know what you are?"

I shake my head. I have no fucking idea, but I can't wait to hear.

"You're a waste of my time. I need a guy who's interested in the long haul. I'm looking for a life partner. So stick that up your admittedly attractive, youthful butt. And I also need to get back to work."

"*Jesus*. Sure, I can take a hint." Trying not to look as freaked out as I feel, the life partner thing has scared the shit out of me, I smirk and stroll to the door. "You'll change your mind. I always get what I want." Which I remind myself is just a fuck from her. Or maybe two or three.

The last thing I see before I turn and walk through the door is her lips narrowing tight and maybe... is that smoke coming out of her nostrils?

Great. I've made her angry. I have a feeling this girl is going to enjoy torturing me with what she thinks I'll never have. Her body. I don't care if she's forty-fucking-four years old. I'm not giving up.

And I am definitely going to fuck her.

At *least* three times.

5

IVY

Here's an Old Guy

"**W**as that Nico leaving just now?" asks Mia as she waltzes through the gallery door carrying our lunch. She sets two deli bags on the desktop and drums her fingers next to them, awaiting my answer.

I feign temporary deafness. "Did they have the smoked-salmon bagels? Gimme quick, please. I'm so hungry I might faint."

She plucks away the bag, holding it out of my reach. "Wait a second. I require information first. I'm pretty sure I just passed that hot-singer guy on the street. The one you kissed at the club last week. Did he come in here?"

I snatch my lunch and free it from the bag and its cute little bagel box. Around a massive bite I say, "Is that a bubble skirt you're wearing? It's kooky and gigantic. But it looks really good with your striped tights."

"Flattery won't distract me. Did he come to see you or not?"

"Yes," I reluctantly admit.

She pulls out a tall metal stool and sits next to me. "That boy is totally into you."

"You're dead right about the *boy* part."

"Give it up, Ivy. You're a sexy, interesting, wonderful woman. I'm not surprised he's chasing you. You shouldn't be either."

"He wants a few rounds of hot, dirty sex, that's all."

"Brilliant. Hop to it."

She makes it sound so easy. And fun. Like I'd be crazy not to chase him down and beg for a taste of his body. I'm sure it would be an incredible fantasy come true—while it was happening. It's *after* that I'm worried about. Since kissing him last week, he's invaded my dreams, my every waking thought. Nico pulls at something deep inside, makes me feel things. Scary things.

"You know I'm not great with casual sex. I'd get too attached."

Mia swallows a big mouthful. "Who says he won't too?"

My eyes bug out. "Get attached? Him? To me? No. Impossible."

"Girl, you need therapy. Plenty of guys get partnered up with older women. It's not a big deal these days. Get over it."

She wriggles her eyebrows suggestively. "And then go and climb all over *him*."

"No way. He's too beautiful. Too young. I'd get my heart broken. And what would people think about me walking around in daylight with a guy like that?"

"They'd probably think—lucky Ivy!"

"And he's a musician. In a rock band surrounded by groupies who want to lick him and kiss him and suck him all over."

"Smart girls." She laughs and pushes my shoulder, nearly knocking me out of my seat. "It's clear you've put a lot of thought into the sucking him all over part. And who cares about the competition? Right now, he wants you! Live dangerously before you become so boring and lonely that you end up looking and *feeling* exactly like one of those sad people in your paintings."

I heave a sigh. She's right. I paint misfits and people with tragic tales. Why? To give voice to their stories. So they aren't forgotten. Ignored. Buried. I want to help free them from their painful pasts, not bind myself to my own.

Tears burn behind my eyes. Will I ever get over my childhood? At thirty-four years old—it's about time I grew up.

I need to change the subject because this one's hit a nerve. "How's the copy writing going for the techno-flower show brochure? Kendra reminded me she needs it finished by tomorrow."

"I know. She's such a sadist. And honestly? It's going badly. I just can't seem to—"

The gallery phone rings, cutting her off. I fumble my head

set on. "Mad Wolf Gallery. Ivy speaking."

"Hey, Ivy," says the last person I expect to hear from.

I only saw him ten minutes ago. His voice is deep and seductive and brims with humor. Maybe he's laughing at me.

"It's me, Nico."

"Um… Hi. How are you? Why—"

"I'm calling to check if you've changed your mind about tonight. Maybe you've decided you can't put off seeing my Diane Arbus for one day longer and you're wishing you'd said yes."

I laugh. "Sorry. It's still no. But thanks for checking."

"You won't come even if I promise not to flirt with you? No pressure at all. Just come and hang out."

"I can't. I told you I've got the pet wedding thing with Mia. And if I don't meet a sweet old man with a hauntingly tragic life story tonight, I'm in big trouble."

He chuckles low. "Right. So I really *am* too young. I'd need to be at least fifty to set you on fire, huh?"

I can't help but laugh, too. "It's not like that. I need this guy for artistic purposes. I desperately want an old man to paint for my exhibition, and I'm running out of time."

"Can't you just find the perfect old-dude photo online and paint from that?"

Mia sneaks glances at me while she pretends to search through her bag, and I draw doodles of curved lips framed by perfect dimples. "I know this part sounds strange, but I need to meet the person I paint. Get their story. It becomes part of the work, the poem that I write into or rather onto the canvas."

"Huh. That does sound weird. But at the same time, kinda intriguing. You write the poems, too?"

"Yep. It's not easy to find subjects. I can't just waltz up to someone who's relaxing on a park bench, ask if they're interested in sitting for a portrait, and then be all *'oh, and by the way, I hope you've had some really bad things happen to you and that you're fully prepared to bare your soul to me. See you at two o'clock tomorrow'* kinda thing. I come off as a very mean, crazy lady."

"Fuck, I bet. Does the type of tragedy matter?"

"Nope. Pain is pain. I extract it from them as gently as I can. And I think mostly it's like a counseling session for them. Sharing their stories removes some of the burden. And they always love the poem that I gift them."

I don't owe Nico an explanation. But my work is unusual, and for some reason, I don't want him to think I'm a heartless monster.

"Hm. Well good luck with that, Ivy. Hey, listen, I've gotta race. Talk soon, yeah?"

He hangs up, and I stare down at the sexy half-face I've absentmindedly sketched on the paper. Nico's.

Brushing crumbs off her bright blue skirt, Mia stands. "That guy really *is* stalking you."

"How could you tell I was talking to Nico?"

"By the pretty shade of Cadmium Red your face turned. You're a fool, Ivy. You shouldn't give two shits what people say about you. Because, I promise you, no matter how well-behaved you are. No matter how nice, how good, successful, smart or whatever, people will still bitch about you. It's impossible to please everyone. The only thing you *can* do day to day is what feels right in your heart."

I pretend I'm impressed. "You're so wise."

"I am! The path to happiness is simple—be kind, don't hurt anyone on purpose, and follow your dreams." After taking a few brisk, know-it-all steps toward the office at the back of the gallery, she turns and winks. "And Nico. It would be good to follow him, too. He's sure to bring you some happy times."

"You don't understand—"

"I do. You're not a drunken no-hoper like your mom. You're never going to be like her, Ivy. And anyone who talks shit about you for dating a younger guy is just an asshole. And it's of no consequence what *they* think."

I throw my bagel box in the bin. "But I'd prefer not to give them a reason to talk crap about me in the first place."

"That's impossible. The only person you have any power over in life is yourself. Your thoughts, your actions, your *re*actions. That's it. Be happy and do what *you* want. And let's get real—if you have some fun with that guy, what's the worst thing that can happen?"

"I don't know." I flick my hand at her. "Go away before I tell Kendra you haven't started her precious brochure."

Mia laughs and disappears fast.

Unfortunately, I *do* know the answer to her question. The worst thing that could happen is that I could fall in love with an over-confident, unbelievably hot man-whore.

And there is absolutely no room for heartache in my life. I had more than my fill of it growing up.

6

IVY

Gregor

Sunlight floods my studio, illuminating the beautiful, bright-green eye I've just painted. Frozen in front of my easel, I'm totally mesmerized by Nico's stunning gaze.

I flick drops of Prussian blue over the sharp angle of his cheekbone and wonder why I'm doing this to myself.

It was a terrible idea to turn the sketch I started of him yesterday at the gallery into a painting. Completely stupid. Imagine if he could see me right now. One moment I'm chasing him away and the next I'm like a teenager recreating his likeness on every possible surface, staring longingly at his image.

Fortunately, I've stuck to my usual style and haven't painted his whole face. The messy hair, the dark slash of one eyebrow, half a strong, perfect nose, and a slice of sensual lips are quite enough to drive me crazy. And I've already mentioned the devastating gaze. Arrogance mocks me from the emerald burn of his eye and flutters my stomach.

Why am I torturing myself with something I can never have? Or rather *someone* I shouldn't *let* myself have.

I tilt my easel to an upright angle and drop my brush on the table beside me. The scarred, wooden surface is barely visible through jars of water, old cans crammed with painting tools, photos, and art paper.

This room is a perfect workspace and the main reason I signed the lease on my tiny, two-bedroom apartment. Through huge, arched windows beautiful light streams in. The ceilings are high enough to cover the walls in paintings, sketches, poems, photos. I'm surrounded by junk—pieces of broken ceramics, feathers, and bones that I've collected for their interesting colors and textures. All ideas and inspiration for future paintings.

Sometimes I dream about having a housemate because paying the rent can be painful. But if I had someone to share the financial burden with, then I wouldn't have my studio, because that someone would be sleeping in it.

Anyway, I've lived here for almost two years now and I can't imagine moving. The whole apartment is a beautiful mess. *My* mess. And only three subway stops from work.

My cell rings, startling me out of my daydream. Unknown

caller I.D. I'm reluctant to answer it, but I take a risk and pick up.

"Hello?"

"Ivy Reid?" says a clipped, male voice.

"Yes, that's me."

"My name is Gregor Night. I'm acquainted with Clarissa Gratton-Alperstein. I saw the collage you did of her in the Long Island house. Very dramatic. I'd like to commission a portrait of myself."

"Fantastic, but I must warn you that I'm not cheap." I've found that it's best to mention price early on in the discussion. Some people hang up when they hear the cost.

"Neither am I. We can discuss the fee in person. I'm not easily put off."

That sounds great to me.

"Did Clarissa explain how I work? I'll need an idea of your story before I commit."

"She did." In a proud voice, he says, "Making money is the only thing that brings me happiness." A few beats of silence. "And I'm thirty-six, and I've never been in love."

That's tragic enough for me. "Can you come tomorrow at two?" Rent is due in a fortnight. Maybe I can wrangle a deposit out of him.

"I'll clear my schedule. How should I dress?"

"Your choice. I mostly paint faces anyway. Sometimes I include the torso. I take photographs to work from and often use pieces of your body from those in the collage. I'll text you the address."

"I'm looking forward to it."

"Okay, great. Thank you, Greg."

"Gregor."

"Right. See you tomorrow."

Huh. No please or thank yous from this guy. I'm very interested to meet him. And also a little worried, because he sounds like a bit of a dick.

I'm about to clean up and turn the partly-finished water-color of my current obsession to face the wall so I won't get lost in memories of how Nico's lips tasted, when my phone goes off again. Another number I don't recognize flashes over the screen. Living dangerously, I answer it.

"Ivy. Hey, it's me Nico."

Nico! Shit, this guy is like a dog with a bone. Or maybe a dog with a boner is a more correct analogy. What does he want now?

"How did you get my number?"

"I called the gallery and asked Mia for it."

For the life of me I cannot understand why she would think it's okay to give my cell number to a guy I'm trying to avoid. It doesn't make any sense.

"Hope you don't mind. It's just... I called to find out if you met your tragic-old-guy at the pet wedding last night. And Mia said that you hadn't. When I told her I'd found one for you, she thought we should speak right away."

"You found me a guy to paint?"

"Shit, yeah. He's perfect. He's fifty-five, but he looks about seventy. And he really wants to do it. He can come by the gallery anytime so you can meet him."

"And he's got a sad story to tell me?"

"Oh, man, has he ever. This poor dude lost his first family —childhood sweetheart and two kids—in a car accident. A head on with a truck that took them all out. Fucking bang. Just like that. His whole life over. After his second wife died of cancer, he lost his job, then the house. He moved the two kids they'd had together into his car. They lived like fucking hobos for a year before his luck changed."

"Jeez. That *is* harsh. And he's okay with talking about it?"

"He's excited. He's one of a kind Red Francis. You're gonna love him."

"Red Francis? Sounds like a pirate."

"And he looks exactly like one."

I laugh. "Wow. That's perfect. How did you find him?"

"He does hip-hop dance classes with my mom."

"Your mom takes hip-hop classes? She must be pretty cool." Or a total embarrassment—just like mine is.

"Mom *is* cool. And the class is hilarious. If you're ever feeling down in the dumps, give me a call. I'll take you to watch. Not only do they work it hard, but they're the biggest bunch of comedians. Like—it's so funny—these guys *want* you to laugh at them. Fuck. They should sell tickets."

"You're not embarrassed for her?"

"Why would I be embarrassed? She's having a great time. If you're at work tomorrow, I'll get Francis to swing by."

"That would be amazing. You're a life saver, Nico. But I'll only be at the gallery from ten until one. Tell him to drop by then or call me instead to tee up another time that suits."

"Done. Hey. And good news—we've got another gig with Up Void on Wednesday. You should come. I can introduce

Mia to South. And you can tell me all about your meeting with the pirate."

Since he's gone and found me an old man to paint, it feels wrong to say an outright no. So I give a vague answer instead. "I'll think about it. Could be fun. And thanks again, Nico. I'm so relieved that I might have a new subject to paint. I was getting desperate and about to start hanging out in hospitals or at strangers' funerals and stalking people."

"You're a weird girl, Ivy. That might be why I can't stop thinking about you. See you Wednesday." He hangs up before I can tell him not to count on me attending the gig.

Did he just admit he can't stop thinking about me?

Freak! This guy is hard-core dangerous.

7

NICO

You Came

This should hurt like hell. But it doesn't.

Adrenaline.

Sweat drips into my eyes as I grate my fingers against guitar strings and scream into the mic.

Electricity.

White light courses through my veins.

Rage.

I'm flying. Free falling, down, down.

So. Fucking. Mad.

She didn't come. She didn't fucking come.

Numb.

I power into the mic, knocking my teeth hard against it,

and sing to the crowd. "Raze me. Free me. Lock on hard and use me. Yeah, take. Take. Take. Yeah take me down."

My throat should be shredded, my eardrums exploding from the stupidly dangerous decibels we're blasting tonight. But I don't feel pain. Only anger. It drives me on, moves my hips in hard thrusts, my heart keeping time with the erratic drum beat.

Our drummer, Patch, seems to be pissed at something tonight, too. Fuck knows what. And right now, I don't much care.

"Down. Down. Down. Buried deep. Yeaaah." I growl out the final word of the last song of tonight's set like a dying beast caught in a trap, enraged at where I find myself—stuck —out of control and unwillingly losing my cool over a girl.

Fuck this shit.

I fling my guitar behind me and it swings off the strap, battering my bones. The crowd screams. I crush the mic in my grip one last time. "We've been Burntbad. And you've been great. Goodnight." I swipe at the mic stand, and it clatters across the stage.

A roadie pitches me a towel, and it hits me smack bang in the face. Bet he did that on purpose. Wiping the back of my neck, I kick a speaker as I pass by, and then get off the stage fast.

"Woah. Keep frowning like that and you'll crack your face," says Up Void's singer, South, as I enter the dressing room. "What's up your ass tonight?" He's slumped on a couch looking at me through chunks of gold hair and plucking his guitar. You rarely see the guy without the damn thing.

Linc grabs two beer cans from a massive tub of ice and throws one at Patch. "Careful what you say, South, Nico might cry. He's very sensitive tonight."

"Shut the fuck up. Where's *my* beer?"

"Get your own drink, sulk-boy." Linc winks, grabs Patch by his lip ring and leads him to the back of the room where the rest of Up Void are throwing popcorn, and I hate to think what else, into their manager's mouth. Fucking animals. Dumb manager for acting like their whipping boy.

I rustle through ice and find the pale ale. "Want one?" I ask South over my shoulder.

"Nope. Right about now I've got the perfect pre-show buzz licking through my veins. Don't wanna mess with it. Where's your bass player?"

"Rob? Chucking up his guts, then heading home. He's got a stomach flu." Our bassist may look like Renton from Trainspotting, but he's a stand-up guy. Always reliable. Even if it nearly kills him.

"Stomach flu. Man, that ain't no fun. Hey, sit down. I wanna talk to you 'bout something."

A big Thor-like dude with a Southern accent that pops in and out, South might seem kinda laid back, but he bristles with something dark and intense that warns you not to fuck with him. And I can't recall ever hearing anybody say the word no to him before.

So, not wanting to break with tradition, I obey his

command and flop down on the couch, cracking my drink open.

Smiling, he watches me guzzle half the can. "It's that good, huh?"

"Feels great on my throat."

"Things okay with your band? I'm detecting some bad vibes floating around."

Yeah. I'm causing them with my shitty mood.

"Nope." The icy can soothes as I roll it over my temple. "Just hanging shit on each other like always. Nothing new."

Shrewd gaze assessing my wrecked state, South nods. "Right. That's almost a shame, because I've got a shit-hot idea. Something I've been thinking on a while."

Laughter breaks out across the room. Linc's on the floor, rolling on his belly, doing the worm. He'll be the one puking next.

I thump my sneaker into the polished concrete floor to disperse excess zing from the gig. The floor is covered in graffiti, mostly dicks and tits and other smutty symbols.

It's a weird feeling to be exhausted but still wired, ready to explode into action—all set to fight, fuck—or scream if I can't.

Sleep would probably be my best option, though.

"You still awake?" South asks.

"Barely. Look Burntbad's going fine. Work's fine. I'm just in a shit mood."

He pulls the sleeve of his black t-shirt up, scratching his bicep. I check out his compass tattoo. Underneath the southern arrow it says *Never Lost*. I think of L and his body work, remembering how jealousy drove me to get my first tattoo when I was nineteen. So I could be like Lightning—an ex-street kid prostitute turned rich-as-fuck male model. What the hell had I been thinking?

I make a mental note to pay a visit to L and Edie soon. It's been at least two months since I've seen them.

"You're not listening to me, man."

"Sorry," I say. "Got lost in a beer-buzz fog. What was your idea?"

"In a few months, when the album's finished, we're doing that European tour."

"Yeah, congrats about the album, that's a sweet deal you cooked up. You got the producer you wanted and everything."

"Yeah. I'm fucking stoked. Record label said we can take a couple of our own crew members on the road. Let Burntbad miss the shit out of you, realize what they are without you. Which is nothing. And come roadie for us. The crew are all rock dogs. It'll be easy to pull a band together. You can play music, too. I'll make the promoter give you spots."

"An overseas tour? Me? That's crazy. I've got my job at the cafe, and I can't run out on that."

"It's only three months. No way they won't take you back. Think about it."

"Why me?"

"We're buddies, aren't we? My bandmates like you, too. I reckon you'll fit in real well." He slides power chords up and down the fretboard, then picks a bunch of pretty notes.

I nod at his Hummingbird acoustic. "What's that riff

you're playing? It's awesome."

"Dragon. New song."

I'm about to tell him Up Void had better play it tonight when someone kicks South's boot.

This brave person turns out to be a roadie. He crosses thick arms over a flabby beer gut, flicking long, wiry hair off his face. "Hey, South, man. I know you don't want any girls back here before the show, but there are these two chicks at the door insisting Nico invited them back to meet y'all. The blond in particular is a pain in the butt."

The guy says *particular* like it's two words. *Parrr. Ticular.* And my brain gets stuck on it, rattling the syllables around and around.

South raises his eyebrows at me.

I shrug.

"Tell them they can come back," South says. "But if Nico doesn't know them, they'll need to fuck off quickly. Make sure they understand that part."

The guy nods and scampers away.

Groupies.

"Doubt I know them. All our buddies are hanging at the bar. They know what a cesspit it is back here and—"

"Hi, Nico!" calls a voice from the doorway. It's Mia, bouncing up and down in purple Doc Marten boots, her eyes fixed on South like she's found a freshwater creek in the desert.

Shit. That must mean Ivy's here.

I lurch forward and get tangled in my own fucking legs. South chuckles. Smile nearly breaking my face, I finally make it onto my feet just as the girl I've been thinking about all night bursts out from behind her friend.

"Ivy! I thought you were a no show," I say, inserting myself between her and Mia.

She gives me a sheepish grin. "No, I've been here all along hiding in the back."

She's wearing a multi-colored mid-thigh dress and black fishnet tights that put my dick on immediate high alert. And she's oozing so much hotness I'm amazed I didn't home in on her from all the way up on stage like a randy bloodhound. Despite how stupid I'm sure I look, I cannot wipe the smile off my face.

"So, how are you doing?" I ask, scanning her from head to toe.

"Good. That was a fantastic show, Nico! I loved every second of it. I could even sing along because I've been listening to your E.P. nonstop."

"That's cool. Hey, did you know that Axl Rose's name is an anagram for oral sex?"

South barks out a laugh and Patch yells, "What's an anagram?"

Ivy gives me a *WTF?* kind of smile that she probably reserves for the clinically insane.

Fucking great. I'm spouting nerdy facts again, which makes sense because my palms are sweaty and I'm nervous as hell. I'll need to concentrate hard, so I don't sound like a lunatic. Or an even *bigger* one.

Mia pushes past Ivy and offers South her hand.

"Hi, I'm Mina." She shakes her platinum plaits. "Shit, I

mean Mia."

"South." He stands and she raises wide eyes to his face, still pumping his hand. "Wanna come meet the band?"

Her gaze rakes his body like she'd rather drop to her knees and lick him.

Excessive head nodding commences. "Yep. Yes, please, I'd love that."

"Consider my offer, Nico," South says as he leads Mia away. "Sure didn't think I'd be seeing those dimples of yours tonight. But it seems like your shitty mood's disappeared." He gives Ivy a smirk. "Wonder what fixed it?"

"Yeah, keep wondering," I say, smirking back at him. "And moving as far away as possible, man."

I point at the couch. "You should sit down, Ivy. I've already checked the cushions. Don't seem to be any critters hiding in them. Want a drink?"

"No thanks. I've got an early start tomorrow, so I need to head home kind of now actually."

Damn it. That's bad news. If I can't put my hands on her soon, I'll go insane.

"You're not staying for Up Void?" I ask, trying not to stare at the succulent flesh on display through the punky net stockings.

"No. But nothing could drag Mia away from watching them. And trying to get into South's pants."

Stretching my arms wide, I say through a yawn, "Yeah, I'd love to split too. I'm shattered. But everyone else is up for a big night, so they won't leave for ages. I might walk out with you and find a cab."

"Oh," she says, clearly not liking the idea of leaving in my company. Tough.

"So, shall we head out now?"

With her face flushing red, she stutters, "Oh. Yep. That's fine. Absolutely."

Bullshit. It's possibly the last thing she wants.

"I'll get my stuff. Come and meet my bandmates."

She gapes like I've invited her to hand feed a tank of white pointers, then launches upright. "No. That's okay. I've got to, um… I'll just meet you in the corridor."

"Uh. Okay."

"See you, Mia," she calls out as she hurries through the door like she's being chased, leaving me dazed and confused.

What the fuck just happened?

"Hey, good job, Nico!" yells Linc. "I think she really likes you."

Every dickhead in the room laughs.

Stuffing my shit into my backpack, I ignore them, and then race after Ivy before she disappears into the night forever.

When I push open the door and see her waiting in the hall, relief washes over me, hot and heady. It's just lust. Nothing more. I've never had *feelings* for a girl before, and there's no reason to start developing them now.

I bend to pick up my guitar case and my hand slices through air. Fuck. Must have left it in the dressing room. I hope Linc takes good care of my instrument. No way I'm going back in there and giving Ivy a chance to escape.

"Hey. You ready?" I ask as my gaze roams over her.

"Yes," she answers, feet planted firmly like she's decided she's in no hurry to go anywhere. Guess the bandroom freaked her out. "I wanted to thank you again for setting me up with Francis. What a fantastic guy!"

I step closer, my body sparking with electricity. "I knew you'd like him. Hey, Mia says you live near the gallery. My place isn't that far from yours. It'd be great if you could drop me off."

Okay, so I'm using her gratitude over the Francis introduction to guilt her into driving me home. It's wrong, I know. But I need to spend more time with her.

Her gray eyes narrow, and she scrunches up her bag strap.

"Then you can tell me what went down with Francis." And I'll have time to work on making her hot for me. I'm not imagining the attraction. A strong current buzzes between our bodies. I feel it. I hear it like a soundtrack crackling through the air. But she's pretending to be deaf, dumb, and blind.

Is the age thing really the problem? She's got a young, creative sense about her. The way she dresses, the sparkle in her intelligent eyes. If she's worried about us not being able to connect—that we're too different—well, I'm not really feeling it.

"So, Ivy, does that sound good?"

Ignoring her wary expression and the fact she hasn't agreed to drive me anywhere yet, I take off toward the exit before she can tell me no.

And I hope like hell she's following me.

8

IVY

His Arbus

"Pardon? What did you say?" I ask Nico as my crappy station wagon idles against the curb out front of his apartment block. "I thought you asked if I wanted to come in." My heart beats like a trapped moth against my ribcage, and even though he's shrouded in darkness, I can see his lips twist into a smile.

He remains silent, forcing me to speak again. "Are you suggesting I come up to your apartment? Right now?"

"Man, so many questions!" Smirk growing, he nods. "Yeah, Ivy. That's exactly what I mean. I'm asking you to come up and take a look at my etchings. Well, to be more specific—my Arbus."

Pulse racing, I gaze through the window at Nico's street. Lots of old brownstones. Cars as dumpy as mine parked haphazardly. Bit of a seedy atmosphere, but the streetlights all seem to work. And I don't mind a bit of grunge. In fact, I thrive on it.

I tap my fingers against the steering wheel and weigh my options.

His husky laugh breaks the long silence, and chill bumps erupt over my skin.

"It's a scary idea, I know," he says, voice laced with humor and more than a hint of sin. "But I'm not planning on hassling you into getting down and dirty if you're not into it. I want you to see the photo you're so keen on, that's all."

Vinyl squeaks as he shuffles a little closer. Not too close. Just near enough for me to study the gleam shining in the dark from the gorgeous gemstones he's got stuck on his face. Those big, beautiful, frighteningly *youthful* eyes.

I really do need to see that photo. And I also wouldn't mind kissing him again. *No.* Bad idea. No kissing. But then again, Mia *has* been insisting that I could do with some loosening up. Live a little before I turn into a cranky, old sourpuss. I don't want my life to be completely boring. Maybe I *do* need to experience a little fun now and then. A dash of excitement.

If I can manage to stick to mouth deeds only and perhaps just send my hands on a small adventure roaming around his sculpted arms and chest, that might be acceptable. Then the emotional fallout tomorrow should be minimal.

"Do you live alone?" My voice sounds ridiculous, all high

and breathy like I've just sucked down a balloon full of helium. Must be the full-blown terror that's quaking inside me, the fear of what I might do to him if we're alone and nobody can disturb us or judge me.

"Yeah, I live by myself. Is that so shocking?"

"But how do you afford it?"

"Wait until you see my place. It's pretty small. I work almost full-time hours at the nursery cafe." He shrugs. "So… you know… I'm not a complete pauper. Come on up. I know you can't wait to see my Arbus."

I have to laugh at the way he says the last part, like he knows full well it's really the Arbus in his pants I'm dying to get my hands on.

"Fine, show it to me then."

The green eyes widen. "Okay. Let's go. You can park right here," he says, before leaping out the car like it's about to explode.

On shaking legs, I follow, admiring the hard lines of his body as we mount the stoop.

"Ready for a climb? I'm right at the top, and they must've built this joint before the industrial revolution, so there ain't no elevator." He flicks his head at the six-story brick building looming over us.

"Must be fun carrying band gear up and down those stairs. And also the shopping. And, well, getting anything up there must get tedious when you're tired. Or sick."

"Yeah. Even lugging *myself* up can be challenging after a big night."

When he gets to the main entrance, he digs keys out of his

backpack, opens the door and directs me in. "But I don't mind. Keeps me fit. And I've been hefting heavy shit around since I was a kid at the nursery, so it's no big deal."

As we clamber up three million stairs, me at the rear—or should I say me at *Nico's* rear?—I study the results of his past manual labor. With his tightly muscled butt, strong thighs and broad shoulders, he's a mouthwatering example of a hard-bodied male in his prime. I can't take my eyes off him.

"Are you checking out my butt, Ivy?"

"No!" I lie.

"Huh. Then what's causing all that heavy breathing?"

"General unfitness." Of course, he hasn't puffed once.

"I'm disappointed. Thought you might have been getting turned on scoping me out."

Great. Thanks for making me feel like an old pervert.

"How much farther? These stairs are brutal."

"See that landing? That's me. So approximately six more steps."

"Finally. There was a moment back there where I thought I was going to have to give up."

"Wish you had. Would've been fun to carry you up."

While he opens his apartment door, I huff, and I puff like I'm about to keel over dead. "I thought you said you weren't going to do any flirting if I came up here?"

He laughs and walks inside, gesturing at me to follow. "I never said that. Flirting is fine, isn't it? I do it with everyone. It's friendly. Hassling you to do something you don't want to do is an entirely different matter."

True. He expresses himself well for a kid. And an indie

rocker. Crap. Listen to my prejudiced train of thought. I like to think of myself as open-minded, but clearly, I've been judging this guy way too harshly.

Leaning around me, he flicks switches near the entrance, illuminating his living room and also my erogenous zones.

"Oh, shit," I say when I enter. I'm not sure why I'm surprised. I hadn't expected him to reside in a crack house, but this is extra-civilized. It feels like a home. A place he cares about.

The room is small and cramped, but full of warmth and signs of a life well lived. A couple of mismatched couches face each other. A small black dining table sits under two huge, vertical windows. Copper-strung fairy lights trail around window and door frames. There's a guitar hung on a wall, one leaning against a dining chair. In fact, the more I look, the more guitars I see. They're everywhere. And, bizarrely, there are actually more plants than furniture. I gape at the bamboo palms and hanging baskets. What the heck?

"It's like a jungle in here!"

"You do remember where I've been working for the last six years, don't ya?"

"Oh, of course," I say, feeling like an idiot. "How cool is that stringy thing?"

"It's a Chain of Hearts. I can get you a heap of plants for your place if you want. No charge." He throws his bag into a corner, then asks, "Do you like vodka?"

"Yes, but—"

"Cool. Sit down. Take a load off."

He ambles into the small kitchen, grabs a bottle out of the

freezer, and pours two shots. He throws his own down in one hit, and then hands me a glass.

"I really shouldn't. I have to drive and—"

"Relax. You deserve a rest after surviving the climb up here. Hey, I need a quick shower. Wash the gig off. Won't take long."

I fumble around the couch, looking for somewhere to dump my drink. "But I've got to get home."

Walking away, he shoots his palm backward in a halt signal. "Stay put." He fiddles with his phone and a Bon Iver song wafts out of speakers, warming the room with low-fi indie vibes, jangly guitars and falsetto vocals. "Don't stress, Ivy. I'll bring out my Arbus when I'm all clean. I wouldn't wanna dirty it up. Or you."

The Arbus. Oh, yes, of course. I'd forgotten what I came here for. I can't wait to see it. Excitement fizzes through me.

Clunking sounds come from the bathroom. Water flows. He's left the door open, and I can see a wedge of tiled floor and blue wall from where I sit.

Doesn't he believe in privacy?

And, wait a second—what does he mean about dirtying me up?

My hands scrunch the fabric of my dress. Oh, God. I shouldn't be here. It's not right. I should leave. And I will— just as soon as I've seen his Arbus.

"You okay out there?" His deep voice echoes off the tiles.

I close my eyes, telling myself not to picture what he's doing right now. Naked in the shower. Wet. Soaping up all those muscles, hand gliding over his...

Oh, stop it, Ivy.

Think about reality. When Nico was fifteen, I was twenty-five. When he was twelve, I was twenty-two. Not good. Not good.

But now... now he's twenty-four. A full-grown man. A funny, smart guy who is plenty old enough to make choices. Careful decisions.

The butterflies flying around my belly get a little crazier, heat zinging to my chest, my toes, and everywhere in between.

Please don't let him walk out here in his birthday suit. If he does, I think I'll die from embarrassment. That's a lie. It will be an overdose of lust that finishes me off.

To rein in my imagination, I look around for a distraction. On the couch beside me lies a notebook, loose scraps of paper spilling over the brown cushions. I peek at a page sticking out of the book. Oh, it looks like song lyrics.

I open the cover, smooth mildly shaking fingers over the paper as the water in the bathroom turns off. It *was* a quick shower.

"Is this your lyric book?" I yell.

"Yeah. Probably. I've got 'em everywhere."

"Can I browse?" I say, knowing full well I'm asking too much. It's far too personal a request. As if he'd want me—almost a stranger—to go peeking through his innermost thoughts.

"Yeah, no problem. Go crazy looking at them."

Surely, he jests. I wait a moment, listening to bathroom sounds, cupboard doors opening and closing, but he doesn't take back his approval. Guess he's serious, then. This guy is an open book—literally. And, unlike me, he's not afraid to let someone peek inside. I start flicking pages, my heart beating faster with every line I read.

The sight of his intimate thoughts spread over the page in messy scrawls makes my chest ache, my skin heat. "Do you play any of these with Burntbad or are they just works in progress?"

"Both."

One song that he's drawn a border of leaves and barbed wire around catches my attention. I whisper the lyrics, savoring the feel of them on my tongue and against my teeth.

ACID SOFT.
> *Yeah, you. Always you.*
> *I won't be the one.*
> *To hurt.*
> *To cause you pain.*
> *I won't be the one.*
> *To take.*
> *To break your soul.*
> *Yeah, love. Love.*
> *Coz I'll never know.*
> *Yeah, you. You.*
> *Are you the one?*
> *If I'm lost.*
> *Yeah, lost. Lost.*
> *If I'm dazed and confused.*

It's you.
You.
Love is overrated.
Yeah, but you.
You.
Is this thing fated?
It'll take the dark to ignite.
To light our spark.
Yeah, take.
Take the night to blow this apart.
Apart.
If I'm dazed and confused.
Will you ever see?
Will you ever know?
Me.
And will you let it burn?
Yeah, you. You know you make me burn.
Yeah, you. You know it's always you.
You.

"OH! I LOVE THIS ONE...."

His head ducks around the door frame. "Which one's that?"

"Um, I think it's called Lost."

"Your kinda misery, huh?" He flashes the dimples. It's unfair the way he uses them. But it's probably better that he whips out the cute face dents rather than something way down lower on his overly-attractive body.

Strands of wet hair frame his granite jaw. His biceps flex as he rubs a towel over his head, making a tousled mess of it.

"You know, I only wrote that song today, but I've already got the melody and everything worked out. I reckon it's gonna be a good one."

I believe him.

He struts out of the bathroom, towel now wrapped around his narrow hips, and I nearly choke on my inhalation as his back muscles ripple their way past me, heading toward his bedroom.

I feel hot and lightheaded. Weak-bodied. And way too fascinated by this man. Correction. By this *boy-man*—I remind myself.

Lost. That song packs a punch. It's ruined me, and now I long to crack Nico open and poke around inside his head— his heart. Find out who he is. Get to know him. And that can't be good.

I bite my lip to stop myself asking what the song is about or—more truthfully—*who* it's about. Swallowing questions, I find my phone and snap a photo of the lyrics. They'll look perfect sweeping down one side of that painting I've started of him.

I'm staring at my screen, wondering whether I'll print and paste his words onto the canvas, distress the paper a little, or if I'll rewrite it in black and purple ink in tiny letters, when he clears his throat.

"Shit," I say, glancing up to find him standing right there in front of me. He's wearing ripped jeans and not a stitch more.

"You're light on your feet," I stutter out. I can't stop myself checking out his body. His height, the broad shoulders, and perfect muscles. Those tattoos. The vision before my eyes is my ultimate bad-boy fantasy come to life.

"Sorry. Didn't mean to startle you." He thrusts out a yellow envelope. "Here."

Bouncing in excitement, I squeal like a fool. Then settle back against the cushions. Taking the envelope from his hand carefully, I ask, "The Arbus?"

"Uh-huh."

Gently, I dig inside the packet and pull out a... *what the fruit?* It's a photocopy. "This isn't an original photo! And this whole Diane Arbus thing was nothing but a big, fat manipulation to get me up here so you could attempt to get your rocks off with probably the only female who has ever said no to you before."

He has the nerve to laugh in the face of my anger. "You should see your expression. Fucking hilarious. I was just teasing. The actual photo is on the fridge."

"The *original?*"

"Of course. Come and see."

I stare at the hand he's holding out. No way I'm touching that thing. It's too large, too strong, too *nice*. Too *Nico*.

Stop gawking, Ivy. The night won't last forever. The sooner I move, the quicker I can get out of here.

Smirking, his fingers thread through mine, and he pulls me to my feet and tows me into the kitchen.

"An original Diane Arbus photo is worth a fair bit of

cash." I try to pull my hand away, but his grip is tight. "I'm sure you wouldn't display it in your kitchen."

"I would. See for yourself."

We hold hands in front of the fridge like we're already lovers, our fingers laced together in a perfect fit. As though his hand was made to hold mine. What am I thinking? My brain is defective, carrying on as if it's a foregone conclusion we'll end up in bed together. A hot wave of *yes please* surges through me.

His warm grip remains firm.

"I think you've got something of mine." I stare pointedly at my poor little overwhelmed hand.

"Huh?" Looking down, he makes a grunt of surprise and releases me. "Did you know that holding hands is a great stress reliever? It reduces cortisol levels… apparently."

I wipe my palm on my stockings. "Okay. Good to know."

Arms crossed over his bare chest, he stares at my legs.

I drag my gaze from his furrowed brow, past the bulging biceps—to the photo on the fridge. Then I gasp.

Lips quirking, he tips his chin at the picture. "Take it, Ivy. I know you want to."

Carefully, I remove the silly sombrero magnets from the corners and, cradling the photo like it's a precious newborn, transport it back to the couch.

The cushions dip as he joins me, sitting too close, blasting me with his body heat. He smells divine. Tangy and musky.

It's hard to concentrate on the photo in front of me, which shocks me a little considering how often I've dreamed of this moment. Of holding this very image. Touching it.

Glancing up, I wave distractedly at his chest. "You should probably..." He cocks an eyebrow as I let my words trail off.

"Yes? Continue."

"Um..." I respond.

His smile grows. "Probably...what, Ivy?"

"Put a shirt on?" My words sound like a question—a dumb one.

He doesn't laugh, only blinks at me. "It's okay. I don't need one. I'm pretty hot."

Yes, he is.

I force my gaze back to the Arbus. "Wow. This picture just gets to me. The Christmas tree, how it's way too big for the space. The room is neat and there are presents under the tree. Taken separately each thing you see is fine and normal. It should make for a happy scene. But it doesn't. Instead it's lonely and unsettling."

"Yeah," he agrees. "I like that thing Diane Arbus said about photos. That they're a secret about a secret."

"Yes." I smile at him, wondering where he heard the quote. "I love that one, too."

"She also said that taking pictures is like tiptoeing into the kitchen at night and stealing Oreo cookies. Did you know that pigs hate Oreos?"

"*What?*" I say, through laughter. "You're a very strange boy, Nico. And you're not exactly your average twenty-four-year old, are you?"

He says nothing as his face draws closer to mine, his breathing slightly ragged and a lot intoxicating. When he tucks a chunk of hair behind my ear, my pulse races.

My name is whispered through his bee-stung lips, blending with the soft background music. I let the photo fall to my lap.

Then he speaks, his voice husky. "Ivy. If you could see how you look right now... *man,* I want to kiss you so badly." He takes a deep breath, swallows loudly. "Can I?"

"No," I tell the picture of the sad Christmas tree. "That's not a good idea."

He sighs. "It *is,* Ivy. It's a great idea. Just one kiss. Nothing more, I promise—not unless you beg me for it."

One kiss.

Just a teeny little taste of Nico. A soft press of my mouth against those delicious lips. It would be so simple. So easy. So *right.*

He stares at my mouth, and I stare at his. Then without any conscious thought, I lean in. "Only one kiss. Just one time."

"Okay. Just once," he agrees, his chest rising and falling fast against my palm.

Nervous anticipation makes me shake. I'm freaking out. What was I thinking before? This is wrong, so wrong.

And then... then our lips meet. His breath is warm and tastes of vodka. The world stops, the music, everything but the feel, the sound of our slow kiss disappears. With a sexy groan, his palms frame my face, changing the angle, deepening the fit.

Teasing, his tongue strokes mine. I love the way he kisses —confident and coaxing, the feel of his lip ring—it's perfect. Perfectly devastating.

After a few minutes of floating on a heavenly cloud, our groove changes, his mouth demanding more.

"Fuck, Ivy." One hand cradles my face, the other urges my hip closer like he's going for groin-on-groin contact. I know this because that's what I want too. Pelvis to pelvis action. I've got an urgent itch that needs scratching so badly it hurts. I ache to melt into him.

No. No. No.

I don't want urgent. Urgency leads to clothes coming off, hearts getting broken. He said just one kiss, and I agreed. But *this*—this is quickly becoming just one *hard-and-fast-fuck*, and as much as I want that, I cannot let it happen. Afterward, I'll pine, I'll yearn, I'll obsess over him constantly. Wanting. Wanting. Always wanting him.

Before I know it, I'm up on my feet, pacing back and forth in front of the low coffee table. I want to run out the door. I want to climb on top of him. Which part of me do I let choose —my brain or my heart?

I can't decide. I can't *think*.

Legs spread wide, he drags long fingers through his hair, torturing it with rough tugs. "Ivy, stop. You're giving me whiplash."

I freeze, caught in the ultra-bright beams of his sultry-green gaze.

"Come back here. Just let me kiss you some more. I'll keep it strictly first base. Okay? You don't have to worry."

I finger my copper feather necklace.

Stretched out like a rumpled, ripped god, Nico makes me want much more than first base. I think only a home run with clapping and cheering and an embarrassment of happy tears will satisfy.

My gaze snags on his chest. "What's that tattoo?" I ask. "The words—what do they say?" In amongst the swirls of barbed wire and red drops of blood a tiny verse—like a poem —lies hidden.

One side of his full lips hikes up. "Come and see."

"Can't you just tell me?"

"Nope." His finger crooks invitingly.

Words are my kryptonite, so I inch closer and bend from the waist, peering down. "Your lovely mood lighting is a bit a dim. It's hard to see properly—"

"Better come closer then."

I give him an *I-wasn't-born-yesterday* look.

"Kneel." He says in a take-no-shit voice and, bizarrely, I obey immediately.

He grabs my wrists and places my palms on his thighs. I move one hand to brace my weight on his shoulder, lean in, and squint at the words. "I can't read that. It's written backward!"

Laughing, he unfolds his big body and stands. "Follow me."

Rising too fast, I trip over my own tangled limbs. He interlinks our fingers and drags me into the bathroom.

I hover behind him, my palms melting against slabs of warm back muscles, pressing him closer to the mirror.

Voice ringing out hollow against blue walls, I read the words slowly, carefully. *"Future mine is yours to hold. Future yours is me. If I lived life over, would I find you sooner? Love is death. Death is love."*

Turquoise eyes pin my reflection.

"What on earth does that mean, Nico? Is it like your favorite poem or something?"

The bolt of green narrows. "It's the first tattoo I ever got. I dreamed the words. Woke up one morning with them spinning around my head. I didn't understand it then, still fucking don't. But I knew it was important, that I needed to see it every day. Every chance I got. The mirror seemed a perfect solution."

"That's weird. And a little depressing."

Nodding, he huffs out a laugh. "Yeah. I think you're right."

Oh, how he slays me with his honesty, the shadow of pain that lurks in his eyes. I want to make it disappear. I want to make him happy.

Wrapping my arms around his waist, I sink my cheek into his back. My fingers rest on his washboard stomach and I squeeze hard. "I think you need to add a final line to that tattoo. Something uplifting. A glimmer of hope that happiness—love even— is real and yours to have should you ever decide you want it."

"Uh-huh. Maybe someday I will. Just gotta find a positive spin on the story, I guess."

Torso twisting, he hikes me up onto the bathroom sink and steps between my legs. Then he's kissing me, and I can only dissolve against his heat, the strange words from his tattoo knocking around inside my brain. Like a spell, it's changing me, destroying my fear of this boy who seems so tough but, as it turns out, might be a little vulnerable. Vulnerable enough to make me do something crazy, like let my fears melt away and have hot sex with him all night long.

Yes. I want that more than anything. Who cares what happens tomorrow?

Hands engulf my waist, and I wish his calloused fingers would touch me everywhere—brand me forever.

I press kisses and soft gentle nips over the words on his chest.

"Fuck," he puffs. "Oh, Jesus, don't do that. Ivy. I promised you just a kiss but, *fuck*, I want you so bad."

"Then have me."

"What?" His heart beats harder against my palm.

Smiling, I look up at his pained frown. "Let's up the stakes. How about just one fuck, Nico?"

His jaw drops and he blinks at me.

"But just one time. One night only."

His eyes slide closed for a moment, grip tightening on my hips. "Really? Is it wrong that, right now, I want to... like... thank you about a million times? That's fucked up, isn't it?"

Entwining my fingers behind his neck, I laugh and bring his head down, and suddenly all bets are off as to who's running this show. Our mouths attack, teeth knocking, harsh breaths heating fever-chilled skin.

He pulls my butt to the edge of the sink and assaults the zip on the back of my dress. "Fuck, it won't... hang on. Got it." He peels stretchy material over my head. I try to help, our limbs raveling together.

The dress sails overhead, landing in a sag on gray tiles.

He steps back. "Oh, fuck. Fuck. Look at you. Those stockings..." Grimacing, he palms the front of his jeans, then tears fingers through his hair. "I'm sorry. I can't stop saying the word fuck. And I think I'm gonna lose it any second just from looking at you. You must think I'm an—"

"Have you got a condom in your pocket?"

He pats his jeans and nods.

The cabinet surface feels slippery under my skin as I wiggle my fishnets down to knee level.

"Fuck, Ivy," he groans, tugging on his hair again. "Oh, man. I said it again. But, fuck, if you could only see what you look like, you'd get why I don't make sense anymore."

I smile down at my black and red bra, the matching panties, and my punk-girl stockings. At this moment, I look like some kind of cam-girl, all ready for a guy to get jacking to. His eyes roam my body, erection straining against denim.

"What are your hands clenching like that for?" I tease. "You want to touch these fishnets, don't you?"

He nods.

"Well, what are you waiting for?"

"If I come near you while you're wearing those, if I touch you, my control will be shot."

"You've got that condom ready, haven't you? So just come here and lose control. It's what I want."

Grinning, he stalks forward. "*Come* being the operative word in that sentence." He brings his smooth, rippling muscles, his broad shoulders, heaving chest, and intense frown up close.

I kiss him exactly the way I've been dreaming about ever since the night in the alley. Deep. Wet. Hot. And he pants into my mouth, his hands trailing over my thighs, my breasts.

Biting his lip, he watches as I undo his jeans' button, then unzip him. I delve into his back pocket and retrieve the rubber. With the packet between my teeth, I use both hands to stroke his dick and massage his balls through the soft cotton of his boxers. He's so hard. And long. And panting like he's dying.

I free his cock, marveling at the silky feel, the slickness of pre-cum.

He frowns harder. "Ivy… I can't…"

"I know. I can tell. You're shaking like a leaf."

The foil tears easily between my teeth. I roll the condom on slowly, making his breath shudder, his eyes roll back. Using his dick like a handle, I tug him forward.

He rubs his shaft against my core, softly, gently as violent shivers wrack over him. "Shit. You're soaking." Through the wet material, his thumb strokes over my folds. Now I'm shaking, too. Plush lips kiss me wetly. Hotly.

He whispers in my ear, "Hold tight, because I'm gonna pick you up and take you to bed. Then you can get these off." A calloused finger catches the netting. "And you'll be more comfortable."

"No," I say. "Do it now. Exactly like this."

"Okay." A massive breath shuddering out, he pulls my panties aside, and pushes in with one hard thrust. His loud groan indicates massive relief—a long battle fought, now over. My bra straps come down with two swift tugs as he thrusts his hips slowly, hands roving between my breasts and where we're joined. The intensity of his gaze sears, burning my skin, setting my heart on fire.

"Nico."

"Fuck, Ivy," he says, moaning and biting back a laugh after he hears himself use the f-word again.

This is the best sex of my life. I have never felt anything like it. The way he fills me, his hard, and dare I say it, *young* body moving in a musician's rhythm—an exquisite rock and roll—that I'd love to dance to forever. It's everything I dreamed it would be. The pulse, the beat, the flame that will consume me.

Heat coils deep in my belly, spreading to my toes, my fingertips. Movements no longer smooth, he hooks an arm through my bent knee, opening me to his hungry gaze.

"I'm sorry... this is..." Letting his words trail off, he puts his mouth to better use, sucking on my tongue.

What is he apologizing for? It's getting rough. And all I want is more. More. More.

His fingers press and pull, urging me closer with each thrust. Teeth scrape. He fists my hair to keep me staked, so he can pump harder, take more, get off.

Harsh breaths pant out through his parted lips, animal grunts. I moan, writhing under his touch, my whole world narrowed down to the fast pound of his hips into mine. God, his cock is perfect. So good. So good. So good.

I grip his forearms tightly. "Oh... no. I'm going to—"

"Fuck, Ivy, do it." His thumb glides over my clit. "Come. Come hard for me."

And with a loud cry, I do. I come violently, splintering apart. My inner muscles clench and release, making me pant and Nico push deep, hips motionless while he shudders. "Fuck." And trembles. "Fuck... sorry," he grunts, then makes a gut-wrenching groan as he comes.

Laughing, I lean back against the mirror while he throbs and pulses inside me.

He laughs, too. "Okay. What's so funny?"

I swipe hair off the sharp edge of his cheekbone. "What were you apologizing for?"

"For sounding like a moron with the constant fuck-stream that was coming out my mouth."

I kiss his dimple, the other one, too, then suck gently on his lower lip. "I liked what you said."

A huge grin spreads over his face. Flinching, he withdraws, removes the condom and throws it in the trash. Then he lifts me off the edge of the basin, prompting me to wrap my legs around his waist.

"Ouch," I say as he walks us out of the bathroom. "I'll have some interesting bruises tomorrow."

"Shit, sorry. Call me and I'll come and kiss them better for you. If you want."

"I'll be fine. A twinge of pain will be a welcome memory of the bliss I just experienced. I'll enjoy it. Where are we going, anyway?"

The living room is a blur of fairy lights as we pass through it, heading for the door at the other end. He opens it. "Back to my lair. Bliss did you say?"

I nod as he dumps me on his bed, wriggling up onto my

elbows so I can check out his room. More music equipment. Numerous note pads. A window. Small desk covered in crap. Old album covers and concert tickets plaster the walls. It's blue and black and messy.

Hands on his hips, he glances around at his stuff too, then says, "Yeah. I know it looks like a bomb went off. Sorry—"

"Stop apologizing!"

"I don't normally ask for constant forgiveness from girls, just from you for some reason."

Chest warming, I smile at him. "I should get dressed and make my way home."

"No! Don't go. Shit, not yet. Give me a chance to act like a man instead of a dick-brained teenager. I can do a lot better than what happened back in that bathroom." He flicks his thumb in the direction of our steamy encounter.

"I have no complaints. When I mentioned the word bliss before, I wasn't exaggerating."

He crawls over me. "You'll stay a while longer?"

"If you kiss me again, I just might."

When his lips touch mine, any notion of leaving disintegrates—along with my *one-fuck-only* vow. Surely I meant *one-night-only*, and if that's the case, I plan to stay right until the end, until dawn's light tinges the sky.

Heart-pain tomorrow be damned.

9

IVY

Gallery Rescue

"Will you answer your frigging cell?" says Mia. "What sort of a ringtone is that anyhow? It's been whistling like a darn prairie kettle all morning, making me think about drinking tea." She pretends to gag. "Yuck. I hate that stuff."

"Sorry. It's supposed to be the sci-fi sound. I'll just put it on silent."

She throws a withering look and a cardboard box at me. "If it's Nico again, please just call him back. What's the big deal in finding out what he wants?"

"You know I can't encourage him, and we're under too

much pressure today. I haven't got time to chat to hot, young stud muffins."

Snip. Snip. Snip go her scissors over the mountain of packaging piled around her. "Do it or I'll phone him myself. Even if you call and tell him you're too busy to talk, at least you'll have returned one of his five hundred calls. You said having melt-your-brain sex with him last week wouldn't prevent you from being his friend. Well, I'm here to advise you that you're acting *very* unfriendly. So are you a liar or just a fool?"

Definitely a fool. Dammit.

"Have I mentioned how much I dislike the face you make when you're right. It's incredibly annoying."

Mia crosses her eyes at me.

The texts Nico's been sending—one per day since I made the mistake of sleeping with him—are hardly stalkerish. More like friendly and weird.

I might have memorized them.

On Thursday I got: *Hey Ivy. I'm thinking too much about last night and I'm getting all the coffee orders wrong. Wanna catch up again soon? X.*

I pretended I never received it.

The next day: *Thank fuck it's Friday. Did ya know Norse Goddess, Freya, rides a chariot pulled by two cats? I'm wondering if the cats were married. Ask Mia, bet she knows. Frowning cat emojis. X.*

Then Saturday: *How fucked up is this? Leo Fender, the guy who invented the Stratocaster, couldn't play guitar. Flame emoji. X.*

Sunday: *Got a gig. Wanna come? Guitar emoji. X.*

By that point, he probably thought I'd lost my phone.

But no, it turns out he's an optimist, because on Monday his text read: *Scientific fact. Movies or sex help beat Monday blues. Netflix ain't doing it for me. Wanna come over? Three prayer hands emojis. X.*

Tuesday: *Apparently, climate change means less redheads will be born. And, also, redheaded women have more sex than blonds etc. Can you confirm if this is true? Five love heart emojis. X.*

Wednesday: *Ivy? Are you mad at me?*

Today, he's abandoned texts entirely and called three times without leaving a message.

I can't handle being rude anymore. It goes against my nature. Mia's right, I need to speak to him. Flopping on the floor against a wall, I pull out my cell, take a deep breath, and press return-call.

"Ivy! Hey! You've finally stopped ignoring me."

My heart sinks. Why does he sound so happy? I'd prefer cool indifference. Then it would be easier to give him the brushoff. "Hiya, Nico. This is just a quickie to apologize for not getting back to you sooner. Work is so stupid busy at the moment that I really can't talk. We're in the middle of an emergency."

"Sounds like a drag. What's going on?"

"Mia and I forgot to book the hangers for an exhibition that's unfortunately opening tomorrow night. Before we leave, we need to get a truckload of artwork on the walls, including some pieces I don't think we'll be able to lift. So it's looking like an overnighter."

"Have you got help coming?"

"We're waiting to hear back from some friends but—"

"I'll be right over. I'll bring extra muscles."

"Aren't you working at the cafe today?"

"Yeah, but that's okay. I'm kinda like the boss. Someone will cover for me. It's cool."

"No, Nico, please don't do that. It's way too much to ask. Just because we've—"

"Don't worry about it. And you didn't ask. I'm offering."

"Yes, please, Nico. Do it. Do it!" yells Mia, her voice clearly audible to the boy whose soft chuckle vibrates against my ear. "Come as fast as you can and rescue us from this hell," she continues.

My penetrating glare does nothing to silence her.

He laughs and says, "On my way."

Grumbling, I get to my feet.

"Where are you running off to?" Mia's brow furrows as I stomp past.

"I don't appreciate that damsel in distress crap you pulled on him. It's manipulative. And I haven't seen him since... since we... so I'm off to the bathroom in case I have to vomit from nerves."

"Don't forget to reapply your lipstick when you're done," she says, unloading a trolley-full of paintings. "That dark crimson color suits you. It's very 1920's silver-screen-goddess."

"Don't *you* forget to staple your lips together while I'm gone. The metal accents your platinum hair perfectly. It's very Lost-in-Space bimbo."

"Done. As long as you don't forget to—"

"Oh, shut up!" I yell, the door thudding closed behind me and cutting her off.

Thirty minutes later, I turn my freshly applied crimson-goddess lips toward Nico and South as they stride through the gallery entrance, bad-boy boots clomping a hard beat over the floor. Mia gasps beside me, our ovaries simultaneously exploding with joy as a double shot of heady testosterone radiates toward us.

They're twin sex-gods clad in worn denim, tight t-shirts, and badass ink—South golden, Nico a little darker-haired, skin paler, his translucent gaze fixed on me, intense and mesmerizing.

"Look who he's brought along," Mia whispers, nearly breaking my wrist in her tight grip. "I think I might faint."

"Let go. You're too obvious. As if South hasn't got a big enough ego," I growl out the corner of a grimace and shake free.

When he reaches us, Nico plants his feet wide and stretches his arms out like a ringmaster. "Well, here we are. Yours to command, ladies."

Oh my piping-hot hell. I know exactly what I'd like to order him to do—in the darkness of the back office. Or over another bathroom sink. My body thrills to his presence, heating and softening internally while my skin tightens against his effect, resisting the spell of his vivid gaze.

"Thank you so much for coming guys," I say, trying not to squirm under his detailed inspection of my body. Maybe I look like mutton dressed as lamb in my jeans and tight, ripped t-shirt.

"It's no problem." South smiles, hands going to his lean hips. "This is what we do. Fucking lug shit around night and day. It's a musician thing."

I pat his shoulder, not missing Nico's scowl as I do so. "You might regret showing up here in a few hours' time when your limbs are shaking. Hanging paintings is a unique torture."

"Hi, South," Mia sighs. "Oh, did I say that already? I feel like I did."

"No. Don't think so," South says. "Hi Mia. How's things aside from the clusterfuck of a day you're having?"

Seemingly lost for words, she giggles.

"How about we get on with it?" I flick my head at the large work table located in the center of the room and guide them toward it.

I spread out papers, point at diagrams, color codes, trolleys, hanging tools, and boxes of paintings. My nerves tingle and buzz each time Nico's elbow, arm—or God help me—hip, brushes my skin.

Mia cannot stop simpering at South, so I pair them off to get things organized before the heavy lifting commences, hoping proximity will desensitize her to him and she'll get over it. Or he'll get his brawny body over *hers* and she'll be satisfied with having him—even if only briefly.

I'm unsure if an attempt at matchmaking is wise, because a dangerous energy emanates from the guy. A couple of years younger than Nico, in addition to the swagger, something hard and uncompromising burns in his eyes.

"What's his story?" I ask Nico.

He shrugs a shoulder. "He won't talk about it. Something bad."

"Should I warn Mia?"

Nico shakes his head, sun-streaked sandy locks falling over his face. "Nah. He probably thinks she's too good for him. He won't go near her."

Okay, then.

My pulse accelerates as Nico steps close. "I'm not that clueless. I *know* you're another universe away from the girls I usually hang out with. And definitely better than I deserve. But that's not enough to keep me away, Ivy."

The sensual curve of his lips lures me forward a little as his dimples begin to form.

Forcing an expression that's the opposite of what I feel— hard and cold—I say, "Are you here to help or harass? I understand sporting a constant boner must be a hardship, but you're not that long out of school, so try and think of me as a favorite teacher. We're on friendly terms, but I'm out of bounds. Okay?"

A stony mask falls over his chiseled features but does nothing to dampen the fire, the anger, in his eyes. "That's not a deterrent. A red flag to a damn bull is what *that* is."

A very horny bull going by the inviting bulge growing against soft denim. I turn away and pretend to peruse the real task at hand before I do something I'll forever regret.

There's only silence behind me. Then warmth as large

hands engulf my arms, searing my skin. He whispers a kiss against my cheek and my heart stutters, contracts, races.

"Truce, okay?" Before I can lean back into his heat, he steps away, lips quirked in a cocky smile. "Tell me what to do."

Oh, boy. I'd like to tell him to… to go home!

No. No. It'd be better if he pinned me against the wall with his sublime, hard dick and kept me immobile until—

"Ivy?"

"Yes?" I squeak.

"Let's get this done." His hands crack together, echoing in the cavernous space, and startling me into action.

"Good idea. Follow me, boy."

Why did I use a dominatrix's voice? Those exact words?

I cut my gaze over my shoulder, wondering if he's pissed. Of course not—his grin spreads ear to ear.

Approximately five and a half hours later, we're nearly done, and I'm ready to be carried out on a stretcher and transported directly to a nursing home.

"Here, Ivy," says Nico, pitching me a beer from the carton he's just cracked open. "Come and rest for a minute. You look wrecked."

Wonderful. I think by wrecked he means—old and haggard. Exactly the look I was going for. *Not.*

Twin beams of fluorescent green track my progress as I trudge over and join the tired trio. They're hunkered over corn chips and dips in the middle of the gallery floor, stuffing their faces.

Limbs aching, I collapse down between South and Nico

and peruse the finished product. The room looks incredible. Between the four of us, we've hung a group exhibition by five up-and-coming painters. It's called Techno-flora, and the flowers look like sexual organs, garishly sensual, mixed with steampunk-style machinery. Surrounded by an excess of dick symbols and dew-laden folds, no wonder I broke out in a sweat every time Nico's gaze smoldered into mine.

"Ivy, could you please pass over one of them beers?" South is weirdly polite for a partial alpha-hole. Must be the Southern upbringing. As he stretches out his arm, Mia leaps up and rushes for the box.

"I'll get it, South." She flutters her lashes at his bright blue peepers, and I smirk at Nico.

Condensation drips down the bottle, mirroring my inner state, as Mia passes South the drink.

"Anything else I can help you with?" she asks, pressing on his denim-clad thigh.

Everyone, including the hot rocker himself, knows what she'd like to give him a hand with. And I can't blame her for persisting. He's wickedly handsome with an overconfident swagger that should shout *jerk* loud and clear, but unfortunately only adds to his appeal. But there's an aloofness, a ruthlessness in his gaze, that chills my blood a little.

He grins slowly. "Nah. I'm good."

Mia's puffy smile deflates. No matter her tactics, she can't seem to spike his interest. Yes, he'll make a joke, laugh with her, but he won't act on the signals she's giving out. Maybe he already has someone in his life and he's the faithful type. Seems unlikely, but miracles do happen.

"South?" Mia asks.

He grunts in reply.

"When I hear your band's name—Up Void—it makes me think of the word *avoid*."

"Good pick up," he says. "It's a play on both *avoid* and the opposite meaning of my name. We liked the sound of Up Void better than North Void so that's what we went with."

"What are you trying to avoid, South?" I say. "Or should the question be, *who* are you trying to avoid?"

He huffs a laugh. "Everyone." Then he gulps beer and wipes his plush mouth, checking out the art-filled walls. "This artwork's kinda hot."

I sigh as Mia's eyes widen and she shifts a little closer to him.

Nico, bless him, distracts her with a question. "So do you attend many cat weddings, Mia?"

Spluttering out beer, South says, "Cat weddings? What?"

"You bet your sweet ass I do. Heaps and heaps of them. And dog weddings too! Not only are they immense fun, but they're quite a lucrative way to support my own artistic endeavors."

South gazes at her in awe. Maybe he thinks she's loaded and that's piqued his interest.

"Last week I got flown to Santorini for an elaborate celebration. It was very charming. The groom wore a top hat and glasses. The blushing bride had the most delicately stunning rosebuds woven into her veil. Well, until she chewed them into pink mush."

"Shit. I really love videos of cats doing funny things,"

South says, all signs of alpha-holism gone. He looks adorably sweet at the moment.

"Cat weddings aren't funny!" Mia scowls.

"Fuck, yeah they are. Maybe you should take me to one someday. Wait until you hear how much I laugh." His cell pings. "Hey, I've gotta split. The guys are waiting at the studio."

South rises, punches Nico's shoulder, then strides to the workbench, dropping tools from his back pockets over its surface. He wipes his hands on his jeans. "Catch you next Friday for a-few-too-many drinks, Nico." He chin tips Mia and I. "Y'all be good now."

I thank him profusely for saving us, but Mia is speechless and stares longingly at his back as he saunters out through the door.

When the door clunks shut, she says, "That guy makes me want to be the opposite of good. There's something about what happens to his eyebrows when he frowns. The shape they make. It's very attractive."

Poor Mia. She's totally infatuated, obsessing over someone's eyebrows. My gaze zips to the dark slashes framing Nico's emerald gems, and I know exactly how she feels.

"I can't stop picturing him up on stage." Mia fans her chest. "One day soon that band will be massive. I'm talking world domination."

I'm sure she's right.

"I think you should give up trying to do *anything* with him, Mia." Nico leans back on his palms "He's got issues for days."

"I could help thin them out a little," she says around a sloppy mouthful of olive dip.

"Doubt that. But, hey, don't be sad. If he doesn't wanna fuck you, it's probably because he likes you."

"*What?*" Mia and I say.

"He doesn't do girlfriends. Or get it on with girls that are potential friends. Doesn't want anyone who might latch on."

"Right," says, Mia, tightening her pigtails. "That's strange. And also good to know."

I give her a sympathetic smile. "I was wondering if maybe he's got a fetish for girls who are the polar opposite of you, Mia. Like investment bankers with black, curly hair who wear power suits and strut around all day in diamond-encrusted stilettos."

Nico laughs. "I don't think he has a type. He's not all that fussy if he thinks he's never going to see the girl again."

"I might have to make myself unlikeable, then."

"Mia! Please don't lower yourself."

With a sickly-sweet smile, she says, "Do *you* do girl-friends, Nico?"

As I pick a loose thread off my top, his intent gaze rasps my skin raw. "Not usually. But I could make an exception for the right older woman."

The right woman! Hang on... I must be hearing things. It sounded like he said *older* woman.

"Oh?" says Mia. "You're into cougars, then. It's your thing, is it?"

"Not as a rule. But—"

"Right!" I say too loudly, leaping to my throbbing feet before Nico can elaborate.

Mia stands to attention, excitement burning in her amber eyes. "Nico, tell us more about—"

I dig an elbow into her ribs. "We'd better lock up and then go home and pass out," I stammer. "We need to be back early in the morning. There's still lots to organize."

The gallery keys jangle as I pluck them from my bag.

"I'm starving," Nico says, rubbing his stomach, the black t-shirt hiking up to reveal layers of deeply cut muscles. "Wanna come grab some dinner?" He scratches his ribs, flicking a hopeful, bright-green gaze between Mia and me.

I glare at his stomach and whisper "no, no, no," a ball of heat unfurling deep in my own belly.

"Do you know that super-cool mariachi restaurant only a block down the way? Let's go there. If we're lucky, we might even get serenaded."

"Sincere apologies, but I'm out." Mia sends a sly wink in my direction. "Thanks for lending us your big, sexy muscles, Nico. Goodnight guys." Then she rushes through the door before I can get a word out, leaving me alone with the *boy*.

The boy I want to squeeze. Bite. Lick all over and use his body as if the world is ending and it's my last chance to feel pleasure before I die.

Hip digging into the front desk, he bites his lip. "Well? Are you gonna come? My treat. You're kinda looking at me like you're really hungry. So, I probably should mention that I'm on the menu, too, if you're interested. Think of me as like… the house special tonight."

A sigh gusts through my lips, the sound harsh and resigned to my fate.

Mia, the deserter, is in big trouble. How dare she leave me and my raging libido alone with Nico.

Doesn't she know how tempting he is?

10

IVY

The Mariachis

I've decided I don't like boys who are funny and kind and overconfident. They think every girl is a sure thing, that any woman they fancy is theirs for the taking—no questions asked. They make our insides hot and gooey with the blow-torch power of their eyes alone. Make us fuzzy headed. Turn us stupid.

I know this because it's precisely how I feel right now sitting opposite Nico. The intensity of his gaze softens my resolve to be sensible and act my age, while his deep voice lulls me into a trance.

As we eat, I spin one question through my head on repeat —*what would be the harm in going one more round with him?* Just for fun. I've had so few skin-on-skin experiences with attractive guys in recent years, I deserve one more soul-blasting orgasm, don't I?

The festive Mexican restaurant must be to blame for my dangerous mood, because I can hardly believe I'm considering consorting with this gorgeous young man again. The crazy color scheme—bright greens, oranges, and reds—are sparking my desires, both artistic and carnal.

I drag my gaze from Nico's and take in our surroundings. The lovely clutter, tantalizing smells. The noisy chatter of happy diners, struggling to hear each other over the live mariachi band.

Images swirl through my mind, and I want to splash them over canvas. My fingers draw patterns over my thighs, itching for a paint brush to hold. Or maybe a guy like Nico to keep them busy instead.

"You seem to be having trouble finishing your dinner. Let me help you out," says the scruffy, inked-up temptation currently driving me nuts as he leans over the table and scoops nachos from my plate. Around a huge mouthful, he continues, "Man, that's delicious. And those chilies! So damn hot I can hardly eat it."

Laughing, I splutter out margarita. "That's exactly how you ordered it—super-hot! And you haven't had any trouble at all eating your meal. *Or mine.*"

Shoulders pressing into the booth, he stretches an arm along the top and lounges back. "So tell me about your last boyfriend. Or husband. You ever been married?"

"No. Although I have attended quite a few weddings—cats and dogs especially—I've never had one of my own."

Salt gets licked from the edge of his margarita glass and I try not to picture what else his tongue is good at. "Had a boyfriend lately?"

"I've been on a few dates, but no one has stuck. The last steady guy I had was back in college. So that was *ages* ago. I guess I'm picky." *Or just old and unappealing.* "And you? Do you have a special girl that you should have told me about before we... before I let you—"

"Inside you?"

My heart rate rockets. Why does he say things like that? He's so brazen. If I were honest, I'd admit that his directness—as scary as it is—is a big part of his appeal.

"Don't really need a girlfriend with the band thing. Plenty of chicks hit up musicians. Some of them get started talking about the love thing—try to suck some sort of commitment out of my dead soul. But I shut that shit down fast. I don't believe in it."

An image of the inky letters on his chest that proclaim—*Love is death. Death is love*—swirl around my mind, hollowing out my chest. It's a sad stance for one so young to take. I feel sorry for him.

"Why so anti-love?"

"My whole life I've watched my mom waste away over my prick of a dad. When I was small, the selfish bastard left her alone in a country where she could barely speak the language. She worked three back-breaking cleaning jobs to feed us. No friends. No money. Just a bratty toddler to take care of. And still she cries over him. Why? If that's love, I don't want anything to do with it."

"She's from Hungary, right?" I ask before bringing the glass to my lips. Tartness washes over my tongue as I sip. "Do you speak the language?"

"A little, but not much. Mom was desperate to fit in, so we mostly spoke English."

"Can you say something in Hungarian?"

"Sure. Let me think…" He rubs his thumb over the glass, narrowed, fiery gaze roaming my face. No matter how much I want to, I can't look away.

"Nagyon szép a mosolyod," he says slowly, sexy accent creating bumps over my skin.

"Nice!" I school my features into a polite mask, hopefully hiding my burning need to close the distance between us and devour his succulent bottom lip. "So, what does that mean?"

"I told you that you have a beautiful smile. I *think*. Maybe I fucked it up and complimented your teeth instead. But I like them, too, so it's okay."

Laughing, I throw a corn chip at his t-shirt. "And your dad went back to Hungary when he left your mom?"

He bites that plush lip, drawing my gaze there again, and stirs the salsa with a chip. "No. He's German. He was like this dumb third-rate actor who ran away to America to follow his dream. Instead of chasing fame and fortune, he ended up just following his dick. Worst decision he made was to swing by my mom's town before he left for the U.S. and then drag her with him."

The German-Hungarian genes certainly mix well, I

muse, contemplating his face—the perfect slashes and curves of bone under smooth skin, the slightly-slanted bedroom eyes full of sinful intent. Those lips I want to suck like candy.

"What's your last name?" I ask. "Something long and hard to pronounce, no doubt."

"You mean you haven't stalked me online yet?"

I might have looked at the odd picture, but I refused to actually read any details about him.

"Nope, I haven't. So is it, Schweinsteiger?"

"Close." He grins. "Wolff."

"No way! Nico *Wolff*. It definitely sounds German, which *means* that you haven't ditched your dad's name. That surprises me since you seem to dislike him so much. But you know what I'm thinking? If he hadn't swept your mom off her feet, you wouldn't be sitting here right now. So you could at least be grateful to him for your existence. I bet your mom is."

"Well, I don't know about that. But I am glad to be here with you tonight. I haven't stopped thinking about you, Ivy. Replaying that night. And if I go anywhere near a sink, bam —instant hard-on."

I strain my eyeballs to keep my gaze raised and not bouncing over his muscular arms and chest.

Leaning closer, he rests his chin on a palm. "Your turn to tell me about your family."

Shit. I attempt distraction by pointing at the band roving two tables over. "Look at that guy playing an accordion. You don't see them around much these days."

"That's true. Weird Al Yankovic got his first accordion when he was seven. You were saying about your folks?"

"How do you know all these weird facts? I assumed the ones you texted me you'd just Googled, but they also pour out of your mouth rather frequently, too."

He smirks. "Ah, you mean those texts you've been ignoring?"

My face flushes hot, no doubt, turning redder than the salsa on my plate.

His laugh is teasing. "Don't worry, Ivy. I know you want me. You won't be able to fight this forever." He lets that comment sink in while he takes a drink, throat muscles rippling attractively. His glass clunks on the table. "I've always remembered useless bits of information. Guess I'm talented. Wait until you see my impressions. I'm great at taking people off."

"And so humble, too."

The hair falling in his eyes as he folds his arms on the table and tilts his head looks adorable. I twine my hands in my lap, so I don't reach out and touch him. "You were going to tell me about your folks."

My jaw muscles tighten. "What's to tell? Mom is an embarrassing alcoholic. End of story."

"Is that how come you're so worried about what other people think of you?"

How old is this guy again? He's more insightful than any of the men my own age I've dated recently. And that only makes me more afraid of him.

"Probably. You might have developed fear of judgment

too if your mother volunteered to help on prom night, executed her duties fairly well until the contents of her hip flask kicked in, and then finished the night humping the science teacher in the lab with half the school looking on. The worst thing is she always means well, and I know she loves me, so I can't even hate her properly. She's just a mess."

"Fuck," he says, his eyebrows arched high.

"Anyway, that basically sums my mom up. I've got a sister who disappeared with her drug crowd five years ago."

His mouth gapes open, and I can see the questions forming.

"That's a long story for another time. And Dad started a new family when I was five. I haven't seen him or my step-brother going on four years now. He's a big guy in the finance world. Mom and I don't fit into his picture of a perfect life."

"So, we've both got douchebag fathers."

I nod. "Sadly."

"Why does your mom drink?"

Before I can answer, the mariachi swoop down. Five guys hover over us, voices soaring in joyful harmony as their fingers fly over guitars, violins, and a deep bodied instrument that Nico can't take his eyes off. The song builds to a ridiculously rousing climax, resolving with a round of loud yelping and foot stomping.

Nico and I clap until our hands are numb.

One of the guitarists leans in, foot resting on the seat next to Nico's thigh. "Your girl?" he asks, flicking his well-oiled head at me.

Nico nods, causing a little chipmunk squeak to chirp out my mouth.

I am *not* his girl. I'm not his anything.

"That insane guitar you've got there has an awesome brassy sound. And, man, there aren't any frets! What's it called?"

"A guitarrón. You play music, senor?"

"Yeah. But just a normal guitar. They're easy."

The guy lovingly pats the rosy wood of his instrument. "This one is easy too! Do you sing?"

"Yep. In a rock band."

The guy's dark eyebrows slash upward, grin taking over his chubby face as he nods at his bandmate behind him.

As directed by his friend, the guy swings his guitar onto Nico's lap. "I think it will be best if you serenade your pretty woman and we listen. Do you know any love songs?"

Fingers clamped over the guitar neck, Nico bites his lip, expression cheeky. "Yeah, I do."

Before I can blink, he launches into La Cucaracha—the cockroach song—the mariachis yelp and play along. When Nico gets to the verses which are in Spanish, he wings it, voice dipping low and singing nonsense, gaining volume in the chorus—as does nearly every customer in the place. I try to sing through my giggling, too.

Applause, hooting, and much laughter from the band greet the end of the song. Their leader's eyes sparkle. "Very good, my friend. But that was *not* a love song. Before we leave, you must honor us with one." He turns a friendly wink on me.

Tap. Tap. Tap. Go Nico's fingers over the shiny surface of the guitar.

Heat lashes through my blood as his eyes land on mine. "Okay. But I've never written a love song, so it'll have to be a cover."

He gets comfortable, sun-kissed hair curling against his jaw as he bends over the instrument. The haunting opening to Chris Isaak's Wicked Game, a brooding song of unrequited love, winds like a ribbon through the air, enchanting every person in the room. We hold our breaths as we all lean closer, waiting for the words to kick in.

Mournful tones vibrate from Nico. My chest grows hot with excess emotion, the final threads of my resolve to go home alone tonight snapping. The mariachi singers chant the part about the girl who's only going to break his heart. My own heart fractures with each second that passes. My resistance dying, dying, dying.

And with a final soft sigh... *gone.*

Mostly, Nico keeps his eyes closed or on his fingers as they deftly pluck strings, but for the last cynical line about *nobody loving anyone* he stares hard into my eyes.

Trust him to choose a love song that fits his pessimistic outlook. It only serves to strengthen my decision to take this sad boy home and show him how amazing it feels to let love in—if only for a few hours.

Tension vibrates in the air for a few drawn-out moments, the only sound the dishes clinking in the distance, then the room erupts.

The band members slap Nico's back and shake his hand.

They tease and they laugh, but I've gone temporarily deaf and can only hear the rough pound of blood rushing past my ears.

I stare in a daze as the mariachis bustle off, singing once again, and then we're alone.

"That was beautiful."

"Thanks. It's one of those songs. It affects everyone who hears it."

And he's one of those boys.

I swallow hard, steel my nerves, and pray I'm not making a terrible decision. Okay. Here goes nothing. Or perhaps everything. "I live close by. Would you like to come back and see my etchings?"

"Waiter! Check!" he yells over the din, giving me a hilarious, urgent look, and shooting to his feet. He grips my wrist and hefts me upward. "Quick, Ivy. Let's go."

Okay. So, I guess I'm really doing this.

11

NICO

Foul Mouth

nlike the ascent to *my* apartment, the one that leads to Ivy's doesn't involve many stairs. Thank fuck for small mercies because, right now, I'm having trouble walking straight, and it's not on account of the tequila.

The short drive over here was taxing enough, my knuckles popping white on the steering wheel as I struggled against the urge to reach out and stroke her soft cheek, a lock of fiery hair... hell touching her anywhere at all would've been good. I ran my mouth like I was auditioning for something, telling dumb band stories to make her smile and laugh, and hopefully not think about ditching me when we arrived at her place.

To say I'm relieved to be standing behind her as she turns the key in the door would be wrong. Ecstatic is more like it.

She looks back at me and grins, hair spilling over her shoulder like rich red wine. "Come in."

Warm light floods her living room as she weaves around couches, bending to flick lamps on. My tightly strung control threatens to snap with each step she takes.

Hips swaying, she crosses the floor with the grace of a dancer and stands in front of me, close but not close enough.

"Would you like a—"

"No thanks," I say as I catch her by the waist, swinging her against the wall, my body pressing close.

Hands in her hair, I take her mouth and kiss her exactly how I wanted to when I saw her today in the gallery frowning hard at a painting of an orange dick that lay in a nest of pubic hair made from sharply bladed leaves. Sorry, not a dick. Apparently, it was a flower.

"Ivy," I pant into her mouth.

Nails digging into my skull, she urges me closer, we lose balance and her head hits the wall with a thud.

"Shit, sorry."

She laughs into my mouth, and her wet lips and soft sighs make me want to believe in… Believe in what? Fucked if I know. Maybe that kindness can heal. Human warmth is real. And that solace can be found not only in the heat of a girl's body but in her *soul*. In the way she looks at me. Dances to my touch like my fingers strike perfect notes and play her favorite song.

My tongue strokes hers. I angle deeper, tug her hair harder. Fuck, I need—

Wait. Is she talking to me? All I hear is: *Something something something, Nico?*

I pull back. "What?"

We pant hot breaths over each other. I nudge my dick into her stomach, just to remind her it's there. And because I'm impatient to get inside her. Because when I am, absolutely everything is okay. The world around us disintegrates and I don't care. Nothing else matters but her.

"I *said*—did you want to see my studio or would you rather get the sex part over with so you can leave? I don't mind either way."

"I would love to see your work." I'm not lying, but as I lean in and brush my mouth over hers, it's a struggle to rein myself in. To remain in control. I'm burning to make her mine again. To fuck her now. Hard and fast.

"Follow me, then."

"With pleasure."

Laughing, she crosses her eyebrows at my suck-up tone of voice and marches off.

Ivy's orange walls rival my walls in the amount of junk she has covering them. There are paintings, drawings, old ceramics, travel posters, but sadly only one plant. I can fix that. Because she deserves to be the queen of a jungle, and I want to make her an awesome one to rule over. That is if she's into it.

The room we enter, her studio, is even more chaotic than the living room. But its beauty drops my jaw.

"Are all these works yours?"

"Yep. It looks more impressive in the daylight."

"I'd better come back soon and check it out," I say. She doesn't even quirk a lip at the way I've invited myself over, and I really want her to smile at me.

She zips around the room, directing spotlight beams over spectral portraits—half faces and washes of dramatic color with all sorts of shit melded onto the canvases.

My dick forgotten about for now, I move slowly and inspect her artwork.

I bend in front of an old man's face. The sorrow in his dark eyes hurts to look at, but his smartass grin causes my own lips to stretch in a smile. "Hey! That's Red Francis! Shit, Ivy, this is amazing. You've totally nailed the bastard. His eyes—the way they're kinda scary, but full of humor, too."

"Thank you!" she says, hurriedly throwing a cloth over a nearby easel like she doesn't want me to see the painting on it.

"What's that you're covering up?"

"Oh, nothing. It's just some… guy. A friend. And I've only just started it." Her hand smooths over the covering as if she's afraid I'm going to race over and tear it off. "Thanks again for setting me up with Francis. He was incredibly fun to spend the day with. Such a great guy. I like him a lot."

"So does my mom. I think they've got something going on."

"Is that so?" She laughs. "Well, your mom's got good taste

in men, then."

Not really. If she knew how to pick good ones, then I wouldn't be alive.

"So, do you make money from selling these?"

"Yeah. I do portrait commissions. And whenever I help Mia out at pet weddings, I make some great contacts. Last year, I painted a wealthy socialite for a hefty sum. And I had no idea that her friends would be into competitive portraiture. They're practically begging to be the one who has the most lavish image hanging over their fireplace. So that's been helping to pay the rent. I can charge a bomb and these people don't even blink at the price."

"So, can you show me the one you just started? It'd be interesting to see a work in progress."

Even across the room, I notice her expression morph into something like guilt.

"Oh, no. I... um. I don't want to jinx it, so it's for my eyes only at this stage."

I slide along to the next painting of a young girl with blond hair. Her brown eyes dance with laughter, and the tiny words of a poem swirl like smoke through a background of silver and gold. The poem is about cats. The script it's written in is so neat and beautiful it totally puts my song books to shame. They're childish scribbles in comparison to the work of this fine calligrapher, who I'm guessing must be Ivy.

Pieces of black and white photos are worked into the painting, long, torn strips that look like they're of...uh... I bend closer and strain my eyes.

"Shit, that almost looks like—"

"A vagina? That, young man, is precisely because it *is* a vagina."

"Fuck! So, does that mean it's—"

"Mine? Well, I really shouldn't say."

Shit. My head spins and my cock hardens at the thought.

I squint harder, turning my head on weird angles.

"Come here you fool." She drags me away from the canvas. "Wouldn't you rather see the real thing?"

"But is it yours? I need to know."

"Why?" She laughs like I'm fully ridiculous. Guess I am. "No. It's not mine."

"Oh, right. Then I've got no further interest in it. But I am ready to see yours."

She smacks my shoulder as I back her into the wall. "Anyway, I'm well aware that it's Mia's."

"How could you know that?"

"The girl in the painting looks exactly like her, just a little younger. The poem is about how animals—specifically cats— saved her life. So including photos of a pussy in the piece is perfect. *Her* pussy, though, not yours."

"Very astute of you," she says, stroking hair off my face.

"So about that offer to see the real thing… Are you gonna show me?"

Breath ratcheting up, her gaze licks over my body. "You show me something first. Take your shirt off, Nico."

I whip it overhead. Then her hands are on my skin, exploring the ridges of my stomach. The way she stares at my muscles makes my dick throb, but something akin to fear slices through my chest. I don't want to fuck this up. "Men get six packs easier than women because we need less body fat to survive," I blurt before I can stop myself. I hold my breath, waiting for her to tell me she doesn't want to do this with a fact-spouting nerd.

"Right," she says.

My fingers go to the hem of her t-shirt, thumb stroking the soft skin at her waistband. Then I take her lips hungrily.

She pushes me away, brow creased.

"I got half naked," I whisper. "Now it's your turn, Ivy."

She slides away from me. "See now I'm a little worried you're going to judge me for my lack of muscle definition."

Fuck I'm an idiot—I should just tape up my mouth and be done with it. "You've got a great stomach. It's really sexy. Perfect. I could touch it forever. And I forgot to mention at dinner that my habit of blurting out weird facts is a nervous tic."

Her gaze narrows but she smiles. "I make you nervous?"

"Shit, yeah." It's probably not very cool to admit that. Thing is—I've always been confident around girls, but I don't feel so cocksure when I'm around Ivy. She's not easily impressed. She's lived a bit. Traveled. Makes amazing art. And what have I done so far? Written a bunch of songs and slept with a lot of girls. Hooray for me.

After staring into my eyes for a few tense moments, she says, "In that case, you'd better come into the living room. If we take this any further in my studio, I won't be able to concentrate next time I'm working."

"Not the bedroom?"

"Shut up and follow."

I don't need to be asked again, so I trail close behind. When we reach the couch, I stay silent and let her press me down into the cushions with her palm.

"Don't move." She walks to the kitchen and pours a glass of water, the sway of her ass in those snug jeans makes my fists clench tight, nails digging into my skin. "Want one, Nico?"

"Sure. Thanks."

Time slows to a crawl as I watch her return. I take the glass from her outstretched hand and gulp cool water down. As she tugs her t-shirt off, I forget how to swallow and nearly choke. Then she wriggles out of her jeans and kicks them away.

"Fuck," is all that comes out my mouth.

Her brain is functioning way better than mine, because she takes the glass before I drop it, clunking it down on the coffee table. Then climbs over my lap.

The black-lace bra is bumpy beneath my fingertips. I pinch her nipples. She gasps, gripping my cheekbones, tugging my face left then right—studying me.

"You're far too handsome," she complains.

I rub a hand over my jaw, smothering a grin. "Am I?"

"Yes. It makes you difficult to resist." Her palm skims down my chest. "And don't look at me like that. As if you don't know you're gorgeous."

I bite my lip ring to suppress a triumphant smile.

She strokes my stomach, looking fascinated by the rack of twitching muscles, the result of hard labor at the nursery and far too much time spent shredding on my skateboard. Then her hand drifts over my jeans, squeezing and massaging just right.

Fuck. Yeah. My head hits the back of the couch as her fingers grapple with my button. The zip rasps down. When she pulls my pulsing dick out, I lose the ability to speak.

"Nico? Where have you gone to?"

"What?" I grunt. Man. This girl's touch transforms me into a bone-headed caveman. Reduced to blazing lust, I'm barely human. I'm nothing but *need* and animal desire. And, Ivy, she's the exact opposite. Red lips parted, rolling curves that hypnotize, she's everything that is good and worthy. A radiant sun. The luminous moon. Her warm breath and slick juices are my only sustenance and the sweet poison of my downfall.

But, right now, I don't care how far I fall or what the fuck happens to me. Devour, take, claim are the only words that fill my brain. All I want is her. This hunger is savage and barbaric, and it feels fucking fantastic.

When she unhooks her bra, I feel sick with joy, my grip on her waist tightening. "Fuck, Ivy," I groan, my eyes trailing over creamy shoulders, the sharp V of her clavicle bones. A song flutters in my gut before flying to my mouth—something about white bones, red hearts, and black souls splintering, burning until there's only pale ash left. My lips press together to seal the whispers in. If I start singing now, she'll think I'm a fucking lunatic.

"Fuck," I breathe out, vision tunneling from lack of oxygen.

On her knees and straddling my lap, her face dips down,

silky sheets of hair tickling my chest. Then, thank Christ, she kisses me. Warm, wet lips sip at my lyrics, removing them, sucking them deep down inside her. But I don't panic. I know I can find them again easily enough—they'll be waiting there in her gray eyes, her slow smile. Something about her face, the way her features are put together, dark and light—a perfect symphony—makes me feel that everything will be okay. I don't need to worry about a thing.

But then she draws back, and I don't like that one bit. I want her close.

Closer.

Closest.

Her eyes narrow. "You have a very foul mouth. I can't believe how often you swear."

I can't deny it, so I just smirk. "You're picking on me a lot tonight."

"I am, aren't I? But you know what? That filthy mouth of yours is absolutely wonderful to kiss."

I'm happy to hear it.

She slides the bra straps down, revealing luscious mounds of flesh with nipples drawn into tight, dark buds. Until I met Ivy, I thought mosquito-bite breasts, the kind that don't require wire contraptions to hold them up, were my favorite. That's no longer true. Holding her perfect-sized tits, I bury my face against her skin, and then set to licking and biting.

The friction from her writhing over my dick sets my heart thumping like a bass drum, and I have to fight the urge to roll her over, to mount and pound and claim.

Just when I can't take it anymore and I shift my weight,

ready to hurl her over, she braces against my chest and says, "No. No. No. I'm driving this bus." Then she grabs my cock like it's a shift stick. "Condom. Condom," she murmurs into my mouth.

While I fumble in my back pocket, she nips along my jawline, bites my bottom lip hard enough to make my breath hitch.

"Fucking hell," I say when she rolls the rubber on firmly. It feels like heaven but is more likely hell. Because this girl— this woman who won't act like all the others, who won't do what I want—is surely gonna kill me. If not tonight, then someday soon.

"See?" she says huskily. "There you go again with the filthy words."

My fingers stroking over soaked material, I say, "These panties feel pretty flimsy. Reckon they'd rip easily?"

"Try."

I get a good grip and tear hard. Then I stare down at lacy scraps of material dangling around Ivy's generous hips. Her beauty laid bare to me. I can practically feel the come surging up my shaft at the sight.

Painfully slowly she impales herself on my tip.

The sight of my dick enclosed in her folds, makes me shudder. Her hips swirl gently, the wet heat so fucking good. But I want deeper. And I want it now.

Gritting my teeth, I lock my muscles so I can't move, because even more than I want to fuck her, I want to know how she takes her pleasure. What she likes. And I want her to use me. I *need* her to fuck me like a toy, so I can watch. That way I'll know exactly what she requires to get off good, and I can be the match to her flame and light her up whenever the hell I want. I have a feeling this girl will turn me into a pyromaniac.

When her hips plunge downward, taking me in all the way to the hilt, she gasps, and I drag her face close for a kiss. She swallows all the bad words on the tip of my tongue as it glides against her own. I fist her hair, smooth tendrils curling around my knuckles, and fuck her mouth exactly the way I want to take her pussy. Hard and with no trace of mercy.

I watch through half-closed eyes as she rises and falls slowly, her thighs shaking, breath rasping. She's struggling for control too.

Hands molding her tits, fingers pinching her nipples, I ask, "Do you want to go faster, Ivy?"

She nods, dropping her head back toward her shoulders.

Oh yeah, she really does.

I stroke the folds of her pussy, wet and clinging around my dick, my thumb circling her clit. "Do it, then. Fuck me fast."

"The things you say..." she tries to scold, then trails off, head falling back again, her hair a crimson wave streaming over smooth skin.

Using muscle power, I push up and flip her backward onto the couch. She doesn't struggle, just melts into the cushions.

I kiss and bite my way down her mouth-watering curves. The smell of her sex drives me crazy as I lick into her seam and eat her up good.

It doesn't take much effort before her thighs squeeze my head and her moans become my favorite new chorus. "Nico. Nico, no. Wait please... I need you inside me. Quick... Please."

"Whatever you want," I huff, giving her nub a final strong suck before I kiss and tease my way over her stomach, her nipples, and then attack her mouth until she's panting. Shaking, I line up my dick and plunge into tight, wet heat. "Oh, fuck, that's so good."

Her legs wrap around my butt, urging me to go for it, to get moving, and I do. I raise her pelvis off the couch, imprisoning her hips, and make her mine. The best fuck I could ever imagine. The only fuck I'll ever want.

What? That idea came out of left field. Whatever. Back to my tight balls, my burning gut, and my hips that piston harder, faster, then harder still.

Legs spread wide, she meets me stroke for stroke. I grunt with each slam, grinding against her pubic bone, her moaning spurring me on.

Wild.

She moves like a wild thing underneath me. A creature that I have no inclination, no desire to tame. No fucking way. I want to own her exactly how she is. Man, I don't know why I want this girl so bad. I just do.

I'm feverish, crazed, my every move jerky, no longer smooth and coordinated. "That's it, baby, take me deep. Oh, man."

She goes still, her inner muscles gripping tightly, then she draws a long, broken breath. "Oh, shit. Ohh..." Her walls clench harder and spasm, clutching and releasing as she comes.

It builds in my chest, pressure, pain, and a hot-poker need for all this to end. And the desire to roll on forever. Like this. Just like this. I stroke faster. "Ivy. Ivy. Fuck. Fuck." Then I break, too, a guttural roar exploding from my gut, shattering my bones, crumbling my soul to dust.

I collapse over her, wrecked and panting, while I wait for her to put me back together.

Warm lips kiss my shoulder, then she giggles into my neck. "Sorry, I really shouldn't laugh, but the way you swear is so funny. And strangely hot."

"Glad to be entertaining. Also it feels incredible when you laugh like that. Ah, shit." A full-bodied shudder wracks through me. Over stimulation. Gotta love it.

"And you're really heavy," she says in a happy voice.

"I'm funny and heavy and you're beautiful and sweet," I counter. Fuck. I think I'm high on the smell of her skin.

She laughs again. "Can you move, please?"

"No." I don't want to let her go. I feel weirdly possessive. Worried that if I get off this pretty fucking uncomfortable couch, she'll disappear. Or run away. Nah, she won't be going anywhere. After all, this is where she lives. But she just might tell me to split—to get lost—so she can sleep and forget about me. I don't want to leave.

"Nico, seriously, I'm having trouble breathing. Hear me wheezing?"

I snap my head up, eyes narrowed, and consider her face. "Liar. You look completely comfortable. Hey, here's the deal.

If you let me sleep in your bed tonight, I'll remove my masculine bulk and you can get up right away. It's a good idea, isn't it?"

"No. And, anyway, why would you want to do that?"

"Do what? Sleep with you? Because I reckon if I spend the night, we should be able to go at least another three rounds. Half asleep sex is the best. Then there's morning sex and—"

"Sh!" she commands, teeth sinking into her lip as she contemplates her options.

I smile, hoping the dimples work in my favor.

"Oh, okay, then," she says. "But only for the sex."

I kiss her quickly. "Cool. Only for the sex," I agree, untangling our limbs.

I get rid of the condom and hoist her into my arms. "Point me in the direction of your bedroom and I'll get straight back on the job."

Her arms wrap around my neck, and she directs me down the hallway.

This feels perfect, warm Ivy snuggling in my arms. Grinning, I set off with big strides, then scowl down at my feet when I trip over a lamp cord. "*Fuu*—I mean, shit! Why am I still wearing my jeans?"

"I can't believe you've only just noticed. I'll be happy to help you out of them in a minute."

"Sounds good to me."

This is turning into a perfect day.

And night.

And, if I'm lucky, tomorrow morning should be pretty good, too.

12

IVY

Zsofia

"When you finish your personal call, Ivy, please ensure you water the Proto-Paradise exhibition before you lock up." Kendra, the gallery owner, flounces past me at the front desk, long black dress trailing over the wooden floor like an oil spill.

I cover my cell with a hand. "Absolutely. No problem."

"Is that your bitch of a boss I can hear?" my mother slurs in my ear.

It's only six-thirty p.m. and she's already blasted, barely making sense. Other moms might be finishing dinner or getting changed to go out and catch a movie on a Friday night, but not Julia Reid. No. *She* sounds almost ready to knock on doors and proposition every male in her seedy apartment complex until she finds one foolish enough to engage in a clumsy quickie.

With her bright-red hair and strangely cheerful demeanor for an old lush, she won't have much trouble obtaining her goal. Her evening is bound to be more exciting than mine. Tonight, I'll be stuck in my studio.

"Of course it's Kendra, Mom. Who else's voice sends shivers of dread running down your spine? Even through the phone."

She cackles. "When are you coming to see your dear old ma, Ivy? It's been months!"

"Not true. It's more like weeks. And I'm flat out getting work finished for my exhibition."

Oh shit. Why did I go and remind her? The opening is in four weeks and I badly want to be successful at something for once. No way am I suffering through her wrecking it. Mom's invite will need to get lost in the mail.

"Oh, of course, sweetheart, I'm so proud of you. I've got the date on my calendar. I see it first thing every morning when I open the fridge and retrieve the milk for my Frosted Flakes. I wouldn't miss your opening for anything. Love you so much Vee Vee."

Vee Vee! *Yuck.* "Please don't call me by that nickname. I'm too old for it. I'm—"

"Hey!" says a deep voice above my head.

Heat zips through my veins. The phone still pressed against my ear, I flick my gaze up and get lost in sea-green eyes and a wicked smile.

Nico presses his palms onto the desk counter and leans down to plant a quick but juicy kiss on my lips.

"Oh, hey!" I splutter, pointing to my cell. "I'm just talking to my mother. Well, finishing up talking to her, really, and—"

"What a coincidence," he says.

"Sorry? What?" I respond.

"Who's that, Ivy?" my mom bleats. "Ivy? Who are you talking to?"

"No one, Mom. I have to go. I'll come around next week. Promise."

Once she has the scent of something interesting, Mom isn't easily put off the trail. "Wait on a moment. Who's the man you're—"

I hang up before she can complete her sentence and lean back in the chair, my whole body buzzing at the memory of last night. And this morning. I kicked Nico out of my apartment nice and early but not before we'd had a final round of incredibly satisfying, half-asleep sex.

"Long time no see," he says, wearing a cocky grin. "How's your day going?" Before I have a chance to answer, he continues, "I spent the morning writing a song."

"Did you now? Well, good work."

Rubbing knuckles over his stubbly jaw, he eyes me lazily. "Yep. It's inspired by that sound you made before I left. In bed. Remember?"

I do recall it. A long, loud moan of intense satisfaction. "Very funny." I smile.

"It's no joke. Did you miss me?"

"Oh, yes. It's been so many hours I'd nearly forgotten what you looked like. What are you doing here?"

Honey-brown locks fall over his face as he swings close again. "Did you know having sex boosts your immune system? So it's healthy to have lots of it."

Unable to stop myself, I laugh. "Like I told you this morning—we're not doing that together again."

His brashness falters for a moment, mouth opening then closing. "And I recently read a scientific study that said marriage actually strengthens men's bones."

"Marriage?"

"Yeah," he nods, dimples framing his grin.

"Nico, are you nervous right now?"

"Yeah. A bit."

The color that stains his sharp cheekbones is an adorably cute contrast to his bad-boy ink and corded muscles encased in a gray t-shirt and black jeans.

I wish he didn't look like that. So beautiful, with something like loneliness simmering deep in his eyes that makes me want to take care of him. Tend him. Use sexual healing.

I mentally smack myself. No. I don't want to heal him. I want him to leave me alone.

Liar.

I want emerald eyes to enslave me forever.

At this moment, I'm the one who should be nervous, but I'm not. I feel powerful. And it worries me how much I like the feeling. This feeling that I plan to fight with all my strength.

"No need to be afraid of me. I won't bite, Nico." I give his arm a quick squeeze, ignoring the bolt of awareness that pierces straight to my core. "So, what were you saying about a coincidence?"

"Ah, nothing. You'll understand what I meant by that later tonight."

"Oh? How will I?"

He gives a mysterious smile. "You're done with work, yeah?"

"Almost."

"Great. I'm gonna take you somewhere. It's a surprise."

"Oh no... let's not do that. Really... I don't think it's a good idea."

The gorgeous smile melts away. "Why not?"

"Nothing can come of you and I hanging out together. I can't do friends with benefits. And in the end, it'll just be a waste of time—for both of us."

"But, Ivy—"

Exiting from behind the desk, I interrupt him with a head shake as I make a quick escape toward the greenhouse, a glass-walled structure filled with plants, in the center of the gallery. Nico's boots echo a hollow beat against the floorboards as he follows.

When I duck inside the large sculpture and start emptying the watering cans over the lush potted jungle, he laughs. "Man, this is awesome. What the hell is it?"

"This is Proto-Paradise. Both strange and lovely isn't it?"

"I want one on my rooftop. The mannequin dressed in fighter pilot gear with plants growing out of his nose is brilliant."

I snort and flick water at him. "You should read the artist's statement. The point he's making with this piece is that nature will triumph over humanity in the end. In the near future, us humans will be long gone, and the earth will revert to jungle."

"I always knew plants were smarter than us." His long fingers caress green leaves, and I try not to think about them stroking my skin.

"Vanilla vine, bamboo palms, Spanish moss, philodendrons," he mutters as he looks around. "I'm friends with plenty of plants, so I reckon I'll survive the apocalypse. I think when it all goes to shit, they'll take care of me. I can put in a good word for you, Ivy."

"That's nice. Thank you."

"Now don't make a fuss," he says, taking the watering can from my grip and placing it on the fake-grass floor. "I'm going to take you somewhere to eat. As a friend. No funny business. I won't even try and kiss you. Or touch you. Or stand too close to you. I promise."

I really want to say no. I really want to say yes. The tiny smile he wears while he waits for my answer tempts me so.

His arms fold over his chest. "Okay. So, what have you got on tonight? Watching a movie? Doing some painting?"

"Yep. I'd planned to paint."

"Alone. Yeah, see that's just sad. This will be a lot more fun. Don't think. Just follow." He interlinks our fingers, his calloused palm warm, and tows me to the desk. "Bag," he says, passing me my backpack. "Walk this way."

Why can't I resist this guy?

Sighing, I tug his hand. "Wait a minute. I need to switch some lights off." I'm going to regret this decision, but my insides crave him. And curiosity has got the better of me. Where could he be taking me?

After a forty-minute drive, during which Nico turns a college radio station up loud enough to rattle my bones, forcing me to sing along to pop-punk classics by the likes of the Ramones and Green Day, he cuts the engine outside a seven-story housing project. He leaps out of his old, brown Dodge, swaggers around to the passenger side, and opens my door onto a wide suburban street.

"Okay," I say when I'm on the pavement staring up at the building tinged pink in the garish light of the street lamps. "Who lives here?"

He chuckles and beckons me to follow him up the steps. "You'll see. No more questions."

"It looks pink!"

"Uh-huh," he says, pushing through the glass entrance door and pivoting to let me walk through first. What a gentleman.

"Hey, Pablo," Nico greets an old guy who smells faintly of piss as he exits the elevator and we step in. He grins at me all the way to the top floor.

"Does every single person you know live so high up?" I ask when we walk into a dingy hall.

"Mostly. We like the views."

He slams a brass knocker three times against a beige door. "Prepare yourself." He smirks.

"What for?"

Before he can answer my question, a high-pitched voice squeals out "My Nico!" through layers of wood, and then the door swings open to reveal a tiny, curvaceous blond woman. Delicious food smells waft around her.

Nico laughs as he gets dragged into her arms. "Hey, Ma."

Ma? *Ma?* No. I must be hearing things.

Smiling broadly, the lady ducks around him. "Oh, Nico! You have friend with you? Hello, darling," she says, enfolding me in a cloud of floral perfume and a warm hug. I'm pondering how old this cheerful, attractive woman might be—perhaps in her late fifties—when her bright, green eyes lock onto mine. Wow. They look almost the same as Nic—

"Ma, this is Ivy. Ivy, meet my mom, Zsofia."

Holy hot crazy guys, I *am* at his mother's house. What is *wrong* with this boy?

I glare at him, and he blinks innocently back at me.

"*Come.* Come inside. I'm so glad you brought your friend. Edie and L had emergency at the farm and canceled. But I have huge pot of goulash." She waves us through a small living room into a cozy kitchen and seats us at an old dining table.

"You like goulash?" she asks me as I take in the cluttered Eastern European vibe, gazing at painted figurines of animals and shepherds, colorful plates and embroideries decorating the walls.

"Yes. I do. It smells wonderful. Thank you, Zsofia."

"You are so pretty." She pats my cheek and grins at Nico. "And how old?"

I stare at her compact shoulders as she goes to the fridge

and brings out a carafe of what appears to be white wine. The shiny material of her purple dress hugs her neat curves.

"Mom, don't start this shit. I'll have to take Ivy away. And question my sanity for bringing her here in the first place."

"Psssht," she scolds Nico as she pours us glasses and sits. "I ask again. You are how old, Ivy?"

"Oh," I say, completely shocked when I finally catch her meaning. Most people I know don't ask about delicate things like age. "I'm thirty-four."

Nico drops his head into his hands, smothering a laugh.

"Yes." She nods, grinning ear to ear and clapping her hands. "And my Nico is twenty-four. Yes. Yes. This is good. We will eat now." And up she springs to crash pots and plates around as she serves our dinner.

Nico bounces up. "Want some help?"

"Yes. You take these to the table, please. My hands shake with too much excitement. I will drop them."

"*Mom*. Settle down or I'll call Red Francis and tell him to get his crazy-ass over here to calm you down."

Zsofia giggles like she's fifteen and squeezes Nico's waist before digging a huge ladle into the casserole pot.

When they stand side-by-side like that, it's clear where his looks come from. With matching high-cut cheekbones, pouting, sensual lips, strong perfect jaw lines, mother and son are a sight to behold. Except she's quite short, the top of her head reaching the middle of his chest.

Nico carries over two steaming bowls and places one in front of me. Without thought, my mouth flaps unwisely. "So did you get your height from your dad, then?"

Nico's eyes narrow, and Zsofia barks out a laugh as she joins us at the table. "Ha! Yes, his height and his big, fat ego come from the German páva who planted him in my belly. My son is beautiful because the father is even prettier than I am. And macho, too. Very big, you know... But a bastard. Nico is pretty, yes? And nice boy, too."

Nico wraps his grin around his spoon. I follow his lead and shovel in delicious stew, smoky paprika giving my taste buds an instant orgasm. "Mmmm. Oh wow. This is the best casserole I've ever had. I could eat bucket loads of this."

Nico laughs. "Don't worry. She won't let you leave until you make good on that declaration."

Zsofia beams at me. "Wonderful. A woman who likes food makes big, strong babies."

I cough out a hunk of meat and Nico kindly slaps my back to stop me from choking to death.

"But how do you answer? My son is very handsome, don't you think? Like an alpha mole."

A what?

The plates clatter as Nico laughs, thumping the table with his fist. "I think you mean alpha male."

"What difference? Mole. Male. Both filthy dirt lovers. Is the same. Give your answer, Ivy."

Clunking down his spoon, Nico stretches his muscled torso back against the chair, making the wood creak. His teeth sink into the corner of his bottom lip and he fixes me with the dreamiest pantie-dissolving bedroom eyes I've ever seen. He's doing it on purpose—unsettling me—because his gaze manages to both mock me and set my pulse racing.

"Better tell her what you think of me. Mom never gives up until she gets her answers. Believe me."

"Yes, I'm like dog scratching at fleas."

Around a large mouthful I say casually, "Your son is very good looking."

Zsofia clasps her hands. "Beautiful?"

"Of course."

"Irresistible?"

"Definitely. What does páva mean?"

"Peacock. Nico's father was an actor from Berlin. Very vain. How did you and my Nico meet?"

"After a gig," he says. "She was in the alley behind the club getting some air and I went up and kissed her."

Zsofia gasps and clutches her chest. My spoon slips out of my hand, splashing goulash over the pretty red and blue tablecloth. Why would he tell her that?

"Then she is your girlfriend! Oh. How perfect. I must call Liliana from my village and tell her Baba Vash was right." She frowns at the clock on the wall. "Oh, no. I think it's maybe two in the morning. I'll call tomorrow."

"Who's Baba Vash?" I ask.

"Hey, Ivy. Tell us about your art." His voice is sharp as his eyes flash something like anger at his mom. "You love artists, don't ya, Ma?"

Zsofia's frown grows. "You have not told her, Nico?"

"She wouldn't be interested in that load of bull. So, Ivy does these amazing watercolor portraits and turns them into weird but brilliant collages. She writes these poems that she puts in there, too, based on a tragic event from the person's life."

"Oh! I would love to see these," says Zsofia.

Now the subject has changed, Nico looks much relieved. This is fascinating.

"She's even done one of Red Francis, Ma. Your very own heartthrob."

"Wonderful. He is interesting man, yes? I like him very much." She slurps the dregs from her bowl. "We do hip-hop classes together. You should come one day and join with us, Ivy."

Nico laughs and his mother elbows him hard. "What? You have joined with us before. You are very good at dancing. Sometimes he helps with the music, too." Nico's laughter gets louder. "Pffft. Don't listen to him. He thinks he is cool rock musician and pretends he does not like to get down with us old ones. But, really, he enjoys it very much."

"I can't picture Francis hip-hop dancing," I say, pushing back my chair. "Can I take your bowls to the kitchen? Thank you, it was so delicious."

"You must have more." Zsofia thrusts me back into my seat and, despite our protests, brings Nico and I another full bowl each. No way I can finish mine. Nico doesn't look the least bit fazed by his mountainous second serve as he bows his tousled head and digs in.

While I attempt to eat a little more, I listen to their affectionate banter, and it fast becomes apparent why Nico is so confident in his charms. He's an only child with a mother who adores him. My mother adores me too. She just has a shitty way of showing it.

"You have big family?" Zsofia asks as Nico and I begin to pack the dishwasher.

"No. It's just me and my alcoholic mom. She means well, but she isn't a very good mother."

I don't know why I revealed that bit of information. Usually, I try to keep Mom's problems hidden, fearing they'll reflect badly on me. Like mother like daughter and all that. Zsofia is warm and friendly. Kindness radiates from her smile, and she's far too easy to talk to. Next, I hear myself say, "I've got a sister, Rose. And she takes after my mom."

Pot dangling from his fingers, Nico turns and stares at me.

"How so?" asks Zsofia, beaming one of those sunny smiles.

"She's a runaway junkie who I haven't seen in five years. I'm not entirely sure, but there's a strong possibility she might be dead." Even though we never got along, my heart pangs at the thought. She may be a bitch, but she's still my sister. If she's alive that is.

Without looking, I grab the first thing I touch from the sink and insert it into the dishwasher.

"Oh, man. Don't put the spatula there. Don't you know how to pack a dishwasher properly?" Nico tickles my waist. "Give it here. Let the expert do it."

"No way!" I laugh, and he chases me across the kitchen to press me against the wall, fingers attacking my ribs mercilessly.

"Stop!" I cry through tears of laughter. He's laughing too, pretending to wrestle the utensil away from me. "Okay.

Truce. You can have it oh Dishwasher King. Just stop tickling me. I can't breathe."

Neither can he.

Strong forearms bracketing my face, a wide grin splitting his, Nico's breath gusts over me. Goulash. Sweet white wine. Then his lips inch closer. I part my own, and suddenly recall where I am. And *who* I'm with. His mother!

My spine stiffens, and Nico and I turn toward the kitchen table. Zsofia's face is a sight to behold—full of glee and something that looks a lot like relief. Maternal relief! This is terrible. We're giving the poor woman the wrong idea.

We leap apart guiltily.

"Well, I'd better get Ivy home, Ma. Dinner was the best. You're the best."

"Could I use the bathroom before we head off?" I ask.

Zsofia leads me down a short hallway and stops out front of a dark room. She flicks a light on. "It gladdens my soul to see him playful like that, Ivy. I am so happy he has finally met you."

My heart sinks to my toes. This isn't good. I can't leave Zsofia with her hopes soaring for no reason.

"It's nice to have a new friend. He's a lovely guy. And he always seems happy like that."

She shakes her head. "When he was a child, yes. But when he became teenager, no. He dislikes very much what I went through to raise him alone. He wrongly bears the guilt for this, for his father leaving. He hates that man. Nico makes his heart hard. You soften it."

Tears burn behind my eyes. I refuse to let them flow.

"You've got the wrong idea. I'm too old for him. He deserves someone young and full of life. An exciting girl his own age. All I want to do is paint and read books in bed. How boring."

"And all *he* wants is you. The way he looks at you is far from boring."

I give her a tight smile and close the door so I can hide behind it.

When I return, Nico is standing over his mother and they're both frowning. She slaps a palm against the table top.

"No," he says, "I won't do it. You can't ask that of me just on the basis of what some lying woman said to you all those years ago—"

I clear my throat and enter the kitchen, eyes dancing over everything in the room but them. "Where did I put my bag?"

"I've got it." Nico kisses his mom goodbye. I do the same. And then we leave.

In the elevator, he's silent all the way down to the ground floor, jaw muscle twitching and arms folded.

We climb into the car and I tell him it's my turn to choose the music. I find a K-Pop station and pretend it's my favorite, singing made up words loudly like I know all the lyrics. At the end of the first song he's laughing. And by the time we pull up out the front of my place we're both killing the fake K-Pop sound and having a ball. Thank God. I couldn't bear to leave him all alone with his dark mood.

He flicks the key in the ignition and turns to me. "So, this is where we part ways I guess."

"Yep." I smile. "Why couldn't you tell me where you were taking me earlier?"

"You survived the experience with poise, but it's best not to have advance warning about Mom. If I told you what you were in for, you would have freaked out."

"But why take me there in the first place?"

Sighing, he scrubs his face with his palms. "Shit I don't know. It seemed like a great idea at the time. And I wanted you to meet my friends Edie and Lightning who were meant to be coming into the city for the weekend. I don't see them much these days. They live on a farm and foster ex-homeless kids. They're both total lost causes turned do-gooders. Edie worked at the nursery with me back when I was a kid. They're great people. You'd like them."

I nod. "Yeah. I'm sure I would."

"I think my mom liked you a lot."

"She's lovely. And she looks at you like you just stepped out of the sun itself. Wow. She adores you."

"She's had a shit life. I'd do almost anything to see her smile." His palm lifts toward my cheek and drops before it makes contact. "It seems a little sad to leave you like this. It feels... inside my chest. It feels wrong. Hollow."

Taking a big breath, I scan his gloomy expression. I can't stand to see it. Can't bear to think about what Zsofia said— that he's not normally the playful, funny guy that I've enjoyed spending time with.

"Well, maybe you'd better come up then."

In an instant he's on me, hands in my hair, lips warm and soft against mine. I feel the shape of his smile on my skin, the cool ridge of his metal piercing, and my heart lifts and beats triple time.

Tonight, if it will save this boy from sadness, I'll ignore my fears of getting too attached—being gutted by my feelings for him.

If I have to, I'll plunge my fist inside his chest, search around the murky depths of his soul to find his smile and drag him back up with me into the light where he'll be warmed. Comforted. Loved. And I'll make him laugh so hard he cries.

Then tomorrow, I'll worry about the consequences.

13

Morning After

Hot water sluices over my skin, Nico's scent swirling down the drain along with the soapy bubbles. One hand wringing out my rope of dark-cherry hair, I shut the water off and press my cheek against the cool shower screen. Reluctant to leave the bathroom, I take deep breaths to settle my heartbeat. It's already past ten o'clock and that boy is still in my bed.

Last night, driven by irrational hunger for him, I set aside my fears and got lost in the raging depths of my need, in the intensity of his heat. Consuming. Ruinous.

This morning, I feel ashamed by the way I reacted to him, by my inability to stick to my guns and keep it strictly friends between us. He must be so confused. My words say one thing and my actions, the very opposite. I tell him to stay away, and then I pull him closer at every opportunity. How irrational and inconsistent I must seem. Well, being a horny young guy, as long as he's getting his rocks off, he probably doesn't mind too much.

I wipe steam from the mirror and stare at the dark smudges under my eyes. My skin is washed out. Ashen. Gray.

Last night, we didn't get a whole lot of sleep. The memory of him moving hard inside me washes in a blaze of colors through my blood. Rich reds for my desire, then every shade of green and gold to match his eyes. I can't wait for him to leave so I can work on his painting.

Rubbing my wet hair with a towel, in my mind I rehearse the different ways I could act toward him when I open the door. It's important that he remain oblivious to how bone-deep he affects me, so I think friendly and casual is the right approach.

I wrap the towel around my body, tucking the ends in tight. As I near the door, his deep laugh vibrates on the other side.

I stop. I listen.

He's in the middle of a phone call. I should open the door, but I don't. I keep listening. No, not listening, *eavesdropping*. I keep eavesdropping like a jealous girlfriend. Like we're dating and I'm justified in feeling cranky when I hear him flirt with another girl. And I'm sure he's speaking to a female, because his voice is low and sexy.

Listening to them is wrong, I know. But, still, I stand here with my hair dripping water over my shoulders and my stupid heart breaking.

"Quit with the Niccy, will ya? I'm real tired of asking you not to call me that." he says, warmth humming through his words. He's silent a moment, then he laughs again. "Is that so? Shit. Ouch. You are one cruel woman. What? Yeah, of course. You know I'd do anything for you, babe. Whatever you need. I'll be there."

My heart thuds four hard beats. Then he says, "For sure. I'll see you then. Yeah. Bye."

Forcing my lips into a wide smile, I push through the door and try not to gasp at the sight that greets me.

He's sitting naked on the edge of my bed, elbows on his knees. When he sees me, he leans back, weight resting on his palms.

My gaze skims over his sculpted chest, the cut stomach, down to his slim waist and the cock that's looking more impressive by the second.

Well, then, I guess he's pleased to see me. Or at least his raging hormones are. What Nico lacks in maturity he certainly makes up for with his constant willingness to get down and dirty. I think I finally understand the cougar thing. If I didn't care what people thought about me, a young lover would be a nice fit for a thirty-something woman. Sexually speaking.

"Hey," he says, smirking seductively, not looking the least bit embarrassed that I might have overheard his flirty phone call. Or about the evidence of his perpetual fired-up state that's inflating in his lap. Perhaps he was talking to his sister and has no need to feel guilty. No, he's an only child. A cousin, then? Or a friend.

My gut says he was on the line to another friend-with-benefits or one of his groupies. He probably has small armies of them all over town, ready to mobilize at the slightest stirring of his dick. Which, going by his dirty smile, is exactly what he thinks I'm about to do.

"Good morning. Did you sleep well?" I say in a level voice, not too cool and not too warm, either.

"Yes, ma'am. But now I'm starving. Should we go out and get some breakfast?"

I step closer. "I'll have to ask you to move along," I say, sounding like the traffic police.

"What?" His brow furrows as he reaches for my waist and tugs me between his legs.

I struggle to remain upright, my body weakening from the heat of his palms through the towel. "My exhibition is coming up in a few weeks, so I've got lots of work to—"

"Oh, *yeahhhh*." He draws the word out like I've just mentioned something a twenty-four-year-old guy would find thrilling. Beer kegs for example. A touchdown. Or maybe suggested we go and play laser tag. "I can't wait for that." His fingers tuck into the towel where it's wrapped around my chest. "You know, my invite hasn't arrived yet. I hope it hasn't got lost."

"Sss...sorry?" I say as he loosens the material, the towel dropping at my feet.

Dick jerking twice, he blows out a long breath and runs

his hands up my sides to my breasts, then slowly down my stomach to finally cup my butt. Warmth gushes inside me as he pulls me against his lips and kisses my belly, his fingers digging in firmly.

Breathing hard, I look at the ceiling and grip his shoulders. I should push him away. "What did you say before?" I ask.

His lips pause in their ministrations. "Huh? Oh... your exhibition..." He trails off, tongue licking lower, hands moving to my hips.

"So, Nico. You should probably get..." My words turn into a moan.

"What?" Hot breath teases my folds as his thumbs spread the lips of my pussy, and he gently kisses and sucks my clit.

"Ahhh... you should probably... go home now," I pant.

"Soon." His fingers tighten on my flesh. "Fuck, Ivy," he groans, and licks into me. "I could live off the taste of you."

The words vibrate to my core and I'm gone, flying so high I want to tear my fingers through his honey waves and push his face against me.

Harder and *more* are the only words I can think. In a hypnotic rhythm his metal lip ring circles over my sensitive skin just as my cell trills from the nightstand.

Automatically, I reach for it. "Nico. I really think you should..." Floating on waves of bliss, I can't even finish a sentence.

Not losing focus on the job, he takes my hand, preventing it from reaching my phone, and presses it against his beautifully mussed hair. Taking the hint, I make fists in the soft waves and press him closer. The sight of his tongue stroking, wet lips sucking, makes me wind my fingers tighter and move my hips against his face.

"That's it," he murmurs.

Wet, slippery sounds overlay rough groans and ragged panting. When my movements become urgent, he lifts my knee and places my foot on the bed, opening me wide to his hot gaze.

I stare at his slick lips as he lubricates two fingers in my juices, then slides inside, curling them just so. I gasp. How does he know the exact right place to press?

"What?" he whispers. "You don't like it?" His smile tells me that he knows I do.

My thighs shake. "I've just never felt anything so..." My head drops back toward my shoulders.

"Fuck, you look amazing like that."

I whip my head up, drop my eyes to his luminescent green gaze.

"Oh, God," I say as he moves inside me, keeping pressure where I want it most. "Oh. It's too much—"

"You can take it." He silences me by putting his lips back on target, his tongue flicking, while his fingers send shock waves through me. The veins on his dick stand out, pre-cum glistening on the head. He's so hot, and what he's doing to my body is sublime. I can't think. Can only feel. And I'm going to come all over his face any second now.

A strong arm snakes around my hips, squeezing me against him. "Look at me," he groans.

I do.

Intense, our gazes flame then lock. His fingers keep working, winding me tighter, drawing me closer to a terrifying abandon. A devastating detonation.

"Ivy." He pants hard, his voice raw and harsh. "Ivy… fuck. You've wrecked me. Stolen my soul. Fuck, this feels like… everything. The whole world wrapped up in one person. One girl. Everything I want. It's you."

What the crap?

Chill bumps prickle my skin, a sharp pain shooting through my gut.

His words sound like a plea. They're desperate. They horrify me. *He* horrifies me. I'm drowning in an icy sea, all warmth leeched from my body. I shut down, numbness spreading outward from my stuttering heart.

I grasp his wrist. "Stop."

Eyes glazed, confusion etching his brow, his fingers slow a little, but still slide in and out of my body. I feel nothing.

"Nico. Stop."

He does. Looking up at me with wide eyes, he breathes the word, "Why?"

I step back.

"I'm sorry. I want you to leave."

Even with his dick softening, most likely from shock, he's panting like he's being chased. "Right *now?*"

Hands wringing in front of my chest, I nod. "I'm sorry, I probably should have let you finish. I didn't plan to work you up like that and then just—"

"Fuck, I don't care about that." His fingers rake through his hair, making an even greater mess. It looks wonderful.

"Why do you want me to go? Just tell me what happened. What did I do wrong?"

How do I explain that he terrifies me, that he makes me afraid of myself? Even now, if he touched me again, I'd unravel. Should I admit how much that worries me?

I'm so grateful he spoke those sobering words. The scary ones that dissolved the lust and yanked me back down to earth.

This boy needs to leave before he breaks my heart. And then he needs to stay away forever.

Because I like him too much.

While I get dressed in painting gear, old jeans and a red embroidered shirt, his dark scowl burns my skin. I can *feel* his confusion buzzing in the air around me.

"Is it... what I said? Did I say the wrong thing?"

Yes.

"No," I lie, pulling a band through my hair and fixing it into an untidy ponytail.

"Are you sure because—"

"Nico. Please. Will you just get dressed?"

"Hang on. Wait a minute—"

"Please." I throw his jeans and t-shirt at his chest. "Last night was lovely. Now it's over and it's time for you to leave."

"Lovely, was it?" He stands, shoving his legs into crumpled denim. The t-shirt gets jerked over his head. He sits again to put on his boots. Then fastening his jeans, he stalks toward me. Soft lips peck my cheek, and I inhale his scent deep into my lungs.

"Yeah, you're right," he says. "It was really *nice*. Thanks. I'll see you soon."

I detect more than a dash of sarcasm in his tone.

He watches me stab amber earrings on. "So, are you emailing invites to your opening?"

My throat muscles tighten. "No. At Mad Wolf we do things the traditional way. We send out pretty hard copies."

He spins away and clomps toward the door. At the threshold, he turns back. "I'll be checking the post then. And if you forget to send mine, I'll have to come looking for it." He exits my bedroom, the door slamming behind him.

Okay. Guess I've pissed him off. It's understandable. Who stops a sex act immediately before blast off? A crazy person, that's who.

Footsteps continue to clunk through my apartment, and then there's another loud *bang* as the front door closes.

Groaning, I flop backward on my bed, limbs spread out in a star shape. Shit. I hate fighting with people.

Why am I acting like a lunatic? So he's a gorgeous groupie-fucking musician who likes to talk deep and dramatic when he's turned on. That's not a big deal. The fact that he's also sweet and funny—now that *is* a problem. A massive one.

I sit up, scrubbing my face with my palms. I need to finish that darn painting of him and avoid the flesh and bone version like he's a deadly disease.

No way I'll send him an invite to my opening.

No way in hell.

14

NICO

Vodka Martini

"Another round of beer for the jerkoffs at table ten thanks, man." With a smirk fixed on me and his usual bad timing, South slides onto a barstool at the exact moment I lift my cell to my ear. Quickly pressing end call before the call connects, I give him a short nod and turn to grab beers from the fridge.

I need to get rid of him fast.

He rests his forearms on the mosaic-tiled bar. "And Linc wants a vodka martini. Said it's his new special drink or some shit."

I throw a sneer toward the long table abutting the back wall of the cafe. It's packed with various Burntbad and Up

Void band members, along with South's growing entourage of groupies and road crew.

The place looks cool tonight. Turkish lanterns swing from the roof and cast a red-green glow around the room, warming the shadows. Candles flicker from every surface.

I stack beers on the tray. "Linc is a finicky fuck. Last week he insisted watermelon vodka was the only thing he'd ever drink again."

South laughs. "He sure likes the fancy stuff when you're at the register."

"And I'm not even officially working tonight." Over the last few weeks, the cafe bar I manage has evolved into a hangout for both our bands. It's a convenient, relaxed environment where we can get drunk and shoot the breeze. I'm not complaining—it's good for business, drawing bigger crowds each Friday, and it's also a lot of fun. Except for the hangovers. They've been a bit intense.

But the best thing about chilling out with the guys is that it's a distraction from thinking about Ivy. Nearly a week has passed since she cockblocked me while I had my tongue inside her and, in revenge, I resolved to ignore her forever. Well, that intention caved about five minutes ago. Thank fuck South arrived when he did, because I really should just forget about her, not call her like a suck up. Move on already. Yeah. He saved me from making a big mistake.

My cell rings. Shit. She's returning my call. Didn't expect that.

I glance at South who raises a smartass eyebrow, clearly wondering why I'm not picking up my phone. With a chin tip at the tray of beer, I say, "Take them over, would ya? I'll bring another load along in a minute."

"Gonna answer that?" He smirks at the photo flashing on my screen—the one of Ivy I took at Mad Wolf last week during our rescue mission to help hang the dick-flower exhibition. Shit. I knew it'd been a dumbass move to save it as her contact picture. Who does that?

"Take the tray over," I growl.

"When I'm ready."

Fuck. I have no choice but to ignore South's wide grin and answer before I miss the call. "Hey, Ivy. How you doing?" I attempt an upbeat, casual tone.

"Other than my cramped neck muscles from painting all day, I'm good. You?"

"Yeah. I'm at the Earth Garden cafe hanging out." Hearing her voice eradicates all sense of logic and self-preservation. "Why don't you take a break and come and have a drink with us? Bring Mia. Tell her South is here." I give him a smarmy smile and watch his lips disappear into a flat line.

"Thanks, but I can't. I've got too much work to do. And how old are your friends anyway? I'm guessing about twenty. I don't think we'd have much in common."

"That's utter *bullshit*." Okay. That sounded aggressive. "So, why'd you bother returning my call?"

"Um. Curiosity? And I don't like to be rude."

"Rude? You mean like how you were the last time I saw you?"

"I am sorry about that, stopping in the middle of... of... You must think I'm such a tease—"

"No, not really. You're something alright. But not that. Come down here and I'll explain in detail what I think about you. Please." South snorts loudly and I taser him with my best electrode glare. "If not tonight, then come by another Friday. Depending on the whereabouts of our gigs, we hang out at the cafe a lot."

"Thanks for the offer, but I really can't. For the next while, my social calendar is fully booked with parties, sadly, mostly fortieth birthdays. I'll need to use any spare time before my opening for those."

I think she's making that up, but I'm not entirely sure. "Need a date to any of those parties?"

"Not a good idea. You'd stick out like a toddler visiting a nursing home. I thought I'd made it fairly clear that dating isn't an option for us, Nico, and—"

"Right. Yeah, I remember. Fine." Heart pounding to the beat of a fucked-up bassline, I end the call without saying goodbye.

"Fuck, man, you're lookin' real desperate there. It ain't pretty." South opens a beer before slugging back a healthy portion of it. "What's the deal with this chick?"

I drag a palm down my face. "Nothing much, really, other than I think she might just be my destiny."

He coughs beer out. "What?"

"You know, like fated mate shit?"

Golden eyebrows shoot high. "No. I don't know about any fated-mate shit. What the fuck's that? Are you on acid?"

"Mom's Hungarian. Back in her village, when she was a girl, a fortune-teller told her I'd end up with a much older

hard. "It's not like you to give up so easy. Either you're in love or you just want to fuck her some more. Whichever it is, just keep trying. South reckons she's hot for you. She'll surrender eventually."

"*South says. South says.* Blah-fucking-blah," I grate out, then heave a huge sigh into my palms. "I don't think South's the authority on girls."

He takes a sip of his drink, eyes popping. "Hey, excellent work. This martini's wicked-good. So, you just need to decide what you want, dude, and then go get it. It ain't rocket science." He cocks his head at me in a know-all kind of way before giving me a two-finger salute and then leaving.

While I pile another tray full of beer, I consider his words. Strangely, for Linc, the advice is pretty good. I'm letting myself get worked up over a bit of resistance. She's thinking and acting motivated by fear. That's always wrong.

The fix is simple. I want Ivy, and I know she's into me too.

I'll let her settle down a couple of days then I'll just go and get her.

No sweat.

Easy.

15

IVY

The Client

After hitting the store this morning, I managed to get all the groceries packed away and my studio set up just in time for my eleven o'clock appointment.

Today is investment banker Gregor Night's second, and entirely unnecessary, portrait sitting.

During the initial meeting with a sitter, I usually just sketch and listen to their story. Then I take photos and use them to finish the work, only having face-to-face contact with my client again when they collect the finished piece. But this pushy guy insisted on another session.

Guess he's incredibly fond of the shiny, gold material I wrapped him up in last time.

In the painting, he's cast as an Egyptian pharaoh wearing a Hermes business suit with a duo of snakes rearing high on his brow, like Tutankhamen's burial mask.

Gregor loves that I'm portraying him as a king surrounded by lots of gold leaf, strips of torn linen, and black hieroglyphic symbols of power floating above his shoulders. I plan to secretly defy his rampant materialism by inserting tiny hand-painted quotes on love that he'll probably never even notice let alone bother to read.

With his neatly clipped, chocolate-colored hair and symmetrical, handsome features, it won't be a hardship to look at him for a few hours today. Although something steely and unnerving lurks in his dark eyes, he's very charming. Flirtatious even.

At exactly eleven, he knocks on the door and smiles suavely at me when I open it.

"You're looking lovely, Ivy."

That's doubtful. I glance down at my ripped, paint-covered jeans, my filthy red apron, hand going to the messy ponytail I've wrangled my hair into. "Oh! Thanks, Gregor. Please come through." I wave him toward my workspace.

The curtains are drawn over the arched windows, leaving the studio dark except for the fluorescent lamp that creates a split lighting effect on his face when he settles on the tall stool, left side in shadow and the right bright.

While I drape gold material over his shoulders his eyes

track over my body, then my face. "You mentioned on the phone we should be finished around one?"

"Yes." I step back and check his position against the Polaroid photos spread over the table next to my easel.

"I'll take you somewhere special for lunch."

He's hitting on me? That's surprising. He's the type of man whose women are usually as shiny and flashy as the brand-new Porsche he drives. Being a not-so-youthful, grungy artist, I'm hardly his regular kind of girl.

Confident I'll agree, he pulls out his phone. "I'll make a booking." He holds his cell in a loving, covetous manner, like it's a baby bird.

"I haven't said yes!" I say with a wide smile, deciding right then and there to paint him in the traditional pose of a pharaoh—his arms crossed, a crook in one hand and his cell in the other.

"But you will." His eyes twinkle, the smile he bestows on me coaxing and pleasant.

I brush thin strokes on the canvas around his mouth, attempting to capture the ever-present hint of smugness. "I don't normally mix business with pleasure."

"Although you'll make an exception this time. I always get what I want."

Ah, now his interest makes sense. I'm a conquest. Another item he can own, enjoy, and then discard when my use by date expires. But, still, Gregor is attractive, wealthy, and mature—all the things I should want in a man at my age. And it's not exactly raining eligible men around here, just pelting down one gorgeous boy from the eye of the storm into my arms now and again.

I mentally shove aside images of glowing eyes and sexy lips.

I should consider Gregor's offer. What could be the harm in just one date? It might take my mind off Nico.

"I'll definitely think about it, but I can't do lunch today. I have far too much work to finish. Maybe something next week?"

Lines crinkling around his serious eyes, he smiles, softening his whole face. "Dinner, then." It's not a question. He speaks like it's a done deal.

"Do you think you can try and keep your mouth zipped for a while? It would really help me paint it on straight, and you are paying a *lot* of money to look good. Let's talk more about making a date when I'm finished."

After that, he behaves, but I still can't wait for him to leave. When I work, I prefer solitude so I can enter the *zone*, the dreamy headspace I get into when the paint goes on just right, flowing onto the canvas like pre-ordained magic.

By twelve-thirty I'm done and have already begun tidying up when there's a thudding on the front door.

"Sorry, I need to get that," I tell Gregor. "You can go now, and I'll be in touch when the painting's ready for you to have a final look at."

"So, we'll do dinner on Saturday, Ivy."

"Okay. Sounds good," I agree without too much thought because I'm keen to get to the door. A delivery of art supplies is late, and I really need it. I rush through the apartment before the courier decides to give up and go away.

Bang. Bang.

"Hang on. I'm coming!" I yell. Patience is a dying art. I swing the door open and my jaw lands on the floor.

Nico.

"Hi." He crosses his arms and leans against the jamb, his black tank revealing swirls of bright ink and hard muscles.

I force a smile. I hope it's a friendly one. "Hey, there."

His gaze flicks over me, then he gives a deep chuckle, pointing to my cheek. "You've got paint everywhere. Does that mean you're working?"

"Yep." I flick my thumb toward my studio. "I'm just finishing up with a client."

"Will you come have lunch with me? We can grab burgers down by the marina."

Every part of me, except for the section of my brain that handles responsible decisions, wants to walk through the door with him right now. Find out how he's doing. Talk to him. Maybe make him laugh. Smell his sunshine-warmed skin as we sit close on the sand, watching the boats pass by on the horizon, and try not to think about kissing each other.

"Ivy?"

"Oh, sorry. Must have zoned out. I'm not sure—"

"Ivy." Gregor strolls into the room making a big show of adjusting his tie and smoothing his hair down as though we've just had intense monkey-sex and he needs to make himself respectable again. As he does this, he fixes a glacial glare on Nico.

"Do we need to make another appointment before I leave?"

"No, I already told you I'd be in touch about that," I say, glancing at Nico whose cheeks have turned a strange color. A rather alarming red oxide.

"So, I'll pick you up next Saturday at seven," Gregor continues. "You'll adore the place I'm taking you. It's a surprise, but I will say this much—there's a six-month waiting list for a booking. However, I can usually get a table on short notice."

I feel my own skin flush hot as he brushes a kiss on my cheek and exits, nostrils flaring like he smells something bad when he passes Nico.

"You're going out with *that guy?*" Nico looks horrified. Wounded. And even though I have no reason to feel this way, guilt swamps me.

"Yep. We have a dinner date booked. Nico—"

"Why?"

"Well, that's what people do when they're trying to find a partner. They go out with each other and see how they get along."

"But what about me? Don't we get along fine?"

"Of course we do. You know I like you a lot, but let's be realistic here. You'll never be in the potential partner category. You wouldn't want to be, either. You've got years and years before you need to hook up permanently. Unlike me. Can't you hear my biological clock ticking like a bomb about to go off?"

Suddenly, he's up close, breathing heavily like I've just

tried to pick a full-on fight with him. My aim isn't to make him angry. I'm just telling it like it is.

"So, I'm not good enough to be a partner candidate. Because I'm not rich enough for you? Or slimy enough like that dickball?"

"Hey, relax." He steps backward, but still looms over me, distress vibrating from his skin. "I don't understand why you're so angry. The idea of us as a serious item is ridiculous. You know that."

"Do I?" he yells right in my face.

I clasp his biceps gently. "Calm down. We're friends who... we like each other. And—"

"Fuck friends. Fuck this *liking* someone shit!"

He tangles his fingers in the hair at my nape, brings my head forward as if he's going to kiss me. His lips are so close. Glowing, bright green eyes narrow. His chest heaves fast. Then he shakes his head, lip lifting in a snarl, and steps away.

My heart thuds, skips a beat, and thuds hard again. "Nico. Wait!" I don't know what I want him to wait for, because I have nothing to give him. Absolutely nothing to say that he'd want to hear. But I can't bear the thought of him leaving like this. The thought of causing him pain.

What if something happens to him? I'll never forgive myself.

If I can just explain how things are. Help him understand that it's not him, it's me. Me and my childhood baggage. Me and the extra ten years I've spent on this earth. The fact that I can't stand people judging me and making fun of me. And if I was with Nico—*really* with him—I'd be a joke. A ridiculous, hilarious, and *old* punchline.

Ready to have a go at explaining, I step forward, but before I can speak, he whips around. Then just like a child throwing a tantrum he makes a strange growl of frustration and exits my apartment. It was probably a wise decision to split before he exploded in a fit of rage.

Upset by his reaction, the rest of the afternoon, I can barely lift my brush to the canvas. I want to phone him, but I know it will go better once he's had time and the headspace to calm down and get some perspective.

Once he thinks clearly about the situation, it will make sense that I need to date. He'll understand that I need to find someone. Anyone but him.

16

NICO

Skatepark

I stumble out onto the pavement and look around like a dumb fuck, blinking in the bright light. I wish there was a little breeze blowing the muggy air around. I badly need to cool down. I'm so fucking angry I shake, palms burning from the stupid way I slapped them against the rough walls of Ivy's stairwell as I made my escape.

Who the fuck does that smooth prick think he is? No way he's her type. Within a week, she'll be bored shitless hanging out with a conservative fuck like him.

Fuck that guy. And fuck her, too.

Yeah. That's exactly what I want to do—fuck Ivy—get

inside her body and disappear. Today, tomorrow, and all the fucking days after that. *Shit.*

Face screwed up, I drop my head into my hands, fingernails digging into my skull. *Fuck.* I need to walk. I have to move and get rid of this damned feeling swallowing me up. I can't breathe.

My sneakers pound concrete in time with the words spinning around my head.

Love is death. Death is love.

Death is love. Love is death.

Great fucking tattoo I've got. I must have cursed myself by etching those words onto my skin. It's like they've penetrated deep into my soul and are preventing me from ever finding peace.

I'm not sure what those words even mean anymore. Did I ever know?

But if that poem is true, if there's no such thing as love, then what the fuck is this painful obsession I have with Ivy? What is the point in stupid fucking longing? A craving so intense for the taste of someone's skin, it feels as though I'll die without it.

Man, this is total bullshit!

Fisting my hands in my hair, I tip my head back and frown at the peaceful, blue sky. A dude on a skateboard bumps past me, and as I stumble sideways, an idea forms.

There's a cool skatepark in the city not too far away. It's the perfect destination. I can shred my body against hard surfaces, give my heart something real to act like an idiot about. Because there's no good reason for an organ to pound so fast at the sight of some *girl.*

From now on, I promise myself, I'm not gonna give a fuck about spectacular tits and sweet, syrupy smiles.

As I walk to the subway, I pull my phone out of my pocket and hit up Linc.

"Dude!" he says, sounding ripped.

"Man, you're hammered already. You do know it's only just past lunchtime, right?"

He laughs lazily. "Yeah. I've been drinking beer with Patch, smoking some weed. But the fucker's left. He went home to have a shower. A shower! What a lightweight."

"Meet me at Lanterns?"

"The fuck... *now?*"

"Yeah, man. Bring your spare board—I want the short one. I'm gonna skate tight places and go *hard.* And your stash. Bring that, too. I need to get wasted, and you need some fucking exercise. You're getting flabby around the middle."

That's not actually true, but I need to inspire him to get off his ass so he'll come and distract me. Help me wipe the mental image of that guy touching Ivy from my brain.

"I ain't had much sleep. How long do you figure we'll be going at it for?"

"All night."

He groans, and I hang up.

Yep, I don't plan on sleeping much tonight.

I boot an innocent trash can as I pass by before scooting down concrete steps to the station.

Fucking suited-up rich fuckers. I hate those guys.

17

IVY

I Deny You

"**I**n my opinion, you ought to consider adding a video installation to the exhibition, Ivy. Soundscapes of bird-song, animals—the opposing beauty and horror of the natural world. Let's get every sense involved, create an immersive experience. It's all the rage."

Turning my head toward the skatepark we're trudging past, I roll my eyes. "I'm not an installation artist, Kendra."

A pack of dudes yell and cheer as they carouse around concrete steps on their boards. I'd rather be entertained by them flying through the air than have to listen to Kendra all the way back to the gallery. When I'm with her, I feel like a second-rate artist with only inferior work to peddle.

Crossing my arms, I stop walking and plant my feet firmly, ready for a confrontation. "I'm not interested in soundscapes. It's just not my thing. I paint. I write poetry. I stick weird stuff on canvas because I think it looks good. That's it. Amazingly, some people even seem to like it, too."

It's only ten-thirty, but the sun burns the back of my head. We've come from a downtown breakfast meeting with an arts council and are making our way toward a taxi stand, then immediately back to the gallery.

I'm glad I stopped in front of the skatepark, because the noise coming from it is a nice distraction from Kendra. The cacophony of skateboards grating over the pavement, the guys' booming laughter and constant swearing are bugging the crap out of her, too. I can tell by her pinched expression.

An extra-loud *clack clack clack* sounds as someone skates close by.

"You fucking idiot, don't do it!" a man yells, sounding thrilled to bits by whatever is about to happen, despite his warning.

There's a suspended silence, then a thundering crack as what could be a board and a body hit the pavement hard. Next comes a whole lot of roaring, clapping, and an explosion of creative cussing.

I think someone has hurt themselves. I keep my eyes fixed on Kendra's even though I'm dying to look over at the skaters and check out the chaos.

"Sit for a moment." Kendra steers me onto the park bench behind us and pins me with a condescending expression. "I was very surprised when Daniel Wanderhaussen confirmed his attendance yesterday. That's a massive boon for you, Ivy. Solo artists' first exhibitions don't normally pique his interest. I think what you need to do—"

"Ivy!"

Kendra puts a hand to her chest. "Did someone just call your name?"

"Hey! Ivy, fuck, I thought it was you!"

I flick my gaze over my shoulder and see Nico crashing through the low garden with a skateboard tucked under his arm. Holy crap. For a guy who works at a nursery, right now, he's showing a shocking disregard for the plants he's squashing under his ripped sneakers. That surprises me.

I leap up and edge away from the seat and my boss. Kendra rises onto her long, skinny legs and follows like a bad smell.

When Nico arrives, he bends to give me a one-armed hug. He's hot and sweaty and smells funny, but I still hold onto him a little longer than is polite.

He laughs. "Hi, Ivy," he says, grinning like a lunatic as he checks out my summer dress.

I have no idea why he's smiling at me so happily, wielding his dimples and everything. Although I'm relieved he's no longer upset, yesterday when he left my place, he wasn't in such a good mood.

"What are you doing here? Want a go on my board? I can teach you how to be a real rad skater chick if you want."

"Um, no, thanks. I'm on my way back to work actually."

Kendra steps in and thrusts her claws out at him. "Hello,

there. I'm Kendra, I own Mad Wolf Gallery. Where Ivy works. And you are?"

"Oh, hey." Wearing a lopsided smile, he seizes her hand and whips it around in an overly enthusiastic shake. "Name's Nico. Good to meet you."

"Nico." She rolls his name around her sour mouth while he lifts his black tank and scratches his rippling stomach muscles.

Speaking of mad wolves, he looks exactly like a predator the way he's grinning and raising his eyebrows at me in a suggestive fashion. Where does the boy think we are? At his apartment? A seedy nightclub?

Kendra notices his wolfish, overly-familiar manner, too. "Is this your boyfriend, Ivy? A *young* skateboarder!"

Shit. Shit. Shit. It's not just my imagination. She definitely emphasized the youth-factor, causing Nico's eyes to snap back to me.

"*Him?* Oh, no. No. He's not my boyfriend." I push out a strained laugh. "Absolutely not. Don't be ridiculous."

Nico's eyes disappear to slits. "I run an organic cafe. And I've also got a band," he spits in a growly voice. The dimples have fully retreated, and he's so pissed off he's slurring. Shuffling his feet, he swaps his board to the other arm and kicks his shoe over the concrete aggressively, like he wouldn't mind walloping Kendra's butt.

Unimpressed, Kendra makes a cat's bum face at him.

Smiling nervously, I say, "We're out on business, so we'd better get back to it. Good to see you, Nico."

Biting his lip, he looks between the ground and my face but doesn't bid me farewell.

"Okay. So, see you..." My brow lifts, prompting him to wind up whatever this is so I can leave.

Silence. More pavement abuse from his sneaker.

I wait a few more seconds for him to say something like, *'Oh, yeah, right. So catch you around'*, but I get absolutely nothing. Just more pavement gazing and foot shuffling.

"Okay. Bye then, Nico. We'd better get going."

He responds with a grunt.

"Shouldn't we?" I say to Kendra who is managing to simultaneously sneer at *and* ogle the hot guy I've slept with. She better not be getting any ideas to take him for a test drive.

"So, there's a chance I might run into you down at Silva's on the weekend. Mia tells me you've got a gig there."

"Yeah. I think it's sold out." Murky sea-green eyes burn into mine.

"Oh." That's weird. It almost sounds like he doesn't want me there. "But if Mia and I decide to go, I guess you could kindly put us on the guest list, right?"

I don't know why I said that. I have no intention of attending his gig, and I probably shouldn't bring it up in front of Kendra. Now she'll be judging the way I spend my downtime and working on an annoying lecture about how a serious up-and-coming artist needs appropriate friends to impress people in the art world. She's so full of crap.

Barely concealing a snarl, he leans close and says, "Nope. Don't think I *can* put you on the guest list."

Okay, so he's definitely upset. Most likely because I made it sound as if being associated with him in any way would be a living nightmare.

Just as I'm about to wish him a good day and run like hell, I notice blood dripping on the concrete. I point at it. "Oh, shit. Nico, you're bleeding." How did that go unnoticed?

When I reach for his elbow, Kendra squeaks and Nico flinches. He stares at the deep gash running down his forearm, the skin around it, grazed and raw. A whooper of a bruise has just begun to bloom over his cheekbone, too. Now that I look closely, it's clear he's a total mess.

Running fingers through his hair, he says, "Oh, yeah. Fuck, I am bleeding. Huh."

"Quite a significant amount, too," says Kendra.

Wearing another crooked grin, he nods like she's given him great news. "Huh. Yeah."

Now that I've recovered from the shock of Kendra meeting him, I'm noticing more details. Perhaps if I hadn't been busy gawking at his sculpted muscles before, I might have detected these disturbing and glaringly obvious things earlier. Things like his unfocused eyes, currently gleaming with fury. The sexy hair, even more disheveled than usual. The way he can't quite stand still. Almost like he needs to keep moving in order to stay upright.

Pretending to stumble so I can get close, I breathe him in deep. *Jeez.* The scent of sweat and alcohol assaults me. Of course! That's why he didn't smell like himself when he hugged me before—when I was in shock and denial and blocking out reality.

"You're completely drunk!" I don't mean it to come out

like an accusation—he's a big boy—and he's allowed to get a little loose if it floats his boat. But I don't hang out much with people who get wasted. Never know what they might do. And they make all those mortifying mom-memories from childhood come flooding back. The sheer embarrassment. The shame and horror.

"Nico, what the hell is going on?" I ask, squeezing his shoulder. The feverish heat of his skin sears mine. "It's only ten-thirty in the morning."

"Yep. And I am *totally* shit-faced."

Wow. He sounds so proud.

My boss's silent disapproval hums through the air, tightening my vocal cords. It feels like a hangman's noose around my neck.

"Why on earth are you drunk at this hour, Nico?" I manage to grate out. "Is this something you do regularly?" It's really none of my business, but I need to know. "Anyone would think you're sixteen."

He laughs, and blood goes drip drip drip onto his red Vans. Leaning close, he whispers, "And I forgot to say that I'm fully stoned too. Pretty sick, huh?"

He's not wrong there. And he sure *sounds* like a sixteen-year-old.

Huffing loudly, Kendra takes my arm. "Let's go, Ivy. This conversation makes me desirous of a shower."

Well, it makes *me* want to take a bath. With *him*. Not to do anything lewd, of course. Just tend his wounds. And hydrate him. Okay, maybe I could plant a kiss or two in a few choice places when he's feeling better.

"Wait," I tell her before turning back to the gorgeous wreck swaying over the pavement—the one whose eyes glow such a dirty green they look like algae bloom. Dangerous. And weirdly sexy. "Nico! I think I should call 911. Or can you manage to get yourself to a hospital? You really need stitches. I'm not kidding here."

Checking out his possibly broken elbow, he mumbles something toward it.

"Sorry? What did you say?"

"Linc's over there. He'll get me where I need to go."

That's unlikely. His friend is probably in a similar state of intoxication and, therefore, practically useless. Oh, hello! Speak of the devil.

Grinning stupidly, dark eyes darting restlessly, Linc sidles up next to his friend. "Hey, Ivy."

"Hi Linc," I say as his hand jets out toward Kendra.

"I'm Linc—"

Nico swats his arm away and points an unsteady finger at my chest. "I don't like this."

"What?" I have no idea what he's talking about.

Anger simmers in his narrowed gaze. "Your body was my refuge. Your smile my only hope. But all you seem to wanna do, Ivy, is put the hurt on me."

Kendra gasps. My eyes bug out and Linc's do the same.

"Your only hope for what?" I ask.

"You sound like a pussy." Linc says, laughing at Nico. "Not bad lyrics, though. Are you working that into a song, man? Fuck, look at the blood coming outta ya. That's gnarly." He grimaces. "Shit. Makes me feel sick."

"Shut up," Nico barks at him.

Black bob bouncing, Kendra tugs me away from the boys. "So you've slept with him," she hisses. It's not a question.

I pull against her tight grasp. "Nico!" I call over my shoulder. "You will go straight to see a doctor, won't you? Right now?"

"Yeah, sure. Whatever. Catch you around sometime— probably in the afterlife," he says, and jogs back to the skate ramp, crushing every flower in his path. Linc does the same. Nico will be devastated about that tomorrow. If he remembers.

Kendra marches us off at high speed, her dramatic, sleeveless dress trailing over the ground like a black shadow. "What does he mean by *see you in the afterlife*? Is that an online game?"

"How would I know? He's completely out of it and not a word he said made any sense."

"Musicians. I suppose they're always like that. No wonder I don't have any rocker acquaintances in my life."

The thought of Kendra backstage among the band room sweat and grime makes me laugh. "But he's different, and he's not normally a loser. I've never seen him act like that before."

"Yes, well, if he's your latest toy boy, I suppose you'd know."

My latest toy boy! What is wrong with the woman? As if I cruise around in my spare time preying on hot young guys.

"I hope he doesn't show up at your exhibition in a debauched state and make a scene. How humiliating for you!

A meltdown from a friend would hardly impress any art world influencers in attendance. In fact, it could ruin your prospects entirely."

I'm so over Kendra going on and on about the *art world*. It's sickening. Surely these people aren't sewn up anywhere near as tight as she is. I ache to mention this. Or poke my tongue out.

I swallow my irritation and say, "I won't invite him."

"That would be a very sensible decision, Ivy. No matter how lovely that one is to look at, he's a loose cannon."

I heave a sigh. "Yes. You're probably right."

But is it sensible to shun Nico? To ignore him? My head says yes, but my heart screams no. *It* wants me to chase after Nico right now and rush him off to a doctor's office—make sure he's alright. Then take him home and deposit him in my bed for some heavy-duty nursing. Or perhaps some hot and heavy petting.

Yes, even in his current state—a condition that both terrifies and embarrasses me—I can't help but want to kiss him better. All over his bruised and battered and annoyingly beautiful body.

18

NICO

Break Mom's Heart

I'm standing out front of the hospital with my phone pressed against my ear. Heat radiates off the pavement and sweat trickles between my shoulder blades. I'm uncomfortable as fuck and… wait. What am I doing? This phone call is a dumbass move. Just as I'm about to hang up and head home to crash in bed, the call connects.

Dammit.

"Hey, Mom."

"My, Nico! This is a wonderful surprise. You phone your mother on a Sunday. Call me amazing!"

"You mean call you *amazed*."

"That is what I said."

She's been in America so long now she speaks perfect English but, for clowning purposes, often pretends she can't.

"You are not practicing with your band boys today?"

Even though I don't like to encourage her, I can't help the laugh that gusts out. "Bandmates, Ma. How many times have I told you they're called bandmates?"

"Band friends. Band boys. Is the same meaning."

"Not really."

"Your voice does not sound right. What's wrong with you? Tired? Too much drinking last night?"

Zsofia never misses a trick. "Both. I'm *still* drunk as hell."

She tsks. "Very bad boy. What does your girlfriend think of this behavior?"

"My who?"

"Your lovely Ivy."

"She's not my girlfriend—"

"Don't worry. She soon will be. Drunk or not, I'm glad you called. I have hip-hop class in one hour. You come and do the music. Celia has called in sick at the last minute. You are good at this."

"You've got cell phones with playlists. Use those. And you need your ears cleaned out. I said I'm *drunk*." And stoned and injured and mad at every single person in the whole fucking world. Especially all the redheads.

"No matter. I need you, Nico. We're still working out the scratches. You will come help." Then she hangs up.

Fuck.

Of course I'll go. But she'll regret guilt tripping me, because even I can smell myself. And I ain't no rose garden.

I stare at my freshly doctored arm—fifteen fucking stitches and an x-ray for glass remnants later and it hurts like a mongrel. Being drunk and high helps manage the pain, but it's my mental state I'm worried about. I can't stop shaking, and I wish like hell I was wearing a long-sleeve top to hide the injury from Mom. When she sees it, she'll go apeshit.

Ignoring all the bemused stares I get from strangers, I catch the subway and then walk fifteen minutes to the community hall where the P.F. Bad Girlz Crew rock out twice a week. The group has five male members too, not one of them under sixty. I have no clue what the P.F. stands for, and Mom refuses to enlighten me. Whenever I've bothered to ask, all twenty-two Bad Girlz (and boys) snicker into their hands.

I make a hard left off the main shopping strip into West-fern Street, then climb the stairs up to the hall entrance, practicing walking straight. I'm not doing such a good job at it. Massive dark-green doors creak as I push them open and stride inside.

It's quite a sight that greets me, over twenty old folks limbering up dressed in track pants, tank tops, and backward baseball caps.

Going for a loud and proud entry as opposed to a quietly guilty one, I plant my feet wide, spread my arms, and holler, "Man, you lot look scary!"

Laughter and shouted greetings assault my ears, and Mom stops canoodling with Red Francis so she can rush over and berate me.

"Nico! What took you so long?" she yells when she's halfway across the floor.

"What? I came straight here—"

"I spoil you too much as a child. You turned out too much entitled bad boy."

And right there we have exhibit A: she does know how to use big words.

Hands wrapping around my neck, she drags me down, squashing me in her arms. For a small woman, she's pretty strong. I squeeze back, and then untangle her bling-laden fingers and set her away before she gets too close a look at me.

"Hey, Francis," I greet the guy hovering cheerfully nearby with the flowing red beard, who's probably boning my mom —not right now, though, thank Christ.

Crossing her arms, Mom shakes her head. "Look at you."

I can only stand there biting my lip, swaying gently and hoping I stay upright.

Her green eyes widen when she finally notices my bandaged arm. "Istenem! Your arm. What happened?" She waves her hands at Red Francis like he might be able to explain what's going on. When he shrugs, she starts toward me, frowning. "Sit down."

"Never mind that." Deisha, the choreographer, appears in the nick of time and links her arm through my good one and tugs me toward the music set up. "Phew, boy! You smell like a damn brewery. What you been putting in your body exactly?"

"I—"

"Don't answer that question," she commands, her corkscrew curls bouncing with indignation. "You're gonna break your sweet momma's heart one of these days. Think about that, will you, baby?"

My face gets hot and I swipe hair out of my bloodshot eyes. "Sure."

She shoves me behind a table that has two turntables and a mixer arranged on top, then plants her fists on her generous hips. "Remember how to use this thing?"

Terrified to speak in case I reveal how truly fucked-up I am, I keep my eyes averted and nod.

"Well, get settled, then. We've got a competition three weeks from now and we barely know what we're doing." She sifts through vinyl records. "For this piece we're using Asap Rocky's *F-bomb Problems* and Beyonce's *7/11*. Today, I'm just gonna run the dance all the way through. So start with Asap and I'll point at your pretty face when I want some scratches. Nothing fancy for now. When I turn my hand like this, switch tracks. Okay?"

"No problem. If you'll just tell me what the P.F. in your crew's name stands for, I'll hop straight to it."

"Good try." Laughing, she slaps my butt and heads for the dancers, walking backward so she can flap her jaw at me. Luckily, I can't understand a word.

Wrapping my hands around my mouth, I create a megaphone to yell through. "Why ya dancing to a track you can't say the name of, Deish? In case you didn't realize, the whole song's full of F-fucking-bombs. Are you crazy or what?"

"Quit spraying sauce from that sulky mouth of yours and get to work," she says as she bosses senior citizens into position.

I organize myself at the desk and pretty soon the room fills with the catchy *oh oh ohs* of the Asap tune and a very sweet beat. The P.F. Bad Girlz, including the old dudes, start shaking their asses. Arms wave, shoulders pop, the whole room goes bounce, bounce, bounce.

Deisha shouts like a drill sergeant over the music. "Step touch, clap. Step touch, clap. Really bend those knees. That's right! Step slide. Step slide. And rock hips—two, three, four." She throws me a huge smile and points.

I go scratch. Scratch. Scratch.

"Yeah!" she yells. "That's what I'm talking about."

I grin at the dancers, my own hips rocking as I pat my pockets and search for a stashed packet of smokes. Frowning at how trashed the cigarettes are, I flip one between my lips and Mom yells, "Nico!"

Fuck. I quickly fling it away. Don't know what she's so worried about. I only get into the cancer-sticks when I'm hammered.

Noticing Zsofia's distraction, Deisha skips up next to her and cracks the whip. "Spin. Reach. Pull. Pull. Come on folks, really get your wiggle on here."

And they do. And fuck it's funny. It wouldn't be so bad if they cut out all the winking and eyebrow wriggling.

"Nico, switch!" Deisha does her hand flip move and I change the track to Beyonce. She points again, and I bust out more scratches.

"Kick it!" she screams, and they break into the running man move.

That's when I really start laughing. The moves don't even

fit the music, which makes it hilarious. Plus those overly enthusiastic facial expressions I mentioned earlier. The way these guys play it strictly for giggles, they should be entering comedy competitions not dance ones.

"Yeah! Let me hear it!" Deisha does the flippy hand thing and I spin the Asap track again, then suddenly they're roger rabbiting like their lives depend on it. "Come join us, Nico!"

What? She's the one on crack. I can barely stand straight. I'm not joining their festival of fools.

I shake my head hard, nearly falling over it makes me so dizzy. "No. No. No. No way in hell." Then I'm attacked by oldies who, squawking like seagulls, tow me out onto the floor. For a moment I stand there scowling, then think, *fuck it*, I like this song. I give the roger rabbit my best shot, and I have to say considering my condition, it's not too shabby.

Then purple-haired Cheryl sidelines me, coming in with her booty aimed right at my hip. I cut her a mean scowl and shuffle along a little, but she won't take the hint and roger-rabbits closer, still trying to do the bump with me. I scoot forward, she humps left, and our feet twist together. Down we go, landing on my freshly lacerated arm with Cheryl over my chest, squeals and laughter from the crew filling the air.

It takes seven octogenarians to lift her off me, my mom moaning in the foreground—one second like she's witnessing my death, the next laughing.

"I'm fine." I wave them all away and, thankfully, most have the good grace to retreat without too much fuss.

Deisha clears the room, telling the crew she's gonna kick their butts if they don't practice their dances hard at home.

"Sorry, Nico. Don't know my own strength," says Cheryl, sounding far too proud of herself for dropping a guy nearly twice her size. Fair enough, I guess. It's an impressive afternoon's work.

"It's okay, Cheryl." I say. "You've got some dangerous moves there. If you were a little bit younger, I'd be thinking up a way to get into your pants right now."

"Nico!" Mom whacks me.

Cheryl waltzes away, her cheeks on fire as she giggles like a virgin.

I have the worst headache of my life, the hangover settling in big time. Groaning, I drop my face into my palms. I feel like shit, and my fingers itch to dial Ivy's number.

I'm so fucking mad with her for pretending not to be into me. For being embarrassed of me. And, yet, all I want right now is to hear her voice, feel her soft fingers stroke through my hair. I let out a pathetic sounding sigh, and Mom pats my back.

"I will lock up," she says to Deisha. "You go wait in the car, Francis. I need to speak with my Niccy."

"Don't fucking call me that."

She grabs her chest like I've shot an arrow through it, then cuffs me over the back of the head. "Language, rude boy!"

"Ow! Gentle. I'm injured here."

Fingers pinching, she grips my jaw. "Looking at your red eyes, I don't think you feel any pain."

Francis bends down and whispers, "I like your girlfriend, Nico. She's a sweetheart. She said my portrait will be distinguished."

"Yeah, she's a real charmer that one. But you've got the wrong idea. She's not my girlfriend."

Gold teeth flash. "If you say so."

Mom drops down beside me. "What's wrong, darling? I'm not talking of your injured arm. I mean what's wrong here." She presses two fingers against my temple. "In your head. What is problem? You're not happy."

Truer words were never spoken.

"No. I'm fine. Everything is great. The band—awesome. The cafe—freaking perfect."

"And Ivy?"

"Ivy? What's *she* got to do with anything?"

Zsofia stares, her silence tightening my chest muscles. Suddenly, I feel like I'm about seven years old. Breath shuddering out, I fold my knees into my chest, face burrowing into my forearm. I just won't look at Mom and she'll go away.

She rubs my back and a horrible heat engulfs my body. "Nico. Look at me."

I shake my head.

"Did I raise you to ignore your mother?"

Eyes swimming in liquid *who-the-fuck-knows-what*, I lift my gaze and watch Mom's eyebrows draw down. She sucks in a quick breath and pulls me into her arms, crooning and rocking me like I'm a baby. I want to push her away. I want to hold on tight.

Moisture runs down my cheeks. Fuck. Fuck. This is crazy. I'm never getting this messed up on booze and shit again.

"Nico. My, Nico. It's okay. Shhhh. Everything will be okay."

What? I'm not making any sound, am I?

She pulls me closer, thumbs stroking over my face.

"It's nothing, Ma." I lie. "It's just... I'm just wasted. My head's fucked. I haven't slept, and I can't fucking think straight. I'm fine."

"You are not fine. I know you like to make parties sometimes. But not like this." Her hand presses against my thundering heart. "Brave men understand it is no problem to feel these things—these emotions that hurt. They open their hearts and bear this pain." She strokes my cheek. "And sometimes, if you let yourself feel this, if you are lucky, you may come to realize that the person causing you this pain also feels it for you. When you understand that your hearts beat only for each other, this terrible feeling turns to joy. What you once ran from becomes everything good in your life. I think it will be like this for you and Ivy."

"No."

She smiles and nods.

"It won't." I drag a hand down my face. "I don't feel that way about her. You're reading it all wrong. I'm just pissed she won't do what I want. That's all. I'll never be stupid like you were and love someone. Spend my whole life crying over them like you did."

Horrified, I watch two fat tears slip down her cheeks.

"You break my heart," she says. "I thought I built you stronger. Not like this frightened boy, too scared to take risks."

I grip her shoulders. "No, Ma. Shit. I'm sorry. Don't cry. I didn't mean—"

"It's exactly like Baba Vash said it would be." She wipes her face with the back of her hand. "You would be the one to break it. Not your father. *You.* How could you be so closed to love? So ready to shut yourself off from happiness like this?"

"I'm not. I've just seen you work yourself raw because of that guy. What he did to you... leaving... and how much you loved him... Look what loving someone got you. Heartbreak. Unhappiness and—"

"And you. It gave me you. You are the one I love. You are the one who breaks my heart. What I felt for the German páva was starry-eyed lust. Never ever love. And now I must watch the only person who holds my heart turn away from their chance of happiness."

The corners of the room close in on me, making it hard to breathe. I can't believe what I'm hearing. "You never loved him?"

"No."

"But, why did you stay in this country working three back-breaking jobs then? I listened to you cry nearly every single night because of him—"

"No. Because I missed home. That is why I cried. And I didn't stay because I wanted him to come back and save me. I stayed for *you*, my darling. To give you a better life here. Love does not break hearts. Stupidity does."

"No." My eyes burn. Her words crush the shit out of my memories, they fuck with everything I believed was true about her. And about me.

"Here, I must show you something." Rifling through her huge, black bag, she locates her purse. "Look." She flaps a dirty piece of paper in my face. "Take it. The Roma's words. You must read them. I think it is time."

I scrub my palms over my face. "Do I have to?"

"Yes. I should have showed you long ago. But maybe you are ready only now."

Exhaling a hard breath, I unfold the paper, my mother's handwriting blurring before my eyes. I struggle to focus, then I read.

LISTEN CLOSELY SWEETHEART, *for what I tell you shall come to pass. You are young, but you must never forget.*

I see three important men in your destiny, but only one who truly matters.

The dark farmer's love is steady and strong, but you will not want his goodness.

The blond voyager's beauty is blinding, and you will follow him far from home. This stealer of joy will crush you, but he will not take your heart. You will keep it safe for the third man. And for him you must wait a long time.

Your only child is the one you see clearly, and you'll name him after your grandfather, Nicholai.

Your boy has a difficult path, for he refuses to acknowledge the truth. He believes only in beats of wild music and discards tender pulses of the heart, locking his soul up tight.

The woman with the key to opening it is older. Yes. So very much older than he.

. . .

FUCK. The fated mate prophecy. My eyes flick to Mom's. Her smile is sad and full of pity. "Keep reading," she says.

ONE DAY *your son will surrender. One day he will understand —only love has the purest pulse and a beat that is ever true. Far truer than any song. Hers are the lyrics he must follow, for the cup of her happiness is his to drink.*

Her happiness is his. You understand?

That day, he will need your honesty, and you must tell him the truth about his father.

Because your son is the man who matters.

Your son, Zsofia, is the one.

"JESUS," I say, handing back the cougar prophecy. "So what's the truth? That you never loved him, is that it?"

"Yes. What I felt for him was of no consequence."

"Bullshit."

"No. I swear it is so. I've waited a long time for you to be ready to see those words. Finally, today is the day you must grow up." She kisses my temple. "These words are the truth, Nico. You are the one. To see you shun love, to run away and not fight for it with your whole being... it breaks my heart. Do you want to be responsible for doing this to your mother?"

"No. Course I don't."

She thumps my back, then stands, her sneakers flashing garish rainbow colors as she shuffles close. I grasp her outstretched hand and let her pretend to haul me onto my feet.

She smiles. "If you want to make me happy, then you must open your eyes." She slaps my chest. "And also this stupid muscle behind your ribs. Come, let's lock up."

When we're out on the pavement, I keep my eyes lowered, feeling like the world's biggest fuckwit for losing my shit. And making my mom sad.

"You want to come with us and I will make you goulash? You will feel well again."

"Better not. I think I really need some sleep. But thanks."

"Yes, my love, you do need a big rest. We'll drive you home."

The sunshine makes my head pound harder as Mom guides my shoulders into Francis' car, like I'm a fucking invalid.

"Promise me one thing, Nico. Promise me you will think on what I have said. Promise that you will not hurt yourself like this anymore."

I roll my eyes. "That's two things."

"And most important—I ask that you loosen up your emotions. Let the pain you feel for Ivy have its way. Do not resist. Let it settle. And if the result is as I predict, then you must work out how to get her. How to fight for what you can be together. Fight for love, kick its butt, and *win*."

"I think that was twelve things."

"Nico," she warns. "This is serious."

"Alright. Alright," I say as I drop into the back seat. "I

promise. Not that I can remember what I'm agreeing to. The list was so long you might need to email it to me."

She slaps my head and slams the car door in my smirking face.

Back in my apartment, I ignore the mess of dishes piled in the sink, swallow some pain killers, and head for the bathroom. Reaching behind my neck, I pull my filthy tank overhead and throw it on the tiles.

The problem with getting fucked-up is not only the stupid shit you do while you're flying high but the comedown. Yeah, the comedown is a total bitch.

I take a piss, and then brush my teeth, the words of my tattoo taunting me in the mirror. Along with all the grazes and bruises and my aching, bandaged arm.

Future mine is yours to hold. Future yours is me. If I lived life over, would I find you sooner? Love is death. Death is love.

What the hell does it even mean? Right now, I hate those words. Hate that I've got them etched into my skin and I can't avoid seeing them every single time I stand shirtless before a mirror. Fuck, I'm an idiot.

Bracing my hands on the sink, I lean forward and stare into my bloodshot eyes. I can't believe Mom never loved my useless father. That news dropped like a bombshell.

So, I do what Mom asked and let my internal walls crumble for a moment—let the feelings I always push down rise up and spread from my chest. All of it radiating out, black and toxic.

The hate I feel for that guy—nothing but a sperm donor. Anger at myself for hurting Zsof. Rage at how much I miss

Ivy. How badly I crave the smell of her hair, the glide of her skin against mine, to see her silvery eyes darken just before she comes when I'm wedged tight inside her.

Heat scalds my chest again, the pressure unbearable as mental images of fucking her right here on this sink flash by. How could being with her feel so good—so right—when she insists it's all kinds of wrong? And that man—that smooth, suited-up guy in her apartment who she's planning on going out with. Fuck. Why him?

I glance down at the hard-on pressing against my jeans, fisting it and giving it one punishing squeeze of frustration. I'm obviously a born multitasker—horny as hell and angry enough to eat nails at the same time. What a genius.

I pad into my bedroom and close the blinds. The sheets feel cool when I slide between them, groaning in relief. I lie on my back with my good arm thrown over my face while I shuffle my legs non-stop.

Fucking hard-on. It won't go away, and I can't relax. Surely, after being awake for over thirty hours, it's not too much to ask to fall unconscious. Anger boils through my blood while a heavy heat coils in my gut, hard dick throbbing.

A mental picture of Ivy's smile solidifies in my mind and I let my palm drift down my chest to my stomach. *No.* Nope. No way I'm gonna jerk off to the girl who's letting another guy wine and fucking dine her next weekend. Nope. Not happening.

I yank my hand up and cover my eyes as I picture taking her nipple into my mouth, grazing it with my teeth. A groan rumbles through my lips. They're so dry I lick them, then keep doing it because it feels good when I pretend it's her lips wetting up mine.

Hard, ragged breaths pant out my mouth as I push my hips into the sheet, imagining it's her wet, tight pussy giving me perfect friction. My hand heads down again, but I whip it back, press it into my chest.

Not gonna touch myself like a damn teenager while I think about her. Husky moans fill my ears, reminding me of the ones Ivy makes when I pick up the pace and thrust hard into that spot she likes so much. Every time I hit it bang on target, her muscles wind tighter. Just like mine do now, my hips moving beyond my control, faster and faster.

"Fuck, that's it. Fuck, yes." To silence myself, I bite my lip and keep fucking her in my head. Her moans get louder, her flesh wetter. The soaked sheet rubbing over my dick feels good. I'm so close to exploding. I picture squeezing her tits, my hips rocking faster.

I won't touch myself. Not for her. Need to think of someone else. Picture another girl when I go over—anyone, just a generic set of tits. Just any pair of—

No. Fuck. *Ivy*—

My heart ricochets against my ribs, vision whiting out. Come floods the sheet and my body convulses, shuddering with the force of my orgasm.

Shit.

I just came without touching my dick. Fucking hands free and a brain full of Ivy. That's all it took.

Painful breaths saw through my parted lips and shame flushes through my blood. I feel like a fucking kid again, shooting a hot load off over a girl who doesn't want me. A girl who'll *never* want me.

My life is so unfair.

I reach into a drawer, grabbing tissues to clean up with. I don't have the energy to change the sheets, so after I wipe up, I shuffle away from the mess I've made and curl into a ball.

Ivy hates drunks.

I don't care. I don't care.

Ivy hates hanging around messed-up people.

Who gives a shit?

Me.

I care. I don't want to, but I fucking do.

Finally, reality begins to dissolve, and the last thing I'm aware of before passing out is overwhelming self-disgust settling like a rock in my gut.

19

IVY

Pet Wedding

"I can't believe you cried during the ceremony," says Mia, hiking her silver dress up over her boobs as we pack away the last of the photographic equipment. "You've never found weddings emotional before. Pets' or humans'."

In her eighties-inspired ruffle dress, she looks like a flamenco dancer with white pigtails.

Eyes fixed on the darkening sky over her shoulder, I fiddle with a light stand to hide my embarrassment. "But the black poodle looked so handsome in his tuxedo and the little Yorkshire terrier draped in her frilly veil was completely adorable. You could feel the love in the air."

Mia quirks her lips. "Especially when the groom humped

the celebrant during the vows. That was so romantic." She links my arm and drags me toward the tables.

The train of the velvety, forest-green gown she lent me for today's special occasion drags over the grass. Thoughts of the dry-cleaning bill terrify me.

Fairy lights and copper lanterns offset the purple dusk, blanketing the garden in a dreamy glow.

"We'll put the rest of the stuff in the car after we sit for a bit. I'm pooped."

"Me too," I agree as we settle in a corner of the temporary gazebo. It's almost empty because most of the guests are whooping it up on the dance floor. With their dogs.

The lavish setup of the garden wedding is beautiful, every detail chic and elegant. White and pink dog roses decorate all possible surfaces. Sophisticated guests slink about, chattering with each other or chasing canine companions. Silver bowls shaped like bones dot each table, filled with something delicious for owner and pet alike. By now, most of the food has been polished off, and I certainly ate my fair share. I don't know why I'm still popping things in my mouth as I sit here.

"I think that boy is doing strange things to you, softening your emotions." Mia shoves some sushi in her mouth.

"Which boy?" I ask, feigning ignorance.

"You know exactly who I'm referring to—"

"Do you think they drugged those poor critters?" I ask, changing the subject swiftly. "Because the bride and groom just sat there like fur-covered blocks of granite during the speeches."

She smacks my arm. "No! Don't be ridiculous. They're just well-trained pets. My clients aren't into animal cruelty!"

"Going by the dogs' expressions, I wouldn't be so sure of that. It was very difficult not to laugh."

"Yeah. It was." Mia sighs. "South would love this. Should I invite him to the next one?"

"No. That's a very bad idea. Why are you so keen to get your heart broken by him?"

"That won't happen. He seems really nice." She absent-mindedly twirls a lock of platinum hair around her fingers. "A night between the sheets with him would be utter bliss."

"Really? I think getting it on with South would be about as blissful as a shark attack. Those creatures keep the females in place during sex with their razor-sharp *teeth*. And how gross is this? The ladies take *weeks* to heal from the so called sexy-times. I watched a documentary on their mating habits yesterday. Put me off my dinner." Spouting wildlife facts, I sound a lot like *he-who-shall-not-be-named*—but thought about constantly.

"South is not a shark. And how about your Nico, I bet *his* fangs are pretty lethal."

"He's not my Nico—"

"Ladies!" interrupts a refined voice, startling me into inhaling a piece of tuna tart. Mia pats my back.

Quentin, the owner of the sprawling mansion we've spent the day in, doesn't even blink as I cough up half a lung.

He's a fashion designer and, accordingly, looks every bit the distinguished silver fox in his tuxedo. "It's lovely to see you laughing and enjoying yourselves." The proud father of the bride settles himself at our table. "Isabella showed me some of the shots you've already emailed her, Mia. Superb work once again."

Last spring, Mia photographed the wedding of Quentin and Isabella's Siamese cats, Dink and Donk, and she gets a lot of referrals from their social circle.

"Thanks, Quent." Mia tugs his sleeve, pointing across the room at the main table. "Look, Isis is getting into your wife's booze."

He glances over and smiles indulgently at the furry bride's long tongue lapping deep into a flute of champagne. "Oh, Isabella won't mind sharing. And fear not, she won't let Isis get drunk."

Thank goodness for small mercies.

Serious, dark eyes turn my way. "I'm looking forward to your opening, Ivy. Are Burntbad going to perform perhaps?"

This time, I nearly choke on my sip of wine. "No, Quentin! How do you even know about them?"

"Mia showed me a video snippet she took at a recent gig. What a wonderful looking boy their singer is. If the opportunity arose, I'd consider jumping his bones, and I'm heterosexual. Sorry, Ivy."

I screw my nose up at him because I have no idea why he's apologizing to me. Lots of people want to sleep with Nico. It's none of my business. "We've booked a string quartet," I say. "But that's about it. Kendra doesn't approve of post-punk indie rock."

"Oh, I thought it would be a perfect fit for your art. And, also, because he's your boyfriend—"

"Whoa, there. He's not my boyfriend. No way. That would be a little on the cradle snatching side."

Chin in his palm, he considers me closely. "But you've dated?"

I give Mia a look that should instantly smote her to smoking cinders. "Not really, no. He's attractive, yes, but far too young for me."

"I'm disappointed to hear you say that." Quentin frowns. "Life's too short to let trivial things hold you back from what you want."

"I didn't say that I want Nico and—"

He slashes his hand through the air, effectively silencing my protest. "When you talk about him, Ivy, your expression says it all. It's as though you're thinking of a tub of the most delicious organic pecan ice-cream and you're dying to gobble it all up but have decided to restrain yourself in order to prevent people from judging you." He wags his finger in my face. "Never a good reason to deny yourself."

I point out the extravagance around us. "Yes, I can see you're not used to renouncing life's pleasures."

He laughs. "I built my success on not giving a damn whether or not I shocked people. And if I've learned anything over my long career, it's that you can't control what others think of you. Even if you speak the words of a saint, plenty will still misinterpret what you're saying. Or they just won't like it and complain and complain and complain. I say, big deal! Don't give sourpusses control of your self-esteem. It's a futile exercise."

Yes, but Quentin didn't grow up with a mother like mine.

He didn't spend his whole childhood being referred to as Drunk Julia's Kid—the town joke.

For no particular reason, I think of Nico coming to my rescue at the gallery. How his eyes soften when I smile at him.

Will I ever meet another guy who looks at me the way he does? One who understands me. Who loves my art. Makes me laugh. Feels like refuge and home.

What if he's the only man who'll ever *get* me?

"He's too young," I say, and skull down the dregs of my wine. "End of story."

"Please don't think me rude, but I can't bear to hear any more claptrap." Quentin rises, kisses both our cheeks. "Remember, Ivy, you may not be able to control what other people think or what they do—but you will always have sovereignty over how you *react*. And that's all that matters. Choose to be unaffected by fools. Choose happiness."

Nodding, Mia raises a superior eyebrow at me. "Amen, Quent. Well said."

I ball my napkin up and throw it at Mia. "What the heck have I done to deserve all these lectures?"

"It's what you're *not* doing that's the problem." She catches the pretty pink cloth and dabs it around her smug mouth. "Let's go. We need to get you home to bed where you can lie in the dark for hours and contemplate all the many ways you're fucking up."

"Fine," I say. "Sounds like a great idea."

When did I become such a liar?

20

NICO

The One

I woke today at lunchtime, feeling about as fresh as a pile of shit that's been baked in the sun.

Because it's Tuesday and I'm not rostered on at the nursery cafe, I did fuck all until it was time to leave for the gig. Other than mope around and think about Ivy, of course.

Tonight's college show was a solid hour's drive from the city, and with our sound tech dude, Skip, driving, the rest of us downed a fair amount of beer in the van. No big deal. Alcohol is a painkiller. How else am I meant to play guitar with a freshly stitched-up gash in my arm?

I cruised through soundcheck no problem, and now we're hanging out backstage, waiting to go on.

Our bass player, Rob, runs his tattooed fingers over his buzz cut and gets comfortable on the couch beside me. "Show us your stitches."

I slug back more beer. "Can you not see the bandage, fuckwit?"

"Yeah. So?"

"Well, unless one of you rejects have recently gotten your first aid certificate, it'd be a bit dumb to unwrap it before the gig. Don't you think?"

Rob gives a lazy shrug. "Maybe."

A packet of peanuts sails toward me. My hand shoots up, plucking them out of the air. "Thanks, Linc. These are my favorite."

"Glad to bring you some joy. You've been a whiny brat ever since your hot cougar sprung loose."

My eyes narrow. I hate the way Linc talks about her, almost crossing the line of decency. If he stumbles over it just once, I'm gonna deck him.

Linc laughs. "Give it up. That ass-kicker look doesn't work on me. If you snap to it, you've got enough time to call her and grovel before we hit the stage."

I glance at the clock on the graffiti-covered wall. Shit. He's right.

Giving him my who-gives-a-fuck smirk, I stand, patting over pockets for my cell.

"Say, hi to Ivy." Rob doesn't even sound sarcastic. Probably because he's the only band member with a girlfriend, and he's hoping I'll join the ranks and take the shit-stirring focus off him. At the moment, I kinda like the idea. And that's fucked up. *I'm* fucked up. Must be the drugs still exiting my system and messing with my head.

As I stride down the hall and into the tiny restroom, I wonder if she'll answer her phone. The cubicle door bangs loudly behind me, and I realize my hands are clammy. It would help if I could remember what I said to her at the skatepark yesterday. I'm a little sketchy on the details, but pretty sure jealousy drove me to act like an ass. And possibly a spaced-out lunatic.

While I clear my throat over and over, her cell rings.

"Hello?"

"So, the word lunatic comes from the Latin word *lunaticus*. It referred to diseases that were thought to be caused by the moon." Fuck! I bang my head on the wall. A simple hello would have done fine.

"Good to know. Hi, Nico! Are you okay? I've been meaning to call. I feel terrible about leaving you with Linc yesterday. Did he look after you?"

"Yeah, I made it to a hospital." I don't mention that he ditched me after receiving a phone call from Janine, who in his words *sucks like a vacuum cleaner*, and I had to find my own way across town to get medical attention. Bleeding all over the train wasn't much fun. "I've got fifteen stitches."

"I bet."

"Wanna come see them? We've got a gig just out past Harrow Beach. Or I could come to you later on tonight."

She sighs. "I can't. I've been helping Mia at a dog wedding most of the day. I'm so tired I can barely move."

My stomach drops, the beer euphoria disappearing.

"Right. Sure." This girl fucks with my head. One minute I'm certain she's into me big time and the next I'm worried this thing I'm buzzing with only goes one way and I've been delusional ever since I met her in that alleyway.

"Did the happy couple have a good time?" I ask.

"Their best ever, I think. The groom humped the celebrant. The lovely bride laid an impressive-sized shit next to the three-tiered cake. Many a crotch was sniffed; dog butts were licked. It was quite a wild party."

I laugh at the mental images she's stirred, then go quiet, trying to come up with something sensible to say.

"Are you still mad at me?" she asks.

"No," I lie. I'm definitely pissed if she's still going out with that slimy douche-suit in a few days. I'll bring that up another time, though, my priority is to keep her on the line. "Hey. I've thought of a way you can make it up to me."

"Make what up to you?"

"Two-timing me with that dead-ass boring businessman and then disowning me in front of your boss." Fuck. How did that spring out of my mouth? During the silence that greets my words, I suck in a breath and hold it.

One beat.

You.

Two beats.

Ivy.

Three beats.

Fucking thrill me.

"Sorry about the thing with Kendra. I freaked out. You're my friend and there's nothing wrong with that. I am, however, still shocked and unhappy about the state we found you in. How often do you do that to yourself?"

"Hardly at all." I'm not excited about being demoted to friend-only status, but it fits nicely with my current strategy, so I won't complain just yet. "This call is kinda like a community announcement, beneficial to all parties."

"I doubt that."

"It's true. I'm alerting you of a rare chance to lecture me at length."

She laughs. "Oh, really? I'm listening."

"Remember my friends with the lavender farm?"

"Vaguely. You haven't said too much about them."

"Edie worked at the nursery with me for years. And L's her partner. He's an ex-street kid turned model."

"That's a very rags-to-riches tale. His name's Al? As in short for Albert?"

That's funny. He'd hate that.

"Nope. It's Leon. Used to get called Lightning out on the streets. Still goes by L, as in the letter."

"Oh, I see. L. It's an interesting name."

"Anyways, tomorrow morning, I'm doing a three-hour drive out to their place. Staying overnight. You should come. You've still got plenty of time tonight to collect your anti-drug-and-alcohol stats so you can inform me of the dangers of my shocking behavior the entire journey. Too good an opportunity to pass up, right?"

"Ummmm," she says, like she's actually considering it. "Probably not a good idea—"

"Wait until you hear the real reason why you need to come."

"Oh, okay. Lay it on me."

"So L's got this awesome yakuza-style tattoo. Flowers, a sword and dragon, wavy breast plate—all interwoven like a mural. It's pretty cool. And he has the saddest childhood story I've ever heard. Sexual abuse. Murder. Homelessness. Moved on to being blackmailed into sex parties. More murder. The whole story is about as dark as it gets and fucking abysmal. I just know you're gonna wanna talk to him, take his photo. Maybe even paint him some time. You're interested, right?"

"If you think he'd want to speak to me, then, of course! At the moment, I'm desperate for someone to paint, and your friend sounds like a dream come true. Text me the pickup time and what I need to bring along. I'm definitely in. Wait..."

"What?"

"This is just as friends. Nothing more. We're on the same wavelength with that, right?"

Fuck no. "Yep," I lie.

"Look, I hope I'm not making a terrible mistake, but as usual, Nico, you tempt me into dangerous territory."

"It'll be fine. As you said, we're friends. Right?"

She sighs. "Right. Okay, so I guess I'll see you tomorrow."

"Catch you, then. And don't worry about anything."

Collapsing back on the filth-covered door, I kill the call, relief washing over me. I was praying the lure of possibly painting *Lightning Boy*, as L used to be known, would snare

Ivy on my hook. And it worked. But instead of feeling triumphant, I'm revolted by the thought of her falling under his spell like most girls do. He's closer to her age, too—and age is a big deal for her.

Wake up, idiot, Ivy isn't *most girls*. L is sickeningly in love with Edie. I have nothing to worry about. The drugs have made me paranoid, that's all. And I'm kinda buzzed on alcohol again, so I'm not thinking straight.

Is it wrong to keep chasing her? Trying to tempt her into getting involved with me. Giving me more.

Bad luck if it is, because I'm not gonna sit back and do nothing while some rich guy schemes to snap her up. So what if the fucker can give her a luxurious life? It may be selfish, but I don't give a damn. No matter how much expensive jewelry that guy lays on Ivy, or how many fancy restaurants he wines and dines her in, he'll never show her the good times like I can. We connect. We make sense together. I totally *get* her.

She just doesn't realize it yet.

And then there's the text her friend Mia sent earlier today while I was in the van. Three words. *Don't. Give. Up.*

Like a lamebrain, I texted back. *On what?*

The answer: *On Ivy, you idiot. If you can wade through her issues, she's yours.*

Never before has a text message made an involuntary *fuck, yeah!* explode out of my mouth like a bomb going off in the van. My bandmates loved it. Me? Not so much.

Going forward, all I have to do is keep my hands off her while I get her addicted to hanging out with me. Make her crave my company. Make her want me so bad she can't think straight.

Should be easy.

Except for the not-touching thing. That could be one of the hardest things I'll *never* do.

See? I'm already planning on failing that part.

21

IVY

Farm

Nico's mouth is dangerous.

Lightheaded from staring at his disturbingly sexy lips, I'm about to lose control of my wits and do something stupid. Like place my hand on his thigh and inch it up over soft denim, slowly, slowly, until he runs the car off the road and we crash into a bush.

So far, the drive out to his friends' farm has been torture. While the wind whipped lovingly through his sandy locks, I've laughed at his jokes and tried to ignore every sweep of his hot gaze over my skin, the whole time battling inconvenient feelings. And by that, I mean extremely filthy thoughts.

This morning, while waiting for him to pick me up in his

old Dodge, I worried that being stuck in a car with him for three hours would be awkward. Or boring. Unfortunately, it's the exact opposite. Fun. And excessively stimulating in the groin area.

Being a perfect summer's day, no doubt the sun looks wonderful sparkling over every golden field we pass. Clouds are probably wisping enchantingly through the electric-blue sky. But I can't say for sure, because my attention has been elsewhere.

And if I had to paint my impressions of the journey, none of those things would feature. My canvas would be covered with Nico's dreamy, green eyes. And those terribly tempting lips—the ones I should never *ever* have let myself taste. Not even once.

Right now, I should be thinking about my upcoming date with the businessman, not daydreaming about painting Nico.

The story he's telling now about how his mom, Zsofia, met Red Francis at a hip-hop dance class is funny, but I can't concentrate on the details. All I can think about is touching him.

"Have I got something on my mouth?" he asks.

"What?" Startled to be caught ogling him, my head snaps backward, hitting the window with a loud thud. "No! I was trying to see around your bulky shoulders. We just passed an abandoned school. It looked creepy. Did you see it? I'd love to snoop around there awhile and get some shots."

His chuckle sends a shiver through my belly. "Want to go back and check it out?"

"Maybe on the return trip. The sooner we arrive at the

farm, the better. I don't think butts are meant to be sat on for two and a half hours straight."

Heat flickers in Nico's eyes as they drift over my body for the millionth time today. At present, I'm wishing for a friends-with-benefits kind of deal with him. Something like the arrangement, I perhaps moronically, just ended. Unlike me, he's the furthest thing from a moron. With confident moves, he controls the car and easily drives me crazy.

One hand releasing its grip on the wheel, he points out the windshield then swipes hair away from his face. That was nice of him. Now I can better admire those sea-green eyes. "See that second hill up ahead?"

I peer into the distance. "Yep."

"We'll take a left on the other side of it. Please inform your numb butt that it should only be about another fifteen-minutes cruising through some pretty cool scenery, and then we're there."

"What a beautiful place to live. Do your friends have much land?"

"About seventeen acres, but they don't farm all of it. Six years ago, when they got it back from the blackmailing piece of shit who held the mortgage, it was a dump. L has sunk a shit-ton of his modeling dough into the joint. And now it's a fully functioning farm, they employ young people who've had fucking nightmare lives and help them get back on track. They run counseling programs—all sorts of stuff. They do tangible good in the world. Change people's lives. So that place is worth a hundred times more than L's spent on it."

"It sounds amazing." I smile at his beautiful dimples. "I

hope L lets me paint him. I need one more portrait and then I'll have enough work for my exhibition. But I've got to find a subject to get started on it, and he'd be perfect!"

"Oh, man, you have no idea."

"But I'm a little nervous to meet him. What if he says no?"

Nico gives an amused huff. "That should be the least of your worries. Wait until you see him. I'm glad you obeyed my orders and resisted Googling him." He shifts gear, tendons in his forearm bulging, and the car powers uphill.

Sighing, I stare at trees out the window—a wash of green, gold, and sepia colors.

It was a bad decision to come on this trip, the endless hours of fighting my attraction to him seem impossible to get through. I should cut ties with him altogether, so I won't be tempted to do anything irresponsible. Such as latch onto his neck like a hungry vampire and give him a hickey.

But the bad news is, I feel good around him. Happy. Basically, I like him too much to ditch completely. As a *friend*—I remind myself.

Yeah, right.

Twenty minutes later, we wind along a tunneled driveway arched by trees that eventually thin out and open onto an expansive, clear sky. The old Dodge cuts its way between the farm's rolling purple fields. The music is off, and we're both silent, taking in the incredible view.

Nico kills the engine in a gravel parking lot out front of a huge, red barn. Insects hum and birds chirp as I exit the car and check out the stunning surrounds, gulping fresh air.

Slumping next to the barn, an ancient hothouse sinks into

the earth and beyond that lavender fields flow into the distance, wrapped by woodland at the edges. Everything teems with life—the air, the grass, lulling me into a sense of peace and tranquility. This place is heaven.

Nico gets our bags out of the trunk, and we follow a coiling path up a hill toward a white farmhouse surrounded by a wild cottage garden, the air between us shimmering with tension.

"I like what you're wearing," he says, his arm brushing mine as he walks beside me.

I squint at my vintage ripped shorts and my black tank top embroidered with silver feathers. "This morning, I let myself be guided by the weather. And travel comfort. Guess I could have dressed up a little to meet your friends."

"No complaints from me." His lips slide into a delicious smile. "Your legs look amazing."

I wish he wouldn't say things like that. Or smolder his gaze all over me. Might be best if he refrained from looking at me period.

As we climb rickety porch steps, the front door flings open, and a heavily pregnant woman rushes through it, yelling his name.

With long, dark hair and dimples sparkling in a friendly face, she's very beautiful. Stripy leggings and a tight black t-shirt dress enhance her voluptuous curves. Her look is sweet and wholesome but with an unconscious sexy edge. I watch Nico's face and, of course, his smile is radiant. I haven't seen him wear that particular expression before—it looks like complete happiness.

He flicks a grin at me and whispers, "That's my first love," then launches himself like a golden retriever at the girl who I'm guessing is his long-time friend, Eden.

I wonder if all his *other* loves are as attractive as she is. Wait a second—what does he mean by *first love?* He seems to have forgotten about that weird tattoo on his chest—*love is death, death is love* and all that rubbish. Is he admitting that once-upon-a-time, he had actual *feelings* for a girl?

He enfolds Eden in his arms and lifts her off the ground, making her squeal, and although the sound should be annoying, it's not. When she emerges from his embrace, she heads my way, wearing a genuine smile.

Wrapping me in a nice, warm hug, she says, "Ivy, it's great to meet you. I'm Edie as you've probably already guessed. Nico talks about you constantly."

Laughing at Nico's frowning face, she waves us forward. "Come inside out of the heat. How was the trip?"

"Hardly any traffic once we hit the open road," he replies. "And I'm guessing it was pretty good for Ivy because she had me all to herself for a real long time. And you know how entertaining I am, Edie."

"Indeed." She winks over her shoulder at me. "Lucky girl."

We enter a long hallway, and with a thump, Nico drops our bags on the wooden floor.

"Wow! This reminds me of a bowling alley," I say, admiring the ornate cornices that go on forever. "It's absolutely massive."

Edie sweeps a fond gaze along the wood-paneled walls.

"Gotta love old farmhouses. All sorts of games have happened in this hall. Most of our young people are at a course in town this week. But you should see this place when we're at peak capacity. Holy heck are we thankful for the space, then."

Brow creasing a little, she turns to Nico. "We've missed you the past few months. How have you been?"

"Great." Challenging the seams of his retro *Mork and Mindy* t-shirt, he stretches his arms overhead and then leans against the door frame.

Through the door is a large living room full of comfy looking couches and an assortment of different sized tables, the walls deep crimson like a wild-west saloon. It looks like a nice place to hang out.

"Well." Edie's gaze rakes Nico's strapping torso, finally settling on his luminous eyes. "You get more beautiful every time I see you."

Jealousy pangs sharply in my chest, which is ridiculous. He *is* beautiful. And it should be no concern of mine if another girl—especially a pregnant one—comments on the fact.

A dark eyebrow raised, he cuts me a cheeky look as if to say, *'there's your proof, Ivy, women everywhere want me.'* He needn't have bothered with the meaningful look. I'm well aware he's a mega-hunk.

Edie leans in to tuck strands of hair behind his ear, thankfully in a motherly fashion. "They must put something special in the bayside drinking water."

"Must do. They grew L on it." His smirk gets wider. "And South, too."

"Good lord." She clutches her chest. "South! Yes, there's definitely something suspicious going on down there. My guess is it's a social experiment on how shockingly beautiful men affect the female reproductive system."

"Now why do you sound like you're complaining?" Nico shoves a hand on his hip, accentuating his shapely bicep. "You love basking in our magnificence."

"He has always been full of himself, Ivy," Edie says in my ear. Then she beckons us down the hallway.

Nico gives me another cocky grin, and I quickly bend and grab my bag before he can get his paws on it.

"You missed Angelo," she says as we follow close behind her. "He's been staying with us but got called away yesterday on a shoot. He desperately wanted to be here to surprise you. I've never heard so much swearing in one sentence when he told us he had to leave."

"Really? Damn. It would've been amazing to catch up with him. Ivy's gallery is so close to where he lives, but he's never in town when I am." Nico elbows me gently, and my skin prickles all over. "Hilarious guy Angelo. And he's a model, same as L. Speaking of your arrogant bastard, Edie, where is L?"

"Out with a crew, checking weed cloth and drip lines. Loves any excuse to work those muscles, but he never misses lunch. He'll be in soon. Let's drop those bags in your room so you can relax."

We turn left into a bright yet rustic bedroom with a high

vaulted ceiling and French doors that open out onto a rose garden. Alongside colorful modern art, photos of Greek islands hang on creamy walls.

Nico throws himself backward onto the massive bed. This must be where he's sleeping, then.

I watch him bounce, limbs spread-eagled and his blue t-shirt a nice contrast against the multi-colored patchwork quilt. He looks lovely, and I'd like nothing better than to crawl all over him. I quickly avert my eyes from the spectacular vision of corded muscle, wavy hair framing chiseled features. Those lust-inducing lips.

Disappointed in my pervy self, I shake my head and catch Edie's smirk as I drop my gaze to the floor. Great. No doubt she can guess what every single one of my inappropriate thoughts are about.

She gives Nico an indulgent smile then turns to me. "Pop your bag down, Ivy, and we can go grab lunch. How does some icy-cold lemonade sound to start with?"

My mouth opens and closes.

A frown crinkles her brow. "Are you okay? Do you need the bathroom?"

"No. I'm just wondering… am I sleeping here? I mean… if I am, then thank you! It's a great room." Shuffling my feet, I quickly check what Nico's up to. Yep, he's still reclining like a king awaiting the arrival of his favorite harem girl. "Shouldn't you get up and find your own bed to wreck, Nico, instead of laying waste to mine?"

"Oh!" Edie blinks rapidly. "You don't want to sleep with him?"

Well, truthfully, I *do*, but I can't admit that, so I wince and shake my head.

"I'm so sorry. I thought you were together, so I only made up this room."

Nico's hand slashes against his throat, trying to shut Edie down.

"We're definitely not together. I hope someone hasn't been giving you the wrong impression." I shoot a glare toward the bed. "Is it possible there's somewhere else I can sleep?"

Edie says, "Of course, would you like me to make up the—"

"Yes, please," I interrupt before I even know what the alternative is. She could be offering accommodation in the barn, and that would be okay. Definitely a better option than lying next to *him* all night long. "I hope it isn't any trouble. I'd be happy with a couch."

Nico sits legs crossed on the bed, leaning back casually on his elbows. "Come on, Ivy. Don't be difficult. The bed's huge. Don't you trust me?"

Edie laughs. "Does she look like an idiot? Of course she doesn't trust you."

"Ha. Ha. Ha," says Nico, launching up onto his knees in a full-on rock star pose—hands on slender hips and his chin raised defiantly. "You're so funny."

Once again, I scan his body. His wonderful face. I really have to stop doing that.

"I wasn't joking." Edie marches to the bed and pats his sharp cheekbone. "Don't sulk, Niccy. You always get what you want in the end. Just be patient."

"Don't call me that." His hand shoots out toward Edie, but she steps backward, causing him to lose balance and tumble headfirst onto the floorboards. "Ow!" Scowling, he rubs his head. "You trying to kill me or what?"

"Or what." Edie wraps an arm around my shoulders, guiding me toward the door. "Let's go find you a more peaceful place to sleep, Ivy. You can help me make up the bed and tell me all about your incredible paintings. I've already checked some out online, and I know which one I want to buy." She tosses a wicked grin at Nico. "And you're not invited."

"What?" Untangling his limbs, he gets to his feet and dashes forward. "But don't you want my help? I'm strong and I can easily lift the—"

"No!" Edie and I say at the same time, slamming the door in his face.

Half an hour later, the three of us are seated at a massive wooden table in the garden, drinking wine and chowing down on French soup. The chunky dish is rich and comforting, full of tasty vegetables and white beans.

Nico is updating Edie on all things Burntbad when a loud crashing sound comes from inside the house. It's followed by a thud, as if something large collided with a wall. A deep voice grunts, "*Fuck.*"

Rubbing her belly, Edie stretches back in the chair. "And that will be L, trashing the place as usual."

I take a big gulp of chardonnay, nearly choking on it when I cop an eyeful of the guy who walks through the doorway and out onto the porch above us.

"Hey!" Ignoring the stairs, he leaps over the railing into the yard and swoops down on Nico, giving him a backslapping hug before turning an expectant smile on me.

It's impossible to form a clear thought while staring at this blond god. Taking in the tall, impressively built body dressed in ripped jeans and a gray t-shirt, tatts twining intriguingly down his arms, the words that come to mind are *sizzling-hot* and *avenging angel*. And never mind that he's blond, I know exactly how I'm going to paint him—as a dark angel. It's a vibe thing.

Craving my sketchbook, I flex my fingers and Edie and Nico burst out laughing. Probably picturing all the flies soon to land in my stupidly gaping mouth.

"What?" L's face twists at them.

Dimples flashing at her man, Edie directs her hand at me. "L, this is Nico's friend Ivy, say hello."

"Yes, ma'am." Blasting me with brilliant turquoise eyes, he catapults forward. My heart pounds in my chest at the thought that he might be about to... yep... he wraps me in a brief but frighteningly tight hug. Thank God I'm sitting down.

"Hi, Ivy," he rumbles in my ear.

"Don't worry," Edie says with a smile. "You'll get used to him. He's not half as scary as he looks."

L struts around the table, plants his hands on Edie's chair, bracketing her between his arms, and leans close. "I'm not sure which is more offensive—the fact that I apparently *look* scary or that I'm not as scary as I *could* be once you get to know me." He strokes one hand over the baby-belly and buries the other in her hair, kissing her slowly while Nico and I openly stare.

After he breaks the kiss, he spends a little too long gazing into her eyes, one side of his mouth kicked up in a *just-you-wait-until-I-get-you-alone* expression. Then his head jerks up, his wide eyes suggesting he'd forgotten that we existed. "You guys started eating without me? Bit rude, Edie."

She laughs as he sits next to her and reaches for the basket of crusty bread. "When a pregnant woman is hungry, she eats. And, anyway, you came back late so, in actual fact, you're the rude one, L."

Smirking, he throws her another *I'll-see-to-you-later* look and gets stuck into the food.

"So when are you due?" I ask Edie.

Before she can move her lips, L replies, "Exactly seven weeks."

"He's not counting or anything." Edie rubs L's back and he practically purrs. Or maybe growls.

L waves his spoon between Nico and I. "So, how long have you two been... you know... hanging out."

Nico chews his mouthful slowly, gazing up at the clear sky. "Three weeks and maybe... uh, about five days."

Our hosts laugh.

"And how many hours do you think it's been, Niccy?" Edie asks.

Nico's brows knit together.

"Sounds like he's not counting either." L grins. "Must be a guy thing."

During lunch, we hear all about the farm—how in five

and a half years they've managed to turn it from a rundown weed plantation into a thriving cottage business. It's been a long journey for them, but one filled with meaning, and hope, and love. And a crazy amount of hard work.

When we finish our soup, L and Nico go inside to collect dessert.

A cow moos mournfully in the distance, and Edie tops my wine up while I refill her water.

"He's different around you, Ivy," she says with a smile.

My face heats. "What do you mean?"

"Well, tell me how you would describe him. Is he light-hearted? A fun kind of guy?"

I think for a moment, then nod. "Yeah, I'd definitely call him fun. He jokes around. Smiles a lot."

She shakes her head.

"What? Isn't he normally cheerful?"

She puffs out a breath. "No. I mean he *can* be that way with people close to him. But grumpy-slash-broody is kind of his default setting."

My jaw drops a little.

"I've known him since he was a smartass teenager, from an age when angry is the norm, but he never seemed to grow out of it. I don't think he ever got over his dad abandoning him. He's stored up a lot of angst about what his mom went through bringing him up alone. Have you met Zsofia yet?"

"Yes. What a character! She's great."

"Isn't she? And Zsof's an optimist through and through. A real battler. She'd love to see Nico fight for what he wants, too, just the way she always has. And you know what she wants more than anything? For him to be happy. That's it—her life's ambition—Nico's happiness."

Wow. Imagine having a mother so devoted.

I fold my arms over my chest and say in the gentlest voice I can muster, "I get how much he means to her. But why do I feel like you're blaming me for something?"

She smiles sadly. "I'm not. Truly. It's just that I've lived through the whole painful scenario of fighting your feelings for someone—running away from them. That was L, obviously. When I met him, he seemed like the worst possible choice for a life partner. And now look at us."

"You look happy."

"Blissfully so. And I don't want to be a busy-body, Ivy, or guilt trip you at all. But... can I share something I've learned?"

I heave a sigh and nod.

"If a person seems too difficult, almost impossible to have, but when you're together, somehow you feel so *right* and *real* —your true self when you're with them—well, you shouldn't run away from that. That person is important, probably the most important person in your life, and worth fighting to the death for. Some would say the greater the battle, the truer the love."

"Yeah, and some say love's a razor that leaves your soul to—"

Edie laughs. "Ah, yes, Bette Midler sang that. Or whoever wrote the song." She reaches across the table and squeezes my hand. "Listen... I can hear the guys coming. But, Ivy, please think about the rest of those lyrics. And don't forget what happens to the seed at the end of the song."

The seed. Of course. It becomes a rose.

A mental image of Nico drunkenly stomping over flowers, crushing them into dirt, at the skatepark taunts my brain.

"Yum! Here come the delicious sweets," Edie says loudly as the boys appear on the porch. She gives me a cheesy wink. "And the dessert course is on its way too."

After L serves us homemade apple tart, he settles back in his seat.

When he takes a big spoonful piled high with sweet cream, I steel my nerves and ask, "So, L, I believe Nico worded you up on the idea of me painting you for my exhibition. What do you think?"

"I don't mind. I'm used to that kind of thing, so if you wanna… sure."

"Your sitting fee is probably way too expensive for me."

He laughs. "What? Nah, no charge."

My mind fires with a vision of L as a golden angel—black wings, wearing a shining vine-like crown and coppery-gold armor that will highlight his tattoos. I need to get a gander at those inky beauties ASAP. "Can I take a few photos when you've finished eating?"

He waves his hand like he's swatting a fly. "Take them now. It's fine."

"Yeah," says Nico. "No need to seclude yourselves away for hours. Just do it out here."

Edie's laugh is a lovely tinkling sound. It makes L chuckle and cast her another one of those looks—full of sexy intent.

He gulps down some wine and raises his glass at Nico. "I'd forgotten what jealously looked like on you, Niccy. It's pretty funny, kid."

"You're only four years older than me, dude. Big-fricking-deal."

L snorts at him. "Go ahead, Ivy. If you're okay with the outdoor light, fire away. We don't wanna upset Nico."

I ignore the comment about Nico. "I'll just take a few Polaroids. But if you happen to be in the city anytime over the next two weeks, it'd be great if you could pop by my studio."

Tapping his boot against the table leg, Nico says, "Do you really think that'll be necessary?"

L and Edie erupt into laughter.

I sprint inside, grab my vintage camera, and return as fast as I can.

When I start snapping pics, I say from behind the safety of the view finder, "Nico tells me you've got quite the backstory, L."

"You bet. Basically, I'm a double murderer, ex-prostitute-slash-street kid." Swallowing his last scoop of dessert, he pushes the plate away. "It's not a PG-rated tale, that's for sure. But if you wanna hear the details, I'll give you the whole sordid story tomorrow before you guys leave. You won't believe how Edie and I first met. That's definitely R-rated."

Oh? Call me interested.

"Will this be like a group retelling?" Nico asks. "Or are you planning on getting together with Ivy alone?"

L smirks at him. "I'm thinking a private one-on-one with her might be good. Probably in her bed." Lips twisting, he shakes his head. "What are you, a fucking idiot? I'm not interested in your girl, Nico, I've got one of my own thanks. *Shit.*"

I gasp. "Oh, but I'm not his—"

Ignoring me, L grunts. "Jesus. Was I like this with you?" he asks Edie.

"Yes." She giggles into her hand.

I expect Nico to go on a rant—explain that they've got the wrong idea about our relationship—but, instead, he gets out his phone and studies it, scrolling through texts or something.

"Got enough shots yet?" L asks.

"Not quite." I take a close up of his dazzling blue eyes, then fan the photo and drop it on the tabletop with the others. "I'd like to see a bit more of those tattoos if it's okay."

Edie and Nico tease him into standing and busting out a modeling pose. He does. The aggression emanating from his icy stare is intense, and the camera worships him. No wonder he makes stupid amounts of money.

"Come on, Lightning, hit her with the good stuff. Show the tatts and the abs," Edie taunts.

With one side of his lips quirked, he stares at her while he peels his t-shirt off. I shuffle close to capture the beautiful artwork covering his skin.

"I want a crisper image of that dragon's face and the sword."

L waits patiently while I swap my instant camera for my phone. Excitement at the idea of a new project knots my stomach. I cannot wait to paint this guy.

Swaggering up next to me, Nico says to L, "Maybe you could ask Ariana to plug Ivy's exhibition."

L nods. "Yeah. Of course. She'll love your work, Ivy. It's very cool."

Nico's chin tips toward me, his emerald eyes glowing in the sunshine. Struck speechless by the sight, I quickly steal a few photos of his dimpled smile. I'll enjoy perusing those later. At length.

Nico bends and plucks a long blade of grass. "L's agent has first-rate society connections."

"I can imagine," I say. "Thank you both for thinking of me."

"You nearly finished, Ivy?" Nico asks. "I want to take you down by the stables."

"*Really?*" says L. "Well, fuck, I'm surprised you mentioned that in company. But feel free to forget we're here. You guys go for it. The horses won't mind. Plenty of times Edie and I have—"

"Shh!" Edie laughs.

I set my cell down next to the photos and start collecting our lunch dishes.

"I meant that I want to take her to *see* the horses. Not..." Nico does something interesting with his hands to indicate some very heavy petting.

Certain parts of my anatomy pay close attention. They have no business buzzing when I've told Nico I only want to be friends. Friends *without* benefits, I remind myself.

"Of course, if you happen to be interested, Ivy, I'm sure

you could convince me to have a crack at offending the horses."

I roll my eyes and pass Nico a pile of plates, careful to avoid skin-on-skin contact. It will only enhance the pesky buzzing in my pants. "Okay, sure. A walk sounds nice. Let's help clean up first. Interested in joining us for a stroll guys?" I ask our hosts.

Hiding smirks, they spout dodgy excuses.

"No. Can't," says Edie. "Gotta wash a cow."

L snorts. "I can't either. Need to read some birth books, because it could happen any day. Edie's labor, I mean. And I don't wanna be useless when push comes to shove."

"I think I'll be the one who has to do all the work." Edie laughs. "You can sit back and eat ice cream, enjoying the spectacle of me pushing out your giant baby."

"What do you mean by that?" L asks, a hard scowl creasing his forehead. "Are my back massages *that* bad I'm not allowed to touch you during labor?"

The smile she gives him fixes a smug look on his face, informing us that his handiwork is more than good enough.

I make an immediate escape to the kitchen, Nico following close behind. It's tough being around his friends. Seeing Eden and L together makes me want what I can't have —or shouldn't allow myself to have.

Nico.

I refuse to let myself become known as '*that cougar woman, Ivy*'.

We tidy the kitchen quickly, Nico joking around and accidentally brushing up against me as we stow pots and pans in all the wrong places.

After we finish, we stroll to the stables, his deep voice lulling me into a contented stupor as he recounts funny tales from Burntbad's time on the road. A few of the stories involve groupies, and even though they aren't about sex, I have to hide the fact they make my stomach nauseous. Darn jealousy again.

The barn door is open. Dust motes circle through dappled light as we enter, a wonderful horsey smell heady in the air. I inhale deep.

"Hey, Daphne," he greets a huge black horse who nods and whinnies at our arrival. We go straight to her stall and Nico scratches behind her ears. "This babe here is a total dream to ride. And she's sweet as honey, too."

Entranced by the rhythmic movement of his fingers, all I can think about is riding *him*. "You must sleep with a lot of girls," I say, absentmindedly stroking the horse's velvety muzzle. "What with all the opportunities the band provide." Oh, God. I sound like a music journalist interviewing him, hoping for a hot scoop.

Wide green eyes cut to my face, then back to Daphne's. His lips thin. The air between our bodies shimmers like a heat-haze.

"Well, I guess I have. But I think it's pretty normal to want to do it a lot. I mean... sex is awesome, right?"

Well, that depends on who you do it with.

Concentrating on patting the horse, he continues, "But, lately, I haven't had any interest in those girls. Since I met you." His fingers drum against soft fur, and he takes a breath like he's going to say more, then bites his silver lip ring.

My chest feels tight, my face hot, and all I manage to say is, "Oh."

His eyes flick briefly to mine. "Did you know that older people who have a lot of sex look five to ten years younger than their actual age? It's a scientific fact." His hand drops from Daphne's coat, hitting his thigh hard. "Fuck. I'm doing it again."

I want to stroke tousled hair from his face. I ache to touch his skin. Anywhere. Everywhere. But I don't. Instead, I say, "I like it when you spout random facts. They're charming." What I mean is *he's* charming. And hot. And perfect.

And so, so young.

His dimples flash briefly before he resumes horse massaging duties. If Daphne's expression of bliss is anything to go by, he may have struck upon an alternative career should things not work out with the band. A horse whisperer.

Without warning, he turns his attentions from Daphne to me and lifts a lock of my hair, running his fingers through it. "Shit. The sun coming through that roof window above is setting your hair on fire."

Grimacing, I reply, "Yep, it often glows like a toxic substance."

"Huh. It's sexy as fuck."

I shuffle my feet and cast around for a change of subject. "Well, your friends' lives will certainly change when that baby arrives."

"Edie and L's? Yeah. Definitely. But those two are rock

solid. Unshakable. Having a family will only make them stronger." The horse snorts as Nico goes silent, angling his body away from me. Then he takes a slow breath. "Do you want kids?"

"Yes. Absolutely." That's one thing I'm sure about. "My mom did a shocking job of parenting. I can't wait to do better —to be there for my little one, stable and reliable, day after day, year after year. I'd like to have a child sooner rather than later."

"Me too."

A cold wave washes through my blood, making me shiver. Why is he telling me this?

"You're a bit young to be a dad."

"Twenty-four? No, I'm not. And by the time you—I mean by the time a girl got pregnant and actually gave birth to my baby, I'd be like a whole year older."

"But at your age and with the band stuff, there's no need to rush into such a thing. You can't just have a kid and then forget about it."

"You mean like my dad did?"

"Well, yeah. And you hate your father. So why would you want to *become* one?"

He drags a hand over his face. "I think when you meet someone and if you… or if maybe they… uh. I think…" His eyebrows scrunch together as his stuttering trails off. "Look I know what I want, Ivy." He shakes his head at the floor, breathing out a soft curse. "I'm not making this up. I'd be okay to have a child soon with the right person."

He must be high.

This conversation is freaking me the hell out. It needs to stop right now. Enough already with the knocking-people-up talk. What sane guy discusses this stuff with a girl he's slept with?

"I'm gonna head back to the house," I say, my voice shaking embarrassingly. "I feel a bit ill. Probably just need to sleep the wine off, then I'll be good as new."

Nico, who's obviously insane, closes the distance between us, fingers lingering near my hip, then dropping away. His emerald eyes shine with longing, and it burns straight to my core. Searing my heart. My mind. Turning my soul to ash.

"I'll come too."

Oh, freaking great.

Sighing, I stride out into the sunshine with Nico following hot at my heels.

"If you want, I can carry you."

Do I look that feeble?

"I'm fine," I say, wondering if I should fake-faint so I can press my face against his neck while his sun-kissed hair tickles my cheek. If only for a few fabulous minutes.

When we return to the house, I withdraw to my room, hoping to verify my not-feeling-well fib, and read.

After half an hour, I feel too guilty secluding myself away and brave the great outdoors to help Edie and Nico tend the vegetable patch.

For dinner, L makes a mean Greek moussaka which we eat by candlelight in the garden.

When we've demolished our food, we retire to the porch,

and Nico grabs his guitar, serenading us into the wee hours. We sing along, laughing and swatting insects.

By two o'clock, I'm all done in and stumble onto my feet and make my goodnights. I feel Nico's gaze follow me as I leave for the bathroom.

I wash my face and brush my teeth then head back to the kitchen to skull down a glass of water before bed.

Muted voices from the porch waft on the breeze through the open French doors, drawing me near. Hidden from view, I peer out from behind a column in the dimly-lit lounge, dragging in a slow breath at the captivating sight before my eyes.

L sinks deep into the cushions of an armchair while Edie straddles him, her big belly pressing between them. Candlelight illuminates their faces as they kiss slowly, stopping every now and again to stare deep into each other's eyes. To whisper secrets. The night air thrums with tension.

How I long to be looked at like that one day—as though I'm the center of the universe, the bringer of death and the font of all life—the only safe place to be.

I can't help wondering what it would feel like if Nico—

"What are you doing, Ivy?" Out of nowhere a warm hand lands on my hip, calloused fingers stroking softly. "Ah, I see," Nico whispers in my ear. "Being a voyeur by the looks of things."

Embarrassed at being caught watching, I push his hand away. "No, I was just on my way to bed and—"

"Shhhh," he breathes against my neck, his body heating my back through my tank top.

I glance behind me. He's wearing nothing but jeans. Top

button undone. And I can smell his skin, musky and mouth-watering. Breathing becomes difficult.

"Nico—"

"Ivy, be quiet." He kisses my neck, gently biting and sucking. I moan as his fingers trail over the skin at the hem of my cutoffs, dipping in. When he finds me wet, he groans softly, his big body pushing my front flush against the column.

Out on the porch Edie rises and falls over L's lap. His breathing is harsh. Loud. He talks to her whilst they're fucking, but I can't make out the words. I'd love to know. I need to know. They'd go perfectly in his painting—in the poem I'll write about avenging angels and love saving the blackest of souls. For him. For them.

Knowing I shouldn't, I widen my stance and Nico's arm tightens around my stomach, the fingers of his other hand working magic over my clit. I pant, and he says, "Fuck, yes. You don't know how much I need this."

"Shush," I say between soft moans. "They'll hear us."

"Doubt it." He grips my jaw, angling my face so he can give me a perfect, wet kiss, his tongue teasing and cock hard against my back. "Ivy. Ivy. Ivy," he whispers, breath hot on my skin, then panting into my mouth. His hands are everywhere all at once, my breasts, stomach, pinching my nipples, driving me crazy. I can't take it any longer.

When my hips roll into his touch and his own press harder against me, a picture flashes before my eyes. A vision, like lightning, of a prideful pharaoh in a business suit. Gregor. Shit.

I gather my self-control, muscles freezing. "Nico, I can't do this. It's not right."

"It's okay. We won't get caught. Listen to them. Unlike us, they're taking their time. Savoring it like they've got forever. I wish we had forever, Ivy."

"Please, this isn't right."

His fingers move through my slick folds again, and it feels so amazing that I have to bite my lip to stifle a moan.

"Let's go to your room, then." His smile is lava-hot. "I'll show you how slow I can go."

I grip his wrist to still his movements. "No. I've got a date with my client coming up, remember? This isn't fair on anyone."

Instantly, he turns to stone.

Silence.

Then his chest heaves against my back, breath fanning my cheek in ragged bursts.

Long seconds pass where I feel him vibrate, his arm around me flexing tight, loosening. He spins me around, eyes on fire in the lamplight. One hand presses into my chest, trapping me against the column, the other skims down my body, quickly unzipping my shorts and disappearing under the denim.

"Nico…" I say in a halfhearted protest as his fingers push deep inside me. He pumps in and out hard.

Lord have mercy. I'm on fire with need, and he burns with a terrible anger. His narrowed gaze fries me to a crisp, but the rest of his expression is ice-cold. Impassive.

"Want me to stop?"

I close my eyes. Pant out three hard breaths.

"Do you?"

"No."

His lips shape victory, more a snarl than a smile, as his fingers pluck a tragic tune from my body—long sighs, helpless moans. The sounds of a heart pulsing, soaring, then breaking.

"Tell me, is this fair?" he asks, working me into a lather.

I'm wriggling and panting, trying to inch closer, but he keeps me literally at arm's length. No kissing, no skin stroking—nothing affectionate—just relentless staring while he fucks me with his fingers.

I blaze hotter every time he speaks. With each whispered word I vibrate harder, like one of his guitar strings stretched to its limits and about to snap.

"Answer me. Is it fair? Is this fair, Ivy?"

I can't speak. I can't even draw breath. Then I explode, crying out as I come hard.

The hand at my chest, pinning me against the column, flies up and covers my mouth. While I shake, his savage staring continues.

My eyes drop to his cock straining through his unzipped jeans. "Let me help you," I mumble as I tug his palm away, then reach to give him relief. Going by his ragged breathing, he needs it badly.

He leans close, his scent enveloping me, soft hair brushing my cheek. For a moment, I think he's going to kiss me, but, alas no, he only looks past me and toward the porch. "Like I said, they're still going strong out there. Taking their time."

There's no warmth in his voice, his anger an impenetrable wall between us, and still I stroke his erection, thrilling when it jerks in my grip.

"Stop." He pushes my hand away.

"Why?"

"Because it's not *fair* on your old-man billionaire, Ivy."

"I don't think he's a billionaire. Or elderly—"

"I don't give a shit. Sleep well," he whispers against my lips, and then disappears into the dark hallway.

The noises from the porch, loud, desperate, and loving no longer entice me. To my ears, they sound mocking and cruel.

On shaking legs, I stagger away from *true-love-going-hard-at-it* on the patio, enter my bedroom, and collapse on an unfamiliar bed. Far away from Nico.

I lay back and prepare for a sleepless night. No matter how comfortable, I always have trouble sleeping somewhere new. And there's that horrible pain in my chest, too. Stupid tears leak out from my eyes, rolling onto my pillow as I attempt to relax and fall asleep. It's impossible. My jaw muscles are so tight they ache, my stomach hollow.

How does Nico have the power to hurt me so badly? His knee-jerk reactions, his inability to temper his anger only prove his immaturity. He's a boy, not yet a man. And this may be prejudiced, but rockers never grow up. Never become reliable partners or good fathers. Do they?

If only I could be casual and make him my toy boy for a month or two, revel in all the pleasures of a quick, hot fling. Let the heat of our attraction burn wildfire-fast out of our systems. Then move on with my art and my life. Marry a guy like Gregor, have a family. Live the dream.

But the problem is, at the moment, Nico feels like the dream I want to chase and Gregor, the nightmare I should run away from.

So the question is...

The question is—concerning Nico—do I chase or do I run?

22

IVY

Leaving Heaven

The next morning, after little to no sleep, I join the breakfasters for L's pancakes—French style crepes, he says, like his mom used to make when he was a child. They're delicious with lemon and crazy amounts of butter and sugar.

The atmosphere is light and fun. Nico acts as though nothing untoward happened between us last night, teasing and joking, but something akin to irritation or frustration stews in the heat of his gaze. I wonder if I'm the only one who notices it.

After breakfast, Edie distracts Nico with a request for help with the horses, and L and I take our coffees into the garden. I can hardly believe the terrible story he relays—abuse, murder, saved from a life on the streets by a modeling agent, then blackmail, Edie, more murder, and finally redemption, freedom, and love. When he finishes his tale, I tell him he should write it all down. It's a horrifying and fascinating narrative and someone out there would want to read it. He laughs hard at the idea.

Just before lunchtime, we prepare to hit the road. Nico has a gig tonight, which I definitely won't be attending.

While I'm stuffing my gear into my backpack there's a knock at the bedroom door. "Yeah?" I call.

"It's me," says Edie.

"Come on in. I'm just packing up."

As she enters looking ethereal in a boho-style shift dress, I flop on the edge of the bed. "Hey."

She sits beside me. "Hey, yourself. Looking forward to getting back?"

"Honestly, I'm a little jealous of your set up here. It's so tranquil."

Her laugh echoes around the room. "Next week, when everyone's back on board, it'll be a madhouse. I'll send you a video of a very different kind of dinner situation. When you see the chaos, you'll be relieved you're not here."

"Sounds fun, though," I say, gazing out at the garden.

Nico and L have popped into view. Two hunks shooting the breeze. Actually, Nico looks a little pissed, arms folded, he's scowling while L talks fast.

"Oh, I think they're arguing." I tip my head in their direction, and Edie turns to look. L is making lots of slashing and pleading type motions with his hands. They both seem angry. "Do they do this a lot?"

"Well, they're as pigheaded as each other, so yeah, they can be a bit volatile. Don't get me wrong, they love each other. When they first met, it was instant hate born through jealously, but now L's kind of like a big brother figure. Trouble is, Nico doesn't like being told when he's heading off track."

I stuff my toiletry bag in my pack. "I wonder what they're fighting over."

"L's probably telling him not to make the same mistakes he did. Advising him to communicate, be clear about his feelings."

"To who?"

"You, Ivy, of course."

"Oh, we're not—"

Edie's palm comes up. "Tell the bullshit to the hand. Speak the truth to my face. We're going to be in each other's lives for a long time, Ivy. Important to each other. I just know it. Let's make honesty the foundation of our friendship."

"*Jesus*," I say. "Poor L. No wonder you turned his life around."

"Can I ask you something?"

Dragging my long hair over my shoulder, I say, "I'd really like to say no."

"You're smiling at me, so I'll take that as a green light. You're a bit older than Nico. He never mentioned that."

My lips tighten. "That's not a question."

"Okay, here's one. How much older?"

"Ten years."

Strangely, her smile grows.

My face gets redder. "It's not what you think."

"Isn't it?"

"We've only fooled around a few times. And each time, I honestly don't mean for it to happen. It just does."

"He's a little irresistible, right? Okay, here's the deal. This is what I make of the situation—you're into him big time. The way you look at him… it's plain to see, Ivy. Your feelings go deeper than lust. But I'm guessing that's the last thing you want. Am I correct?"

I nod, staring out the window at a willow tree. The boys have disappeared.

"But why is it a problem? You think he's not mature enough for you? At first, I thought maybe you were worried about the band thing. All the girls. The rock singer man-whore issue. But it's the age difference that you can't handle, isn't it?"

"Yes," I admit. "But the hot rocker stuff isn't ideal either. Not long ago, one morning after a night that shouldn't have happened, he was on the phone to one his *chicks*. He was all flirty and sweet and *don't call me Niccy* and *anything for you babe*. And there I was standing right in the next room!"

"Eavesdropping!" She muffles a laugh with the back of her hand. "If that was a couple of Saturdays ago, that was me he was talking to. I was teasing him that if I went into labor while L was away on a shoot, he'd have to drive me to the hospital."

"Oh! That kind of makes sense that it was you. But, even

still, girls constantly fall all over him. I've seen it. And then there's the age thing. It's sort of almost okay now, but I'll be forty soon."

"But you're thirty-four now, right? I wouldn't call six years *soon*."

"Okay. Sure. But I want a child, and if he goes along with that just to make me happy, then we'll be stuck with each other, involved forever trying to rear a family amicably even if we're no longer a couple. Besides, will he still want me when I'm forty-five?"

She threads her fingers together over her big belly. "Well, he'll be older too."

"Yeah. He'll be the same age I am now. And still gorgeous. And I'll be a wrinkly old hag."

"I don't think a few wrinkles will bother him," she says, her hazel eyes serious. "He's not that shallow."

"But they'll sure as heck bother a lot of other people who see us together. And they'll no doubt feel sorry for him." I'm picturing my boss, Kendra, shaking her head at us, warning me that he'll run off with someone his own age the first chance he gets.

"Ivy, I think you make him happy. You change him. Make him a better person. And you're happy, too, when you're with him. It's obvious. Don't throw love away because you're worried about what other people think. That's insane." She smiles down at her baby-belly, stroking it lovingly. "When people fit together, they just do. What some sourpuss thinks won't change that. Never let unhappy people steal your joy."

Oh, my God. I'm getting the same lecture from virtual strangers—over and over.

"Love?" I scoff. "You *have* seen his tattoo, right?"

"Like feelings, ink can be changed. You've heard the fated mate prophecy his mom's raised him on?"

"What? No."

"When Zsof was young and living back in Hungary, she visited the local soothsayer, Baba Vash."

"Baba Vash? Gee that sounds totally authentic."

"But she is. Or *was*. I'm not sure if she's still alive, but back in her day she was famous for being accurate. Amazingly, she predicted Nico's asshole father—that he would abandon them. And, more importantly, she said that Nico's great and *only* love would be an older woman."

"That actually explains a lot about the night I went to Zsofia's for goulash. She thinks I'm the fated mate."

"And Nico *knows* you are."

"No. No. No. No. No." I shake my head while Edie nods, her dimples twinkling gleefully at me.

Struggling with the weight of her stomach, she pushes off the bed and massages her back. "This baby is getting too heavy. I can't wait until he or she pops out."

"On the nights when the baby's screaming instead of sleeping, you might long for it to go back in. I've been talking to friends with children. You can say goodbye to getting any beauty sleep for the next few months. Or years."

"True. Life is gonna change." She waddles to the door. "And maybe it's time for yours to change too. Take a risk. I can vouch for Nico. I know him well, and he's one of the good guys. Don't throw away your chance at happiness. What if it's your only one? Take Nico, he's yours if you want him, and keep him and love him wholeheartedly—"

"Please stop!" I laugh, dropping my head into my palms.

"Anyway, you can't run away, because that boy needs you. I promise you won't regret taking him on, Ivy. See you out at the car."

I flop over the bed. The ornate plaster ceiling rose would look amazing with some gold paint applied to the petals.

I mull over Edie's words. I might not regret taking Nico on during the blissful honeymoon phase of a relationship, but what about in the long term?

He's out on tour. I'm home with a baby.

He's thirty. I'm forty.

I'm fifty. He's forty.

Would we even make it that far? And would he still look at me the way he does now? I highly doubt it.

Sighing, I launch onto my feet and twist my hair into a messy bun before grabbing my backpack and heading out the door.

When I arrive at the car, Edie and L have Nico wrapped up in a tight group embrace. Stepping back, L swats Nico's mop of sandy hair and says, "Don't be an idiot, kid."

Nico rolls his eyes. "Yeah. Yeah. Yeah." He gives me a halfhearted smile then takes my bag and dumps it in the back seat. Arms folded and leaning against the car, he watches me hug his friends goodbye.

"Thanks for everything," I say. "I had such a great time."

"Don't thank us." Edie smiles. "Just send us invitations to your exhibition instead. We'll keep our eyes on the post."

"Oh, sure!" Freaking hell. Now I'll definitely have to invite the big lug of muscle who's currently holding the passenger door open for me.

Doors slam, shutting out the gentle hum of insects, the sound of distant whinnying from the stables. The engine sparks and we roll down the driveway and through the archway of trees in silence.

When we hit the open road, Nico's palms strike a steady beat against the steering wheel, his boot thudding against the floor as he sings. "You say no. No. No. It ain't right. Right. Right. I turn left. Yeah. Yeah."

"What?" I ask.

"Shh! You turn mad. Bad. Sad."

"Are you making a song?"

I get a crooked grin from him, and he croons the growly rockabilly-inspired tune even louder. "Poison Ivy. Ivy. Ivy. It hurts so good. Yeah, you. You. You. The meanest green. The reddest sky. Girl, you're the finest pain I ever did feel. Fill my cup. I'll drink you down. More. More. More. I ain't gonna cry. No. No. I ain't gonna cry."

By the end of his little ditty, he's laughing. I laugh too, but my heart hurts as I wonder how many girls he's sung to like this. I ache with the desire to be the only one. Cringe at how hard I wish I'd never walked out into that alleyway behind Silva's that fateful night.

We spend the rest of the journey singing along to hilarious

old-time hits we find on country radio stations, idle chitchat at a minimum.

As the heat of the day turns into a balmy afternoon, Nico's shoulders grow tenser the closer we get to the city. I think he's stewing on something, working up to a lecture maybe.

Finally, with his face serious and no sign of the dimples, he says, "So last night, things didn't go so well. Maybe I over-reacted a little—getting pissed at you. You did the right thing, reminding me that you're not exclusively mine. That there's another guy in the running. A guy who you think is better suited for your... purposes."

"My purposes? Wow, you make me sound like some kind of ruthless man hunter."

"I don't really care what you are, Ivy. It won't change anything. I just want you to know that I'll be here waiting." Switching lanes to get out from behind a slow truck, his chest rises on a big intake of breath. "I'll be waiting for you to realize that this suit guy isn't the one who'll make you happy. I know you. When you smile, I know why you do it. Every single time. I don't have to puzzle it out, because I've known what makes your skin heat, your laugh burst out, your voice sing for-fucking-*ever* because I've always been waiting for you. It's meant to be. When will you stop fighting it?"

"Nico—"

"Please, Ivy." Emerald eyes shine as his eyebrows draw together.

His longing is a painful current that connects his heart to mine.

Burning. Burning.

In the silence, he searches my face for something—a sign that I'll give in maybe? When he doesn't see what he wants, his lips thin, then his brow smooths, and he flashes the dimples. It looks forced. Fake. "Okay, so maybe I laid that on a bit heavy. Let's just have some fun then. Finish what we started last night. Come over to my place?"

"I can't."

"Well, how about I come to yours?"

A sigh gusts out. "No, Nico."

"But what's wrong with just having a bit of fun? Forget what I said before and just use my body. I'm alright with that. I promise. My insides feel bad when I picture you getting outta my car and walking away from me."

"I *can't* ignore what you just said. Shit! What a ridiculous request." My fingers scrunch up the fabric of my summer shirt as I consider taking the leap, coming clean and being honest.

Okay. I think it's time to act my age and hit him with the truth. "Look, I want to be with you too. I really do."

A blinding smile blazes over his face.

"But the age thing is a big problem for me."

His teeth sink into his lip ring.

"I can't get past it, Nico. The humiliation. I'll obsess constantly over what people will be thinking about me walking around with such a beautiful young man."

"Great. At least I know you're attracted to me. That's something, I suppose. Anyway, fuck what people think."

At the next traffic lights, he takes the turnoff to the bay

area where I live. We're mostly silent until the car rolls to a stop out front of my apartment block.

His whole body angles toward me. One hand grips the steering wheel and the fingers of his other dig into the car seat like he's keeping himself in check. "Can I come up?"

I click my tongue at his persistence. "Haven't you got a gig to get to?"

"Ah, that's ages away. Come on, Ivy. I know you want me bad."

He's right, I do.

"It's stupid to start something that has no chance of a happy ending. Aren't you going away next month, anyway? On tour with Up Void?"

"I don't know." The heel of his palm drags over his face. "Shit."

"Look, thank you for taking me to meet your friends. And for giving me my final painting subject. L and his story are really something else. He and Edie obviously love you a lot. Not everyone has friends like that you know." I lean in and kiss his cheek.

His arms enfold my waist and he squeezes me hard. I sigh and melt into his heat, his scent drugging me. To escape his grasp, I start to squirm, but he takes the hint and lets me go without trying for more.

"I'll call you soon," I say. "I don't want to lose you from my life entirely. I just have to learn how to be satisfied with the friendship thing. Not let you tempt me so." I swing the door wide and step out of the car, then collect my bag from the back.

Arms braced on the open window frame, my skin sticking to warm metal, I lean in. "Okay?"

"Well, it's a start. Like I said, I'll be waiting for you to come begging for my body. Should the temptation become too much of a burden, give me a call anytime. I'll lighten the load."

"Don't hold your breath. I'm still going on that date with smarmy Gregor on the weekend. See ya, Nico."

Bright-green eyes light up. "You just called him smarmy! Unbelievable. That dude's fucking toast. He's history."

As I walk away, he calls through the open window, "Hey, Ivy? It's not the love of my friends I care about right now."

Shit.

I fling a weak wave behind me and start up the stoop.

"I'm still going on that date. I'm still going on that date," I chant with each step I climb.

Even if it's only to prove how wrong for me smarmy Gregor is.

23

NICO

Sorry South

Yesterday, at work I was useless. Hungover from the previous night's gig, I fucked up so many food orders that even the junior cafe staff advised me to go home and get some rest. But, plagued with thoughts of Ivy, I knew I wouldn't get any shut eye.

So when my shift ended, I made the bad decision to go to Linc's place. We drank beer and smoked pot until four a.m., and he talked band stuff all night, world domination and the like, keeping my mind off my troubles. Well, mostly. The redheaded problem still vexed me.

I passed out for roughly three hours on Linc's hellishly

uncomfortable couch, then left his cockroach infested hovel early this morning.

With my nervous system shot—limbs and thoughts jittery —I've been wandering the streets like a zombie since seven a.m., tortured by mental images of Ivy's impending date tonight.

Right now, I'm drifting down a city alleyway wondering if she'll enjoy being wined and dined in luxury by that rich prick, treated like the queen she is. Maybe she'll love it so much she'll end up sleeping with him. I picture wrapping my hands around the skinny neck of Hector, or Trevor, or whatever-the-hell-his-dumbass-name-is and squeezing hard.

And if she decides to let slimy-dude touch her, will she ever want to slum it with me again? Probably fucking not. And that idea kills me.

I know I should want what's best for her, but *hell* I hope she doesn't screw him tonight. Or any night. If I had my way, she'd only fuck me. Always. And that's nuts, right?

Chain smoking until my lungs hurt, I keep ambling along. I only ever smoke when my head is a mess, or I'm wasted, and it seems I can tick both of those things off my to-do list today.

The sound my boots make scuffing over the dirty pavement is a mournful, scratchy soundtrack that goes nicely with heartache.

A drop of rain splashes my nose, and I stop walking and look skyward. The air may be warm and humid, but gray clouds loom overhead. Yep, looks like it's gonna piss down any minute.

My bleary eyes track over rundown warehouses to an old hat factory sign, black paint peeling on the brick wall.

Unbelievable. Up Void's rehearsal space is on the fourth floor of that building tucked away at the back, so noise doesn't filter down to street level. How the hell did I get here?

Wonder if any of the guys are stupid enough to be up this early?

I pull out my cell and check the time. Huh. I've been brooding and roaming for nearly four hours now. Still, a quarter to eleven on a Saturday is way too early for musicians to be out of bed and working, but miracles do happen. I'll text South just in case.

Me: In a bizarre stroke of fate, I find myself out front of your monstrously Gothic rehearsal room.

South: Hey. Good timing. I'm here alone. Come on up.

Me: Good timing because you're by yourself? What the hell are you doing?

South: You'll never know unless you get your ass on up here. Elevator's broken. Take the stairs.

It's dark when I step inside the tiny foyer, the damp stench of rotting wood filling my nostrils. An insane guitar riff, with South's raspy vocals raging over the top, rattles from above. It's fucking loud.

Luckily, the building's only other residents are a bike repair shop—a front for drug dealers—and a handful of squatters who happen to be the bike shop's best customers.

By the time I reach the landing, a heavy foreboding has settled like a boulder in my gut. Statue still, I stare at the wrought iron elevator gate. Hell, I think I know why I'm here.

Her name crashes through my chest—an urgent heartbeat.

Ivy. Ivy. Ivy.

Guess I'd better get it over with then.

Puffing from jogging up four steep flights of stairs, I push open the door that's decaying off its hinges, enter Up Void's rehearsal room, and confront the noise head on.

Like always, South stands at the center of chaos, nearly swallowing the microphone. Surrounded by band gear and general mess, his arm pumps over his axe, eyes screwed shut as he screams out a repetitive refrain. It sounds like: *Black black blood is rain. Black black I ain't insane. Ain't insane.*

Not sure if I want to be the one to break it to him, but he *does* sound fucking demented. And he's so lost in the song, he hasn't even noticed my arrival.

I bend and unplug his guitar from its amp, the immediate decibel reduction a relief to my aching brain. His head jerks up, and he laughs as his raw vocals bounce off the walls. Even without accompanying music, it sounds fucking good.

Letting out a howl any self-respecting werewolf would be proud of, he steps back from the mic and chin tips me in greeting. "Lucky I had to take a piss before. Otherwise, I'd never have heard your text come in."

"New song?" I ask, powdery shit crumbling onto the floor as I lean against the wall.

"Yeah. It's called Lined Black. What do you think?"

"Cool as fuck. Manic riff. Vocals are a bit Cobainy but in a good way. Why are you running it through the amps without the band?"

"I always do that with a new one. I write them on my

acoustic, but I've gotta feel it vibrate my bones, loud and elec-trified, to finish it properly. You know, kinda like riding the wave right into shore."

"Yeah. I totally get that."

South loves to surf. And talk about it way too much.

Abandoning the microphone, he picks up his acoustic and flops over the ripped-up couch, gray light from the high window opposite illuminating him like a spotlight. Specks of fuck-knows-what float through the air and sparkle like magic dust.

Barely able to walk straight, I weave clumsily around the drum kit—I really need some sleep—swipe a guitar from a stand, and sit across from South on a plastic crate.

Hands moving fast, he runs through the new song and my fingers automatically follow along, easily picking up the rhythm. We play it over and over until I know it so well, I could jump on stage with him and kill it, no problem.

"This is why I want you on the road with us, man. You pick everything up so goddarn fast. Anyone's too fucked up to play or whatever, you can take their place. Easy."

"It's because your hooks are strong and lethal. I only need to hear them once and they snare me quick and never let go."

He laughs. "Nice complement coming from you. You're no slouch in the song writing department, either. So, you didn't get any sleep last night?"

"What makes you ask that?"

"You look like hell, man. What's going on with your hair?"

I rake shaky hands through my wild mane. "I got *some* sleep. Been at Linc's and—"

He snorts. "Stop right there. The word *Linc* explains everything. So did you come bearing good news? You've decided you're gonna come on tour with us, yeah?"

I keep my fingers moving and my eyes on South's fretboard.

Seconds pass in silence. South lets the question fade into the music and doesn't hassle for a reply. Instead, he whispers the words to his song. Most of them I can't make out. But I hear the word *black* over and over again.

And then *beat* and *pulse* and *cup*.

My own pulse kicks up its pace, my breathing choppy and unsteady. The sick feeling in my gut churns harder. Something about those words he's crooning get my brain ticking. And searching.

I picture Ivy looking beautiful out with that dickhead tonight, smiling at him from across a fancy table, her silver eyes shining bright over the rim of a glass of fancy red wine. Those three specific words from South's song race through my brain, tugging at a memory.

BEAT.

Pulse.

Cup.

Cup.

Pulse.

Beat.

. . .

SOUTH'S VOICE GETS LOUDER, my head spins faster, and words from Mom's Romani prophecy come flooding back to torment me.

ONE DAY HE WILL UNDERSTAND—ONLY *love has the purest pulse and a beat that is ever true. Far truer than any song. Hers are the lyrics he must follow, for the cup of her happiness is his to drink.*

Her happiness is his. You understand?

THE MEANING STRIKES ME COLD. Her happiness is mine. Of course. Of fucking course! Ivy's happiness *is mine*.

And if that's true, then maybe it goes both ways. Maybe *my* happiness is hers, too. Maybe like planets doomed to collide and explode, merging into one mass, we *are* fucking fated. Me and Ivy. Ivy and me.

Meant to be.

Lovers.

In love.

For always.

All my organs are freaking out so bad, I can hardly draw air into my lungs. "South. Hey, listen. I'm sorry, but I can't do it. I can't tour with you guys. I need to stay here."

His eyes shoot up. "Why the hell not? Come on, man. Up Void is about to crack it big time. People are losing their shit over us. Come ride the wave. And if you want to amp things up with Burntbad, you'll be able to make all the contacts you need while you're hanging out with us."

"I can't leave Ivy."

His eyes narrow to slits of blue ice. "Why not? I thought you were just friends." The twist of his eyebrows tells me he thinks I've lost my mind. Maybe I have.

"The friends thing was her dumb idea."

"Right," say South, his fingers changing tempo over the guitar strings and thrashing out a punk tune. He sings, "I really don't wanna dance. I just wanna get into your pants," over and over until we're both laughing. "Bit like that, huh?"

"Yeah," I agree, omitting to mention that it only felt like that in the beginning. Because not long after meeting Ivy, I was interested in a lot more than getting her clothes off. Her thoughts, her dreams, heck, her whole life fascinated me. And I'd be willing to tap dance all the way down Main Street right now if it would stop her from dating that dick tonight.

Knee jerking up and down, I force myself to hold his gaze. "But it's weird... It's like I've been sleepwalking and now I'm awake. She woke me up! And now she's like the only thing I can think about. I don't know how to explain it, but there's something about the way she moves that makes me feel like I can't live without her. Like I wanna stay around her forever."

"Something about the way she moves... stay around forever..." His fingers stop dancing over the strings. "You sound fucking nuts! But you should probably write that down. Not bad lyrics."

I bury my face in my palms. "Fuck, man, fuck! Shit. I think I'm in love."

"Don't say that." South drops his guitar on the cushion beside him. "Are ya sure it's not a stomach flu coming on or the hangover fucking with your mind?"

Grimacing, I nod down at my boots.

"Man, that sure is bad news. So, what does it feel like? An intense case of gas?"

"It sucks." Burying my fingers in my hair, I pull hard at the roots. "Feels fucking terrible... and also totally *right*." Chest warming, I stop tearing my hair out and grin up at him, my eyes wide. "And fated. It feels fated."

"So she's the prophecy chick that you never believed in. The one your mom's been banging on about."

"Yeah, it sounds crazy as hell, but I think she is. That Baba Vash knew her shit alright." I bolt to my feet, the guitar bouncing over the rotting wooden boards.

"Hey!" South says. "Go easy on the equipment."

"What?" Luckily, the Hummingbird acoustic lying on the floor is still in one piece. "Fuck, sorry." I bend toward the guitar like I'm going to pick it up but change my mind halfway there. "I've gotta go and find Ivy before she makes a big mistake."

Frantically, I look around the room as though she might be hiding behind a bass amp waiting to jump out and surprise me.

"She ain't here, man."

"I fucking know that," I say, backing away from South and falling over the kit. Cymbals crash into the snare drum.

"Shit! Get out of here before you trash the place," he says as I spring upright.

"Take a good look around. I don't think this place could get much worse." I salute him then flee down the stairs like my life depends on how fast I can descend them. Maybe it does.

Outside on the pavement, I look toward the main street, sucking back big lungfuls of air. The rain has stopped, and Saturday shoppers crowd the sidewalks, searching for bargains. My stomach rumbles. It feels like lunchtime already.

I quickly check the time on my cell—twelve-thirty—and then I call Ivy. She doesn't answer, her voicemail kicking in almost immediately. Fuck. Fuck. I wait for the beep.

"Hey, Ivy, it's me. Uh… I need to talk to you." I have to bite down on my tongue to stop myself from saying something like—*hey, remember don't sleep with strangers!* I wait a moment until the dumb urge has passed, and then say, "Call me ASAP. It's important."

Okay. What do I do now?

My cell pings.

South: Maybe take a shower before you go anywhere special.

Huh. How did he know I needed guidance? Must be psychic.

Me: Good idea.

But before I head home and clean up, I need to call my buddy, Sam, who owns a tattoo joint. I've got an urgent job for him.

After a painful visit to the Pierced Lung studio, I catch the subway to my apartment.

When I hike up the six floors to my front door, I find our emo-kid drummer, Patch, knocking on it. I cough loudly.

"Oh, hey, Nico, good timing," he says, then does a double take from the cell phone in his hand back to my face. "What the fuck happened to you?"

I shrug a shoulder, then dig my keys out of my pocket, grinning as I open the door. "I think I'm in love."

"Come again?"

"I *said* I'm in love." I pitch my keys at a huge black bowl on the kitchen bench. Its sole purpose is to hold crap. Reminds me a little of Linc. "Ever heard the word before, Patch? Love. L.O.V.E."

"I know how to spell it. Do I look that stupid?"

Best if I don't answer that question.

He stands in the living room while I open blinds, smoky-colored light flooding in. "Bit of a mess in here," he says.

"Given the dump you live in, I'm not sure you're qualified to speak on the art of housekeeping."

He's kinda right though. There's shit everywhere. Lyric notebooks. Clothes. Empty junk food packets. And my neglected jungle-plants are drooping sadly. Where's my head been lately?

"Who are you in love with," Patch asks. "Is it Ivy?"

I cut him a sharp look. "Of course. Who the fuck else would it be?"

He nods sagely. "Knew it. Your plants look thirsty."

"Your powers of observation are genius today." I fetch a jug from beside the fridge, fill it with water, and wander around watering my leafy-green friends. All seven hundred of them. Okay, so I don't have quite *that* many. But almost.

Patch tops up an old beer bottle from the sink and trails behind me, double dosing the plants I've already watered.

"Hey, don't overdo it. Too much water nukes them the same as too little does."

He scowls at me through thick chunks of dyed-black hair, three metal rings shining on his bottom lip. His red-flannel shirt flaps open revealing his inked torso. Just looking at his tatts makes my fresh one hurt like a mother.

"Hey, my thumb is fairly green," he grumbles. "I know what I'm doing. No need to talk down to me nursery-boy."

"So, what brings you here anyway?" I ask.

"Left my practice pads on your couch the other night. My neighbors are banging on my door crying because I'm making so much noise practicing the new songs. Thought you'd be home so I could retrieve them."

"You got a kit set up at home?"

"Part of one. I need to—"

"You need to own more than one set of pads. Then you can leave some here permanently." I snatch the bottle from him and dump our watering equipment back in the kitchen.

Riffling around inside the cupboards, I ask, "Want a stale bagel?" I glance over my shoulder. "We can have butter on them, but that's about all I've got. I really need to go shopping. Damn. I hate that shit."

"Same. Store dudes always check me out like they're afraid I'm gonna steal something."

"And don't you?"

He grins. "Fuck, yeah, sometimes. Otherwise I'd starve. Money's tight, you know? So, yeah, make me a bagel. I'm always hungry."

After I toast our lunch, we climb up the fire escape stairs and eat on the small rooftop garden, studying the clouds and making up songs about their weird shapes.

When Patch notices me look at my cell for the hundred and twentieth time, he swipes butter from his chin and says, "Go ahead, call her. I don't mind."

So I do.

Once again, my call goes straight to voicemail. That's fine. I'll leave another message. "Hey, it's your favorite hot rocker checking in. I need you to call me back before tonight. Okay? Please? Don't go on that date with the douche. Just call me. I'm trying real hard to hold back from relaying all the statistics I know about S.T.I.s and first dates. Infections happen a lot more than you think. Just saying. So be safe and abstain. Then come see me for relief."

Patch kicks my boot. Yeah, I should probably hang up—quit before I get any further behind. "Choose me, Ivy, I'm clean. And much better looking than that stick-up-his-ass dude."

I click off and stare at my cell, biting my lip ring.

Patch snorts. "Jesus. You *are* fucked up. Hot rocker! Christ."

"Yeah, probably should have put a little thought into what I was gonna say before I called. More romance less diseases would have been good."

"And you're also a liar," he says, pointing an accusing

finger at me. "You ain't looking so clean at the moment. And you smell like funky moonshine."

"And you look like a bagel. You should see the mess you've got smeared all over you. What I was *meaning* is that I'm clean *sexually* speaking."

Eyebrows raised, he stops chewing and says with a full mouth, "Really? You don't like it dirty? I had no idea you were a vanilla sex kinda guy. Damn surprising that is."

I shake my head. "No, you jackass. Clean as in I don't have any sexual diseases. Do you follow?"

"Oh, yeah, yeah. Right. That kinda makes more sense. But you should still take a shower if you're gonna go see her. And a nap could be a good idea, too. You look ragged, man." Brushing crumbs off his clothes, he stands up. "I'll find my pads and leave you to it, then. Good luck nailing your chick."

Nailing my chick! The whole *love* concept is obviously foreign to him. Just as it was to me only a few weeks ago. "Yeah, thanks, man. Catch you soon."

After Patch leaves, I pace around my apartment for half an hour, checking my cell every few minutes. Finally, I decide to take both my friends' advice and wash the hangover from my skin.

When I'm dried off, I stare at my cell like the answers to the universe and everything in it are about to appear on the screen. Still nothing from Ivy. So I call her again but, this time when she doesn't answer, I don't leave a message. I plan to crawl into bed and crash for a few hours then I'll track her down in person.

With the shades pulled over my bedroom window, darkness enfolding me, I drop into an immediate dead sleep.

Hours later, the sound of my own moan and an accelerated heartbeat wake me from a dream. Panting, I bolt upright and smack my head on the wall, hands feeling around the sheets for my cell.

In the nightmare—or daymare—I was in an all-white room, gagged and tied to a chair, watching a naked Ivy ride a guy reverse cowgirl style on an oval-shaped bed, her eyes locked on mine the whole time. Normally, Ivy featuring in a dream like that would result in a mega case of waking-wood, but not today, because that guy she was fucking sure as heck wasn't me.

I click my phone open. Hell, yeah! There's an hour-old text from the girl who's making me crazy.

Ivy: Hey! Sorry I haven't called you back yet. I'm at home working way too hard. I'm totally under the pump. But I promise we'll speak soon, okay?

What the fuck? No mention of whether or not she's going on the date. No comment on the sexually transmitted diseases issue I highlighted in my text. Thought she might at least make a joke about it, but nope. Nothing.

There is one good thing about her text—it's given me a destination to head to, because I'm almost certain the little workaholic will still be going hard at it in her studio. And after nearly three hours sleep, I feel sharper and ready to plead my case. I only hope she's willing to hear it.

This is it. Two sentences: Age means shit. I'm her guy.

At a quarter to six, time's a wasting. I need to get over to her joint before that guy Trevor (or whatever he's called) does.

Heart banging against my ribs, I throw on clothes—my favorite ripped jeans because I've caught her checking out my butt when I've worn them, and a short-sleeve shirt with lots of turquoise mixed through a retro-geometrical pattern. She says it turns my eyes into green wildfire. I don't know about that—but I'm not ashamed to throw glowing eyes in my arsenal if it helps keep her attention on me.

Now, what else might assist? Better check a mirror I suppose. I sprint to the bathroom and run my fingers through my wavy hair. It's a mess. Guess I shouldn't have slept on it wet. There's no time to tame it now, though, I've got a girl to win.

I retrieve my keys from the black bowl and zoom down the stairs.

As my car door clicks shut, I think of something else I need. Flowers. I need fucking flowers. I've never in my life bought any for a girl before, but hey there's a first time for everything, right?

Hopefully there'll be a florist open somewhere between my place and hers. No way I'll stoop to purchasing those shit gas station bouquets. The douche-suit would never give her those.

Ever.

24

IVY

Love

"I don't like it," says Gregor, frowning his well-polished brow at the large portrait he's standing rigidly in front of.

The final threads of daylight shine through my studio window onto his face, highlighting the scowl lines around his pursed lips.

The guy may be sophisticated and handsome, but when I look at him, I hardly feel a thing. Okay, maybe some mild irritation. But that's about it.

"Oh?" I say, my curiosity the only thing that's aroused right now. "I'm really happy with this painting. I'd be interested to know what you don't like about it." I'm sure it's the subject he's having difficulty with—because it's of Nico.

Sucking his teeth, Gregor's jaw ticks as he folds his arms over his expensive suit jacket and squints at my work. "Well, firstly, nobody has eyes that vibrant a color. I think you've exaggerated the shade excessively. And he looks far too... *pretty*. It's as though you've tried too hard to make him appealing."

I almost laugh at his blatant display of jealousy. I haven't exaggerated anything. That's just how Nico looks. Incredible.

Anyway, Gregor is wrong. It's not the sharp planes of Nico's masculine but beautiful face that makes the painting compelling. It's the way his soul bleeds through the brilliant emerald color of his eye, penetrating deep into your chest and seizing your heart. What shines from his gaze is something both tough and fragile. Something rare and wonderful that I want to nurture and protect forever.

"Ivy? Are you listening to me?"

"Sorry, I'm a little tired. I must have zoned out there for a moment. What did I miss?"

He huffs and bends to inspect the canvas. "*My* painting, which I am immensely pleased with by the way, features lots of symbols and individual words spread throughout. The effect is elegant. Sophisticated. But the writing on this one invades the space. Why did you paint such a long poem on it? It occupies over half the canvas."

"It's a song. They're Nico's lyrics. I only meant to pick out part and weave it through the work, but in the end, I had to include the whole song. The words belonged together. I couldn't separate them."

"Is that so? Well I'm certainly no connoisseur of rock music but by my reckoning, they're not very good."

To my great surprise, he reads them aloud in a grumpy, staccato voice. It's bizarre to hear Nico's words coming out of Gregor's mouth.

ACID SOFT.

> *Yeah, you. Always you.*
> *I won't be the one.*
> *To hurt.*
> *To cause you pain.*
> *I won't be the one.*
> *To take.*
> *To break your soul.*
> *Yeah, love. Love.*
> *Coz I'll never know.*
> *Yeah, you. You.*
> *Are you the one?*
> *If I'm lost.*
> *Yeah, lost. Lost.*
> *If I'm dazed and confused.*
> *It's you.*
> *You.*
> *Love is overrated.*
> *Yeah, but you.*
> *You.*

Is this thing fated?
It'll take the dark to ignite.
To light our spark.
Yeah, take.
Take the night to blow this apart.
Apart.
If I'm dazed and confused.
Will you ever see?
Will you ever know?
Me.
And will you let it burn?
Yeah, you. You know you make me burn.
Yeah, you. You know it's always you.
You.

"I DON'T LIKE IT," he says. "The words are naive and pedestrian. They remind me of a child whining and—"

A loud thumping sounds on my front door. Gregor arches an eyebrow as if he can't believe anyone would dare to interrupt him.

"I love that painting. It's probably the best thing I've ever done. And before I put it in my exhibition, I might have to put a big fat sold sticker on it so no one buys it."

I dash out of my studio, tripping over my laptop cord in the living room in my haste to see who's knocking. When I swing the door open, I make a silly-sounding gasp at the sight of Nico standing on the threshold. His hair is a hot mess, and he's clutching a sad-looking bunch of roses to his chest. He looks absolutely adorable. And the way his gaze penetrates through my skin and flesh, marrow-deep, straight to my core... dear God.

Heat flushes through my body, an irrational hunger flooding my brain. I want him so badly at this moment that I don't care two hoots about how old he is. I only want to drag him inside, tie him to my bed, and have my wicked way with him for hours. Or forever.

"Hi," he says, thrusting the flowers forward. "These are for you. Obviously. Sorry about the plastic wrapping... and their general shittiness. I was in a rush, so I didn't—"

"Thank you!" I take the fake-purple colored flowers and hug them. "They're the nicest ones I've ever received."

"Really?" His amazed expression hints at disbelief.

Nodding, I stare stupidly at the floral travesty then return my gaze to his radiant smile.

After a long period of me smiling back, he finally seems to realize that's *all* I'm capable of doing. "So, how about I come in?"

"Ivy? What's going on?" Gregor calls from the studio.

A scowl darkens Nico's face. "*He's* here already! Fuck—"

"It's okay," I say quickly. "He's only picking up his painting—"

"Ivy?" Gregor calls again.

"Yes. Hang on. I'm coming."

Nico struts into the living room. "I'm not leaving."

"Fine. Good. Gregor's only here to—"

"Ivy!" My name is boomed from the studio like a thunder clap.

"Stop bellowing at her!" yells Nico.

A moment later Gregor's head appears in the hall doorway. "Oh. It's you." He sneers first at Nico then the flowers.

Nico glances at them too. "Sorry again about the flowers, Ivy. But I had to get over here fast before you made a big mistake." Planting a hand on his hip, right over the slice of black boxers popping enticingly out the top of his low-slung jeans, he frowns at my client. "Oh, hey, Trevor. How's it hanging?"

"Gregor."

Nico smirks. "Sorry, Greg."

"It's *Gregor*, not Greg."

"Great. Good for you." Nico's narrowed eyes, framed by luxuriously long lashes, glow a stunning translucent green.

I glance at Gregor, checking if he's noticed the phenomenon. No. He's smoothing down his lapels and preening like a self-satisfied cat.

"Quick, both of you need to come into the studio. Right now!" Gently, I place the roses on the kitchen bench. "I want to show you something, Gregor." I weave my fingers through Nico's and pull him along behind me. His palms feel a little clammy.

With my hands on Nico's biceps, I maneuver him until he's standing in the only remaining patch of light in my studio, then push a little. "Bend down, Nico. Wait. Yep. Stay right there. Gregor, come closer."

He does.

"Look," I say, pointing at Nico's eyes glowing like sunshot willow leaves—gold and green and every color in between. "See? In actual fact, his eyes are even more spectac-ular in real life than in the painting." My hand slides from Nico's shoulder to his chest. His breathing accelerates, pupils blowing wide.

Gregor's back stiffens. "Hm. I'm sure he's wearing special contact lenses."

"What?" Nico's laugh is soft and husky. "You can't go out with this guy. He's a dick."

"We aren't going out tonight. Ivy canceled on me."

Squaring his shoulders, Nico says, "That's because she's mine."

My lips stay sealed. I can't bring myself to disagree, because I think Nico is correct. I *am* his.

"Well, I'd better collect my painting and leave you to it, then." Gregor gives us a remarkably kind smile and retreats to the other side of the room. He tucks his wrapped painting under his arm. "I'll send you a photo of this masterpiece hanging over the fireplace. It's going to look very impressive. Thank you, Ivy. I shall be sending more business your way very soon."

I kiss his cheek and shuffle him out the door.

Before I can turn around, Nico is pressed against my back, arms snaking around my waist, squeezing tightly. He buries his face in my hair and breathes deep. My knees go weak.

"What am I going to do, Ivy? I'm crazy in love with you."

What? I wish I could see his eyes, but I'm trapped facing away, staring at a blank wall.

"In love with me? You might be getting a little carried away there. Infatuation is the correct word."

He spins me around. "No. It's love. Nothing else can hurt so bad and feel so good at the same time. I swear it, Ivy. Look at this... wait." He unbuttons his shirt, my favorite because of how bright it makes his eyes shine.

I cover a hysterical giggle with my palm. "What are you doing?"

"You need to check out my tatt. I got new sentences added to it today. Now it finally makes sense. But it hurts like hell."

Covered in clear wrap, the tattoo on his chest is red and swollen but still readable. Below the original words that dismiss love as a ridiculous, impossible concept there are new lines, written twice by the looks. First backward so he can see them in the mirror. Then the right way around for all the world to see.

I press my palm on his chest and lean close. He smells of sandalwood and a hint of vanilla. Delicious.

While I read, he sucks on his lip ring and breathes unevenly.

The old words say: *Future mine is yours to hold. Future yours is me. If I lived life over, would I find you sooner? Love is death. Death is love.*

And the new: *With every heartbeat, I die willingly. Resurrected eternally. Forever yours.* And the whole tattoo is now surrounded by an intricate border of Ivy leaves.

"Do you believe me?"

I shake my head in wonder. I desperately want to believe him, but I'm scared. Going by his pained expression, he's taking my stunned silence as bad news. But it's not. I think I fell in love with him the moment he smiled at me back in that dingy alleyway. I've just been fighting it. Not believing that he could ever feel the same way.

But he does.

He does.

His palms frame my face, but I push them away. "Wait. You need to see something." I beckon him over to his painting and watch his mouth drop open and naked chest shudder.

"That's my song!" His gaze intense, he scans the canvas. "And that's me! Jesus, I look like some kinda prince of the fucking forest or an apocalyptic hero-guy. Is that really how you see me?"

I smile. "Yeah. It is."

"*Unbelievable.* That is so freaking cool. I can't wait for Linc to see it. He's gonna be sick with jealousy." His excited expression darkens as he turns to me. "But you know what, Ivy? I think there's room for a little improvement."

I swat his arm. "What do you mean? I love this painting. It's perfect."

He gives me a wicked smile. "But I can't see any ivy. You didn't include it."

"What ivy?"

"You took a photo of my lyrics on your phone, right? Show me. I want to see it."

I locate my cell and swipe through photos. "Here it is."

He snatches it and stands close, stooping a little so we can both see the screen. His scent envelops me, drugging me.

"Look." He enlarges the photo. "See my drawing around the lyrics? The border? I'm an artist like you."

I pinch his cheeky smile. "What is it, barbed wire?"

"Are you blind? It's *ivy!* This fucking song is fucking about you! How did you not get that?"

I think I *did* understand on a subliminal level.

My heart has stopped beating, but I force myself to speak. To joke. "Jeez. Enough with the swearing already."

I stare at the photo. I wouldn't exactly call him an artist; his work is too messy. Inconsistent in style. Nonetheless, the leaves trailing around the border are definitely ivy leaves mixed with barbed wire. There are even a few tiny hearts sprinkled in with the foliage. The hearts are a surprising touch.

Slowly, I meet his frustrated gaze. "Well, now that you've pointed it out, it's obvious. I must have known. But it didn't compute. Or register that it might have had anything to do with me."

"I think you didn't want to understand, Ivy." His dimples have disappeared now, his voice turning dark. "How long did you spend looking at this piece of paper while you were transposing it onto canvas? A fucking while, yeah?"

"Yes. Of course. Hours. Days."

"Fuck!" He throws my phone on the couch. "Fuck," he says again, collapsing against the cushions and burying his head in his palms.

I don't get what's happening—or why he's freaking out so badly.

He makes a sound halfway between a groan and a growl. I creep forward and drop to my knees in front of him.

"Nico? What's wrong?" I pull at his wrists, but he won't

raise his head.

"You don't feel the same way." He looks at me, eyes shining with emotion.

I take in a slow breath, making ready to admit the truth. "I do. I do feel the same."

His lips part, air rushing out his lungs in a loud gust.

"I just wish I didn't, Nico."

Grimacing, his gaze lowers. "Ivy. Ivy. Please. What am I supposed to do? You're the only one for me. I know it. That fucking fortune-teller was right all along. Wait until I tell Edie. Her and L are gonna laugh their asses off."

"I think they already know."

His head whips up. "What?"

"Edie told me about the older-woman prophecy at the farm. I tried to make fun of the Baba Vash thing, but her eyes went all scary. She vouched for you, told me I'd never regret choosing to be with you. She even tried guilt tripping me. Your friend can be pretty scary—even when she's smiling at you."

"True. She's almost worse than Mom." Eyes soft, he blows out a shaky breath. Then he cradles my face between warm palms. "It will only ever be you, Ivy. Only you who makes my heart beat like this. Always and forever. I promise you that."

Hot tears spill down my cheeks, and he wipes them away. "You can't know how badly I want that to be true. But how can you be so sure? When I'm older—"

"Shh. I know it, Ivy. I know it because the first thing I want to see every morning is your face. This feeling, it overtakes me, lifts me high and smashes me low. Shoots blissful arrows through my skin and kills me. Then you resurrect me. It's everything. *You're* everything."

"Nico—"

"Take a chance on us. Please, Ivy? I know we can make this work. I just need you to try."

"Nico."

Before I can say another word, he takes my lips gently, his mouth moving slowly over mine. Deeper. Rougher. Then he pushes my face an inch away, his expression both pleading and calculating. "Listen. I'll give you my Diane Arbus photo. Anything, everything I have is yours. If you want something and I haven't got it, I'll find a way to get it for you. Just say you'll be mine and I'll do whatever it takes."

This boy slays me with his beautiful heart, his ardent words, and I feel my resistance, all my worries dissolve on a breath. He's worth the risk of heartbreak. He's worth everything. "What about going on tour with Up Void? Even if we give this a shot, you still need to do that. I *want* you to do it."

"Fuck Up Void. Fuck those Europeans. Anyway, Linc rang on my way over here with good news. A rep from String Power Records is coming to next week's show, so Burntbad are about to hit our strides. And I don't want to go anywhere without you until I've cemented myself in your life so fucking hard, your faith in me couldn't be jackhammered out."

I'm laughing through tears now. "But what about when I'm fifty-something? You might not be so into me when I've turned into a sack of annoying complaints."

His smile is light and dark, heaven and hell. Pain and pleasure and all I want.

All I'll ever need.

"You'll be way too happy to complain. *Together*—we'll be happy. And, hey, I'm just like the French president. That guy walks around with a constant boner for his wife and she's like *forty* years older than him."

"I think it's more like twenty years."

"But the truth of what I feel about you, why I feel it, is in here." He presses over my heart. "It's your smile. Your laugh. The way you move. Your art. How much you care about things. Justice. Fairness. Your fucking kindness. I love *you*, Ivy. You're my heart. And it can't beat anymore without your love." He takes my hand, pushes my palm into his chest. "A few wrinkles won't ever change that."

"What about when people laugh at you... or say something horrible about us?"

"Who gives a fuck? They'll just be jealous because they're not as happy as us. I don't care."

Between sobs, I breathe his name out.

"Stop crying and kiss me." He strokes my hair, softly, reverently. "You okay?"

Nodding, I inhale deep. "Yes. Never better, I think."

His lips meet mine, pressing gently, coaxing out the words I've kept locked up tight in my heart.

It's time to be brave.

True to myself.

True to Nico.

"I love you," I say in the tiny space between our kisses, feeling his lips stretch into a wide smile against mine.

Strong arms wrap around me—too tightly—squeezing my breath out. "I love you, too. I love you," he whispers. "Put me out of my misery and tell me again."

"I love you, Nico."

"Again."

"I love you."

"Keep saying it with my name. It's better. Because when you do that, the love shoots straight to my dick."

I laugh and slap his shoulder. "You're an idiot."

"I'll be anything you want me to be."

I hold his face, taking in every beloved feature. "I love you, Nico. Please don't break my heart."

"Never," he says, pulling me onto his lap.

I run my hands all over his muscled chest, avoiding the healing tattoo, and rock over his hardness.

"I won't ever hurt you, Ivy," he says through a groan. "I promise I won't. I'll write you amazing songs so you can stand in the middle of a crowd and hear everyone sing them."

"The only person I want to hear sing those songs, is you," I say.

Weaving my fingers through his hair, I press my tongue inside his mouth while my other hand works on getting his jeans undone.

He sighs. He moans.

And then it's a very long time before his words make any sense at all.

25

IVY

Exhibition

"Congratulations, Ivy!" says Nico's mom, bursting through the gallery crowd to squeeze me against her bountiful bosom. "Everything is so beautiful." Jutting out her hip, she runs a hand over her body proudly. "I am, too. Look at the outfit Francis picked. Very sexual, yes?"

The way the red dress clings to her generous curves, she looks like an old-style Hollywood starlet. Perhaps Jayne Mansfield rocking a gorgeous Hungarian accent or a smoking-hot Doris Day.

I've made it three quarters of the way through my exhibition opening, my first one ever, and the night couldn't possibly get any better. Sales are booming. Friends are smiling. And Nico is close by.

Two weeks ago, he moved some stuff into my apartment, mostly band equipment, so we could be together every night, switching between my place and his jungle tower depending on what was happening with work and gigs. It's been joyful, but I do feel a little sorry for him.

In the lead up to the opening, I lamented on repeat that nobody would likely turn up or be interested in buying my work. The poor guy. A night apart might have been a welcome relief for him. But not for me, because I couldn't be happier in his company.

Living with him is utter bliss. Baba Vash was right—Nico and I were meant to be.

Zsofia smooths a hand over her blond waves. "You look more beautiful than me, of course, Ivy. How stunning your velvet emerald dress is with your fiery hair. And when Nico stands next to you, your outfit makes his eyes go *pop!*"

"That's why he made me wear it."

She gasps and clutches her throat.

"No, Zsof. I'm joking. He wouldn't dream of telling me what to wear. Although, he did hint several times about this one."

She flashes her dimples. "Hinting, like Francis does, is no problem."

Mad Wolf Gallery is packed to the rafters and buzzing with good vibes. "I can't believe it. I think every single piece has been sold."

"I believe it," says Zsofia. "If I could, I would have all of your paintings in my house. Especially the one of my Nico." She smiles at Kendra who has just flown in like a black-caped ghoul and landed beside me. She's added a dramatic cloak to her usual Gothic-gown ensemble and looks about as approachable as a grave robber at midnight.

Touching my boss's arm, Zsofia says, "You must be so proud of Ivy."

Oh, crap. Here we go.

Kendra sniffs loudly. "Yes. Indeed. It's a very successful opening for a first show by a solo artist. I believe she's worked quite hard, too." She swirls her cape in Nico's direction. "But I must ask you, Ivy—was it a wise decision to bring that skater boy along to such an important make-or-break event?"

Zsofia's eyes narrow but she remains silent.

Bracing myself, I stand tall. "Why wouldn't it be, Kendra? What's wrong with him?"

Sounding as pleasant as a chainsaw, she grates out a chuckle. "As anyone with eyes could tell you, there is nothing wrong with the young man physically. He's quite something to behold. Hence why you appear a tad sad hanging off his arm like a desperate cougar cliché, don't you think?"

"And who brought you up?" asks Zsofia. "A pack of nasty hyenas?"

Kendra's mouth gapes open. She's not used to people calling her out on her rudeness. "I beg your pardon?"

"You should beg Ivy's pardon. Do you know the proverb that if you don't have anything nice to say, then keep your mouth closed? It's golden. Be kind and you might make some friends. I'm sure you could do with some more, no?"

Braying like an affronted donkey, Kendra tosses her sleek mane and trots away. This won't be the end of it. Somehow, she'll find a way to make me pay for having a successful opening night. Jealousy is a real bitch.

I turn to Zsofia. "She's going to be so pissed when she realizes who you are."

"That I am the mother of mister skater boy? Yes. I hope she will be. Unpleasant woman!"

"Speaking of Nico, look at him over there checking his phone every few seconds. I wonder if he's had any news yet on Edie's baby."

Looking edible, Nico stands near his portrait with my mom close by laughing and making fun of him. She's a little drunk but he knows exactly how to handle her. They make each other laugh, and he somehow manages to bring out the best in her. It's miraculous, really. Right now, he's smiling at her jibes while staring at his cell, living up to his new nick-name—*The Julia tamer.*

I think as long as Mom doesn't try to sleep with him, they'll continue to get along famously.

"Edie and L were very disappointed to miss your open-ing." Zsofia pats my arm. "They made it almost half of the way here. What kind of baby tries to be born in a car? L nearly had a heart explosion and drove across that thing in the road. What is it called? A medium stripper?"

I laugh. "Close. A median strip."

"No problem. Means the same."

"Poor L. It was lucky no one got hurt."

From across the room, Nico glances our way and smiles. Then leaving my mom in the safe hands of L's modeling agent, Ariana, he makes a detour to the bar before heading toward us. Upon arrival, he hands us glasses of champagne and then plants a soft kiss on my cheek.

He smells divine and looks delicious wearing black jeans and a charcoal shirt, folded up sleeves revealing strong forearms. As usual, the wavy locks on his head are a disheveled mess.

"Thank you, Nico. Now I can make a special toast," says Zsofia, grinning at us. "Ivy, tonight I must give thanks to you for two things. One—for the beautiful smile my son wears. I've never seen so many dimples before. And two—for making such a wonderful painting of him. You paint only half his face, but in it shines all the love he feels for you. I see it. I feel it. And my own heart is changed because of it. So I raise my glass to you, Ivy, for taking big chance on him. And also to fated love."

"To my fated love," says Nico, eyes smoldering hotly at me as we all clink glasses. "Hey, good news. Ariana wants to commission a portrait, and she's bought not one but two of your pieces tonight."

"But she'll need a tragic story to have portrait, yes?" asks Zsofia. "Why do you only paint sad people, Ivy?"

"They don't have to still be sad when they sit for me, but the stories they tell inspire the poems I write. This sounds weird, but I think pain molds us into who we are. It's the truth we carry in our eyes, in the shape of our bodies, and that's what I want to capture—people's truth."

"There is nothing wrong with weird," she says. "Life is boring if we are all the same. Be proud to be different and say big fuck you to people who don't like it."

Nico frowns. "Hey, hey. Watch your language, Ma. Seems like that hip-hop music is turning out to be a bad influence. I might need to have words with Deish."

She smirks. "I've learned all the rude words from you, my Nico. Oh, Ivy! You should have asked the P.F. Bad Girlz Crew to perform tonight. We would have been honored to entertain."

Choking on a laugh, Nico spurts champagne back into his glass. "Yeah, well, in case you haven't noticed, this isn't a comedy festival." He pulls me closer. "And, Ivy, Ariana does so happen to have a tragic story to tell you about the death of her first husband. It features a jealous lover, some cross dressing, and enough prescription medication to run Wall Street on for a week."

"Sounds intriguing. Was one of the paintings she purchased *Lightning Boy* by any chance? L's portrait?"

He laughs. "Of course. She had tears running down her face when she first saw it and was all like... *oh, Nico, it's horrifying. Shockingly beautiful and lethal—just like L is.*"

I laugh at his excellent impression of Ariana's cultured voice.

"She's planning to give the painting to them as a birth present. Edie will love it and L will tolerate it for her sake. *And* she texted a photo of it to a buddy of hers, an editor at

Vogue. They're looking at doing a story on you, featuring that painting."

"What? Are you serious? Wow! I'm so excited I feel sick. Imagine all the work I might get from that kind of feature. That's possibly life changing."

"You wanna know what else is life changing?" he asks, inching his face closer. "You are."

I stroke his cheek, and his eyelids slide closed for a moment. "You're so sweet," I say.

Zsofia squeezes my arm. "I will go rescue South from Mia. She has not left his side all evening and he looks like a lion in a cage. Hungry. Ready to kill."

"Shit. Good idea, Ma."

"I'm really going to miss your painting," I whisper against Nico's lips. "It's my favorite."

"Lucky you've got the real thing then, huh?"

"I am very, very lucky."

His huge smile is dazzling as he brings it closer and kisses me. He draws back and asks, "I wonder who bought it?"

"I did."

"What? How can you miss it if it's still yours?"

"I'm giving it to your mom."

"Man, she'll love that—"

There's a crashing sound across the room, and I look over Nico's shoulder. My mother, in typical Drunk-Julia style, has managed to knock a tray of drinks over. Tiny glass shards sparkle around her silver heels. I shrug at Nico. That's no problem. Drunk-Julia can deal with her own mess.

Kendra stares at me, her jaw hanging low. She's probably

shocked by the sight of me wrapped up tight in the sexy skater boy's arms. Who cares?

For the first time in my life, I don't give a damn what anyone thinks.

"So, I know this is a super-special night for you, Ivy, but I can't help wondering… Is it wrong that I can't wait to take you home and get you out of that hot dress and naked beneath me? Or on top of me. Any way, really, as long as you don't have clothes on and you're looking at me like that."

"I think that's exactly the right thing to want."

He gives a contented sounding sigh against my lips. "Yep, it is. We'll sneak out soon, yeah?"

"Nothing would make me happier, my love."

I flick my gaze around the room at the bevy of distinguished gentlemen who Mia would normally be falling over herself to set me up with. Not one of them interest me.

I can only see emerald eyes sparking fire, curved lips fanning flames. One beautiful heart beats and keeps the embers glowing red hot. He's all I want. All I need.

Because just like the prophecy predicted, it's always been him. He's the one.

Nico is the only man who matters.

And that's how it's going to stay.

THE END

Thank you for reading Tempting Ivy! Saving South, South and Mia's tale, is available now.

You can catch up with Nico and Ivy who also appear in it. Keep turning for details on other books in the series and an excerpt from South's book.

OTHER BOOKS

Books in the Damaged Souls Golden Hearts series:

Finding E, a heartbreaking prequel to L and Eden's story. Check it out - it's usually FREE!

A street boy who doesn't know what love is. One night, one girl changes everything.

Loving L, a full length HEA to L and Eden's story. Can be read as a standalone.

An ex-street boy. The girl who'll be his first and last. P.S. Nico appears as Eden's rocker buddy and co-worker!

Saving South: South and Mia's story

Most secrets cause pain, but sometimes they heal.

As a pet wedding photographer, Mia is used to handling large temperamental creatures. All she wants is one hot night with the sexy blue-eyed rocker, not to accidentally fall pregnant.

And if you like enemies to lovers stories about cursed fae princes falling for feisty mortal girls, check out my paranormal romance series, the Black Blood Fae.

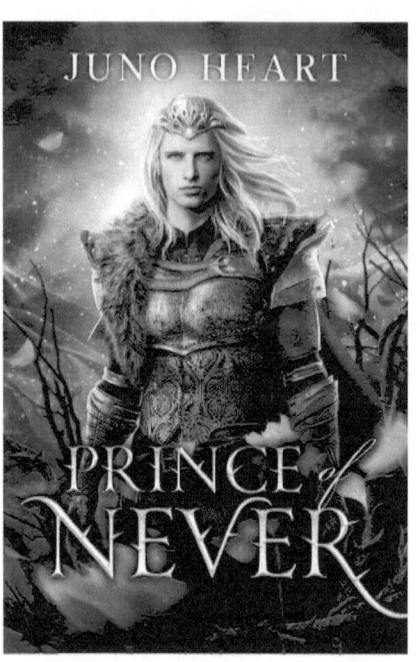

For general release news and deal alerts sign up to my newsletter.

SAVING SOUTH PREVIEW

Mad Wolf

Mia

No one grows up planning to become a stalker. It happens quite by accident. How do I know this? Because I am one. An accidental stalker. Let me back up a little and explain.

The first time I saw South, I spilled coffee over my favorite dress. It was lunchtime, and I'd just parked my butt down at a cafe near work, flipped over a music magazine, and *boom* there he was on the cover. One tiny glimpse of him and along with my glittery eighties frock, I was ruined.

The coffee spillage was a sign. A warning to look away.

Run fast.

Scream loudly.

And did I?

Nope.

Why not? Because it was love at first sight just from gazing at two photos of the guy.

The article inside the magazine featured a small black and white picture of South onstage, his bee-stung lips making out with the microphone. On the cover was a close up of his face framed by golden hair, his azure eyes gazing into the camera lens like he was about to declare undying love to it.

Being a photographer myself, I appreciated the artistic lighting, the details of the composition. But as a single girl, I salivated over the sharp cheekbones, the square jaw, and fluorescent glow of his eyes. Poetry in motion, South as a complete package shook me to the core, and in all of three seconds I was a goner.

In.

Love.

Forever.

The article that I rabidly devoured revealed Up Void was a local band on the rise, and from that moment on, my enthusiasm for hot, sweaty gigs increased. I attended as many of their shows as possible, swaying in the front row with all the other girls who went along to make desperate eyes at the singer.

Sometimes, while his hips rocked to the pounding of the drums, our gazes would lock for a few magical seconds. I'd suffer a blast of that intense frown, and then his eyes would drift away.

It took a grand total of four gigs before I faced the sad fact that no matter how seductively I smiled, I couldn't hold his attention for longer than a few heartbeats. Platinum blonds with quirky long pigtails obviously weren't his type.

"What are you staring at, Mia?" asks my friend Ivy, startling me back to the present moment.

The crowded art exhibition opening that I'm plonked in the middle of comes into focus. Ivy's stunning artworks, our friends' happy faces, people dressed in flashy, crazy clothes, and loud chatter fill the gallery where we both work.

I clutch my champagne flute tighter. "Oh, just that amazing painting of yours." I point across Mad Wolf Gallery to the opposite wall.

She turns her smirk toward it. "You mean the painting of Nico that South's currently standing under?"

"Yep," I squeak, flushing a guilty shade of red.

She huffs. "Quick, silly, look away before he calls the police. As I've been telling you for the last few months, you need to stop being so obvious."

She's right, because here I am once again—accidentally stalking South. Thankfully, I'm not at all dangerous. I'm more of a friendly neighborhood stalker. Kindly and opportunistic, rather than sinister and devious. But still, I never in my wildest dreams imagined I'd be so obsessed with a guy. A guy who's a friend. Well, sort of.

See, not that long ago, Ivy met Nico—another hot rocker—and that event caused my love life to go from crap to tragic. She's ten years older than Nico and he had to work hard to wear down her *anti-cougar* resistance. Now they're together, madly in love, and I couldn't be happier for them.

The problem is, Nico happens to be great buddies with South.

So now that South and I attend the same parties, my comfortable crush has evolved into a raging case of unrequited love. It's not my fault he's a tall, tatted, entitled alpha male with a Southern drawl hot enough to melt the boulder holders off a grandma. I want him. I've sworn that I'll have him.

Just once.

One long, steamy session between the sheets is all I want. ASAP. And why not? Okay, so he's super intense and something dangerous brims within those brilliant blue eyes. He's obviously damaged and doesn't do girlfriends. Oh, yeah, and have I mentioned I'm not his favorite person?

"Mia? Mia!"

Whoops. I must've zoned out again.

"Sorry, Ivy, I got distracted."

Frowning, she flips her wavy, red locks over her shoulder. "Yes, I can see that. Move on, girl. He's not interested. You deserve to be adored, not ignored."

"I know." My palms smooth over my velvet cocktail dress. It's red—South's favorite color. "You're absolutely right, but you can't reason with a pining heart. Believe me, I've tried."

"Maybe you should skip the Up Void gig next weekend. Let yourself go through withdrawal. Tonight, you've followed him around nonstop, and it's too much. Have a break for a couple of weeks and see if it reduces the lust. You'll feel better."

"We'll see," I say, avoiding her gray eyes.

I fully intend to go next Saturday because, at a gig, I can stare at him all I want. Everyone else will be doing the same thing, so I won't look like a crazy stalker-girl.

Anyway, as if I'd miss an opportunity to see him on stage. It's thrilling, the pull of his emotional agony, the effect it has on the crowd. And when his eyes meet mine, it's like I've been plugged into a hazardous power source that, at any moment, might spark into flames and burn the venue down.

But no matter what Ivy says, I'm determined to hook up with him soon, and she needn't worry about the fallout, because I won't allow myself to get hurt. Growing up with wealthy parents who were too busy to take care of me themselves means I'm quite used to being ignored. As long as I get what I want, I can handle it.

And what I want is South. Only for temporary sexual purposes, of course.

I'll never let myself be a man's pawn, shuffled about and discarded when I'm no longer useful. No way. Like a master chess player, I'll make bold moves and stomp across the board until I've gotten back power.

Still, bedding South won't be easy because, unfortunately, he dislikes me. Well, at least I think he does. Why else does he run in the opposite direction whenever he sees me?

Sighing, I place my empty glass on the table beside us. "I'm going to head out, Ivy. It's been quite a week. Massive love and congrats on your awesome opening. You've sold every single piece!"

"No one's more surprised about that than me." She laughs and kisses my cheek. "Over the last five days, you've photographed two pet weddings as well as worked tirelessly to help organize tonight and didn't miss one day of work. No wonder you're beat. I'll call you tomorrow. Sleep well, honey."

As I duck through the crowd, the string quartet in the corner of the room shifts from a Beethoven piece to the breakout hit single from Up Void's debut E.P., *Lined Black*, and the crowd laughs. Everyone knows the song.

I can't help noticing South laugh too as he slides his hands into the pockets of faded black jeans. Then he looks up and, from only two meters away, glowing blue eyes stare into mine. Scorching me.

Time slows to a crawl. Sound warps. My heart beats faster.

I stare, too. But this time, I look away first.

Gig

South

"Zave, go harder!" I yell at our drummer. The rage burning through me needs feeding, requires more heat and speed.

Sticks flying, Zave responds by pounding the kit as if he hates the damn thing. Perfect.

Spinning back to the mic, I scream until the veins in my neck almost rupture.

The crowd charges forward like soldiers, battle cries spewing from their lips. They've all been waiting for this song—the one I saved for the encore just to fuck with them.

Panting, I lean into the mic. "This is *Lined Black*."

They go nuts, their roar of approval surging like a rogue wave through the room.

I smash my fingers against my strings and laugh at our lead guitarist, Nate, as he trips on leads and bends his torso deep into the distorted riff.

The sound swirls like a hurricane and—me—I'm the eye of the storm, feet planted, hips pulsing and spine flexing beyond my control.

"*Dirt. Black. Huh. Yeah, grind me clean.*"

The audience moshes hard, bouncing together and writhing like an almighty beast that grows bigger every second, taking over the room.

"*The sea's my midnight. Water chokes. Black shine. Yeah, shine.*"

A sudden flash of silver in the mosh, illuminated by a roving spotlight, catches my eye. Mia's shimmering pigtails.

She's leaving already?

Whenever we play a local club, Mia comes, stays until the end. Comes backstage with my buddy Nico and his girl, Ivy. Always smiling. Always staring at me with those big golden eyes.

With the music shuddering through my bones, I watch her

push her way to the bar, and I miss the cue for the chorus, coming in three seconds late. Shit.

"*Black black blood is rain. Black black I ain't insane. Ain't insane.*" Actually, I feel pretty fucking crazy as I let loose another blood-curdling yell, stretch my guitar high, and then slam it down hard into my hip.

I'll regret that tomorrow.

Sweat drips into my eyes, and I swipe my face against my t-shirt sleeve to clear my vision.

Mia.

Mia.

Sweet Mia.

At least five guys scope her out as she waits in line to be served, their sleazy gazes tracking over her legs. Her sweet ass.

Fuckers.

I lean in to sing the chorus three more times, laughing as I try to shout louder than Nate.

Once.

Twice.

Then the last line, "*Black blood makes dirty rain. I ain't. Ain't insane.*"

The drums crash three, two, one, then disappear. Feedback screeches. And screeches some more.

Wild applause and screams rain down on me while I stare into the abyss, hypnotized by the lights. Then seek out those white pigtails once more. I'll look away after five beats. I swear it.

Five.

Four.

Three.

Two.

One.

I'm still looking.

Then Nate says, "Night, y'all. Thanks for being awesome. We'll catch ya real soon."

People yell and whistle and chant the usual shit.

More. More. More.

Up Void. Up Void. Up Void.

South. Fucking. South.

I'm miles away. Planets out.

"Take your guitar off, dickhead."

"What?"

Nate stands in front of me, scowling and dripping sweat. "What are you doing hovering there like your brain's shorted out, man?"

Before I summon the sense to look elsewhere, he follows my line of sight to the bar and laughs.

"Right. You idiot." He shakes his rockabilly quiff at me and bumps my shoulder. "Just bone her already, will ya?"

Easy for him to say.

"Come on, man. You look fucking crazy. Get your ass off stage."

I shrug out of my guitar strap and hand my '72 over to a roadie. He throws me a towel.

Crew members slap my back and *hey-great-show* me all the way to the dressing room. Toweling off, I push through the door and check out the scene. The room is packed with booking agency and String Power Records staff and, worse, the label's managing director, Vince.

Shit.

The guy's a certified lunatic. Barely sleeps, drinks like a fish and constantly shoves powders and pills in all the wrong places. He's tall and lanky with a wild mane of frizzy hair, and he's a real pain in the ass. Luckily, he's also hilarious. I kinda like him.

The second he sees me enter the room, he darts over, rubbing his hands together like a mad scientist. "Amazing show, South. Amazing. Got me so fired up I'm not gonna bother sleeping tonight. You coming out? We're gonna hit that weird bar that's hidden behind a bookcase in that fake store downtown."

Yep, there's no way he'll get any sleep tonight. He's in constant vibrating motion. Eyes bouncing like pinballs. Legs juddering. Not so relaxing to stand next to.

"Do you know if Ivy's friend Mia is going?" I ask.

Vince nods. "Yep, that whole crew's coming."

Which means I'll decline.

I squeeze his shoulder and show him a face of fake regret. "Nah, not tonight. I'm heading home. Need some sleep."

Ben, our bass player, sidles up fussing with his man-bun. He loves to look pretty, and with his half-Japanese super-symmetrical features, he nearly always does.

"What's that you're saying?" Ben asks. Just like a thirteen-year-old girl, the dude cannot stand to miss one word of gossip.

"I *said*, I'm outta here."

"Why's that? Taking a chick home?"

"Nope. I'm beat."

His eyes bug out like I announced I've got a terminal illness.

The door bangs open, and a blast of shock erupts in my chest as Mia walks through it with Zave, laughing at him juggling drumsticks like a clown and then threading one through his long, wavy locks like a hairpin.

Our eyes meet, and she gives me a sunny smile. Same as always, my gut clenches, so I chin tip her, then quickly glance away. Lost for words, l look from Vince to Ben.

Yeah, it's the same old Mia effect. Fuck knows why it happens.

The buzz in the room gets noisier, increasing the claustrophobic feeling. Fifty sets of eyes penetrate my skin like a million needles… prick, prick, fucking prick. These people are getting ready to swoop down on me. Talk my ear off. Entertain me. Become my newest close buddies.

And Mia—she's getting ready, too, glancing over here every few seconds thinking I don't notice.

I notice.

I've gotta get out of here before I do something stupid.

To *her*.

Speaking to as few folk as possible, I work my way to the opposite corner and grab my duffel bag. Only takes twenty minutes. Finally, with a sigh of relief, I turn toward the exit to make my escape.

And bang. There she is standing right in front of me. Big smile. Platinum hair. Golden eyes. Hot body dressed in the kind of edgy clothes you'd expect an artist to wear, revealing just the right amount of skin.

She leans close. "Great show, South."

"Hey, Mia. Thanks." I try not to breathe so I don't get fucked up on her scent. It's like roses on a hot summer's day. Sexy.

She keeps smiling, silently offering up the usual bounty. Kindness. Laughter. Friendship. A sweet fuck. All the shit I'm not interested in. Well, that's a lie—I want the fuck.

Oh, man, do I want the fuck. But I don't want it sweet. Or fun.

I like it savage. Dirty, merciless, and completely unemotional.

I try to smile, dig my hands into my pockets. "Been well?"

"Yeah, I have." She squeezes my arm, and a bolt of lightning shoots straight to my favorite organ. "Oh, South, I went to the funniest cat wedding last week—"

"Yeah, right. Sounds great." I grip her shoulders and move her off to the side. Shit, I really don't like it when she tells me her pet wedding stories. They make me feel weird. Lighter. *Interested.* Ignoring the blast of heat radiating through me from touching her, I say, "So, yeah, I've gotta go. I'll see you around sometime."

Her smile drops away. "Oh."

As I slide past her, I give her a crooked smile and a wink. *Fuck.* I hate winking. I hate *winkers* even more.

"Guess I'll see you tomorrow at Nate's party," she calls to my back.

Double fuck. I forgot about that.

Without looking, I fling a thumbs up in her direction.

Why the heck did Nate have to organize such a stupid-ass thing? And it's funny how Mia calls it *Nate's party*, knowing full well the event at our house has nothing to do with me.

Even though Nate's mom, Abbie, practically raised me up and he's more brother than best buddy, sometimes I wish I didn't live with the guy.

I keep walking.

As I wind through backstage passageways, insanely loud rock music vibrates out of the club's sound system, thumping through my chest so hard it feels like a near-death experience. I fucking love it.

What I don't love is the idea of Mia at my house tomorrow and so close to my bedroom. It's dangerous.

I bang through the metal door at the backstage exit and out into a beautiful crisp night. I take a minute to suck fresh air into my lungs, then head down an alley and onto the main drag, all the way feeling eyes on my back, like someone's standing in the shadows, watching, staring. I look around but see no one. That's weird.

The smell of meat sizzling from the souvlaki van parked under the bridge makes my stomach rumble. Groups of drunks roam, laughing and yelling like losers. The street vibe is festive—a bit like a Friday, not a Wednesday night.

I need a cab.

Scanning the road, I consider how best to avoid tomorrow's party. To get out of it, I'll need to do something drastic, like poison myself so I get carted off to hospital. Sometimes I like the idea of flirting with death but I'm pretty sure I won't be in the mood for it tomorrow.

Anyway, there'll be so many people at Nate's dumb shindig that I probably won't even have to speak to her.

Yeah, right. Who am I kidding? Ever since I met her through my friend Nico, she's been following me around like a bad smell that, come to think of it, actually smells pretty darn good. Like I said before—hot summer roses.

Truth is—Mia is supremely fuckable.

And totally untouchable.

She's too good for me. I don't sleep with friends. I don't sleep with friends of friends. I don't fuck nice girls or ones who look like they might break too easily. End of story.

So, yeah, even though I'm horny as hell, there's no way I'll touch Mia. *Ever.* I'll continue to keep my distance.

Even if it kills me.

The queue at the taxi stand is ten people deep. Sighing, I look right, then left. Hey, it must be my lucky night. A car full of hipsters approaches, crawling along the road in the right direction. I stick my thumb out, and they pull over.

Whenever I hitchhike, people always stop for me. Don't really know why. *I* wouldn't stop for me.

I stroll toward the beat-up sedan, lean on the roof and pop my head through the open window. Two guys and a girl stare back at me. They look wired.

"Hey. You lot heading east?" I ask.

The driver tucks jet black hair behind her ears and says, "We're going anywhere you want, gorgeous."

"Cool." I climb in and thank fuck that she's not sitting in the back seat. She's not my type.

Sadly, I like blonds with golden eyes, husky laughs, and great big massive hearts.

Damn it.

If you'd like to keep reading South and Mia's story, go right ahead. It's available now!

ACKNOWLEDGMENTS

I'd like to give a massive shout out to Anna, Joanne, Ken, Lorna, and Terry for your amazing feedback. I can't thank you all enough, and I'm so grateful that you gave so generously of your time and energy to Nico and Ivy's story. Thank you!!!

And big hugs to the very talented Aubrey at A.T. Cover Designs for the gorgeous cover!

I adore helping golden-hearted girls and broken boys find redemption. I also love indie music, mad hair colors, nuclear-strength coffee, Siamese cats, and long-haired boys. And not in that order!

Sign up to my Newsletter

Facebook

amyjheart.com

BookBub

amyheartromance@gmail.com

www.ingramcontent.com/pod-product-compliance
Lightning Source LLC
Chambersburg PA
CBHW021406110726
47901CB00008B/2082